Date: 2/14/17

LP MYS MYERS
Myers, Tamar,
Tea with jam and dread

TEA WITH JAM AND DREAD

A Selection of Titles by Tamar Myers

The Pennsylvania Dutch Mysteries

THOU SHALT NOT GRILL
ASSAULT AND PEPPER
GRAPE EXPECTATIONS
HELL HATH NO CURRY
AS THE WORLD CHUMS
BATTER OFF DEAD
BUTTER SAFE THAN SORRY
THE DEATH OF PIE *
TEA WITH JAM AND DREAD *

* *available from Severn House*

TEA WITH JAM AND DREAD

Tamar Myers

Severn House Large Print
London & New York

This first large print edition published 2016
in Great Britain and the USA by
SEVERN HOUSE PUBLISHERS LTD of
19 Cedar Road, Sutton, Surrey, England, SM2 5DA.
First world regular print edition published 2013 by
Severn House Publishers Ltd.

British Library Cataloguing in Publication Data
A CIP catalogue record for this title is available from the British Library.

ISBN-13: 9780727894922

Severn House Publishers support the Forest Stewardship Council™
[FSC™], the leading international forest certification organisation. All
our titles that are printed on FSC certified paper carry the FSC logo.

MIX
Paper from
responsible sources
FSC   FSC® C013056
www.fsc.org

Typeset by Palimpsest Book Production Ltd.,
Falkirk, Stirlingshire, Scotland.
Printed and bound in Great Britain by
T J International, Padstow, Cornwall.

This book is dedicated to Kate Lyall Grant. Her keen editorial eye and her brilliant observations were much appreciated.

One

My name is Magdalena Portulacca Yoder Rosen and I have a heart full of Christian joy, but I am not a happy woman. This may seem like a paradox, but please allow me to explain. The joy comes from the certainty that my sins are forgiven, and that I will, for a fact, be going to Heaven, but how can I be happy when my only sister faces a twenty-year prison sentence for aiding and abetting a convicted serial killer? Even more damaging to my psyche is the fact that the serial murderer, Melvin Stoltzfus, our erstwhile Police Chief, is not only my brother-in-law – he is my biological half-brother!

No one would guess that we are related just by looking at us, because I resemble an upright mare, although with pinned-back ears and somewhat larger teeth, whereas Melvin is the spitting image of a praying mantis. At any rate, through some inexplicable means, Melvin was able to cast an evil spell on just about everyone he met. The result was a bizarre cult known as Melvinism. Its adherents worshipped him as if he were a deity. Someone 'discovered' a complete set of scriptures called *The Book of Melvin*, and a second volume titled *Sacred Hymns to Melvin*, both wrapped in a feed sack and tucked away in the far reaches of a hayloft of a long-abandoned barn. The book's contents were nothing more than a bunch of fairy tales in which my bug-eyed, bobble-headed brother performed a series of outrageous miracles – stuff impossible to believe. However, that didn't stop the local yokels from falling for it. Not only did they fall for this clap-trap hook, line and sinker, they proselytized others as if tomorrow was the end of the world. In a way, it *was* the end of my world, because when Melvin turned into a killer his cult followers protected him wherever he went.

Truly, my tale of Melvin is tragic enough to sadden any good woman, but my unhappiness did not begin then. Even now my face burns with shame as I confess that some years ago I became what *I* refer to as an 'inadvertent adulteress.' Yes, I know, there are others who will always call me just plain *adulteress*, and I suppose that is their right to do so, but it is also my right to suppose that they are just plain *envious*. Anyway, it happened like this.

I was a young woman and a virgin. I had no idea what a naked man looked like, supposing that they all looked similar to Michelangelo's Statue of David, a photo of which I'd chanced to come upon in a travel magazine. You can imagine then, that when I did espy the real thing on my wedding night, as it wobbled straight at me like a headless turkey neck, that I screamed and dived under the covers. After that traumatic night I could never look at a real turkey without blushing, and Christmas dinner was forever ruined.

But wait, if only the horror of my tale ended there, it would at least remain *my* private

2

nightmare. Alas, that was not to be. Just as the ex-virgin (that would be me), now the newly wedded and bedded, freshly minted matron, was on the verge of experiencing marital bliss, her husband, Aaron Miller, blurted out the name of his *first* wife. That's right: his *first* wife, a woman to whom he was still married!

'I signed the divorce papers,' he whined. 'How was I supposed to know I needed to show up in court? It was my first divorce.'

We all make mistakes, and I might even have been able to stick by Aaron through all of this debacle – I had promised 'till death do us part' – except that within a matter of days he confessed that there was a child involved, a daughter by the name of Alison.

Long story short: my marriage to Aaron was annulled and I met and married Dr Gabriel Rosen, whom I call the Babester. Several years ago, Gabriel and I ended up formally adopting Alison, now age fourteen, because it turned out that neither Aaron, nor his first wife, really wanted her. One year ago, at age forty-nine, I gave Alison a younger brother, delivered in quite the more usual way.

There you have it, if only in a rather large nutshell: the history of my unhappiness. Given the extent of my suffering, please indulge me by permitting me one last observation: a woman with two husbands is an adulteress, whereas a man with two wives is merely a bigamist! Why, you might ask? It's because all three of the biblical patriarchs were *poly*gamists. Forsooth, being an inadvertent adulteress, I was the victim of *rape*. My maidenhood was stolen from me by an act of deception; there, that's putting it plain and simple enough, is it not?

One would think that I had done enough suffering to make Swedes in winter as giddy as schoolgirls in comparison, but that didn't stop the Good Lord from testing me further. Despite the fact that my younger sister, Susannah, was in prison for aiding and abetting a man wanted for murder, I was finally getting the hang of the one skill that happy folks of all mindsets must finally get around to mastering, that of *compartmentalization*.

So what if my half-brother, who resembled a giant praying mantis, was the alleged murderer, and that I'd witnessed him skipping town dressed in a nun's habit, riding in a bus full of fake nuns? And so what if my sister, who had too many bad habits to list, was also wearing a nun's habit when she was caught by the long arm of the law, and that, as per usual, there was a tiny, but vociferous, odoriferous, and vicious Yorkshire terrier nestled in the right cup of her oversized brassiere? It's my contention that just about every family has at least one psychopath, if not two, clinging to the limbs of its ancestral tree. What sets my family apart is that the dearly demented sit next to each other on the same branch.

So there I was, on the verge of becoming happy once more, when Sheriff Felonious Stodgewiggle, our county law enforcement official, paid a surprise visit to the PennDutch Inn. It was early summer and I was shelling green peas whilst sitting in an Adirondacks-style rocking chair on

4

the front veranda in the cool of the afternoon. My hunky husband, Gabe, the Babester, was at that moment driving our teenager, Alison, over to spend the night at a friend's house. Gabe had taken our infant son, Little Jacob, with him.

Our village has its own police department, so the sheriff's people normally just do 'drive bys.' So when I saw the car turn up the gravel lane in my direction, I instinctively knew it was trouble. When I saw that it was Felonious who was driving, I knew it was *big* trouble.

'Whatever it is, Felonious,' I said as he got out of the car, 'I'm going to have to take a rain check.' I glanced at my wristwatch. 'How about, say, two o'clock on the Twelfth of Never?'

Poor Felonious Stodgewiggle. His were the shaggiest eyebrows I have ever seen. Truly, they are like a pair of black Persian kittens that someone has glued to the skin of an otherwise baby-smooth face. His so-called five o'clock shadow would be the envy of any Hollywood actor's weeklong attempt at growing facial stubble. The thatch that manages to escape from the slight V at his throat hints at grave but marvellous consequences for any woman fortunate enough to undo another button. Oops, perhaps I have said far too much for a married woman who has promised to remain faithful to her husband, even in her mind, to the bitter end.

Being all man, Sheriff Stodgewiggle doesn't possess a shred of humour. He is the kind of man who would hit a woman over the head with a club and drag her back to his cave – if he were a Neanderthal. Of course, I'm only joking, because Neanderthals never existed, given that God created Adam as a white man with a prominent jaw and a straight forehead, and that was around five thousand years ago, not hundreds of thousands of years ago, or whatever. And we certainly didn't evolve from apes, or even a common ancestor of apes, which is what my husband, Gabe, believes. I know for a fact that the sheriff doesn't believe in this scientific nonsense.

At any rate, since Felonious is humourless, and neither is he a Mennonite like myself, nor married to a secular music lover like my husband, he was stumped by my answer. He scratched beneath his voluminous chin with his thick, broken nails and sniffed the air, as if those actions might bring clarity.

'Uh, is that one of youse Mennonite holidays?' he asked.

'Forgive me,' I said. 'I was being facetious.'

'Yeah.'

I set my bowl of peas aside, along with my attitude and my bad manners. 'Would you care to take a seat, Sheriff? These rocking chairs are actually more comfortable than they look.'

Sheriff Stodgewiggle settled into his proffered chair with a smile. 'Yeah, this is nice. I've been wondering what to put on my porch ever since Ma broke the hammock. Her doc's been after her to stay under three hundred pounds, but you know how she loves her sweets.'

'When I offered you a seat, dear, I didn't mean that you could actually *keep* the chair. It belongs to my husband.'

6

'Oh. I knew that; you bet I did. Magdalena, I'm here because I have some bad news.'

My heart leapt into my throat which, given that I am vertically enhanced, meant that it had a long way to travel. 'It's my sister, Susannah, isn't it? What did she do now? Try to sneak out of prison in a laundry bag? Dig her way out with a teaspoon? Feign death so well that she was taken to the prison morgue? Because she's done all of those twice already, except that last one—'

It was only then that Felonious raised a hairy paw to signal me to stop blithering and to start listening. 'I got an email today from a woman in Charlotte, North Carolina, by the name of Maggie Peerless.'

'Hmm,' I mused, 'Maggie. Do you suppose that is short for Magdalena? Sadly, there aren't that many parents naming their daughters Magdalena these days – at least not out in the general population. It's still pretty popular among the Amish, though.'

Felonious shook his thick salt-and-pepper mane and roared like a lion. 'Magdalena, I swear I don't know how your husband puts up with you.'

'Why I never!' I said.

'This woman's name wasn't the point,' he growled. 'I thought that you might want to know what her message said.'

I could feel my hands grow cold and clammy as my throat constricted with dryness. 'Well, since you drove all the way out here from Bedford it must be something rather important. So yes, I do want to know. I very much want to know.'

Sheriff Felonious Stodgewiggle knew by then

that he had me hook, line and sinker. The satisfaction showed in his eyes and what little bare skin he had on his face, but I didn't care; I was his for the telling.

'She claims to have spotted Melvin Stoltzfus on television doing a commercial,' he said. 'It was an advertisement for Adorhim: those pills that are supposed to stimulate the female libido. The adverts feature handsome, bare-chested men lounging next to a pool. They're speaking directly to the TV screen and their message is that all a woman needs to do, in order to get her engine racing again, is to start swallowing those pills.'

I burst out laughing, which was like jabbing the lion with a white-hot poker. When the beast had calmed down enough to pay attention to my words, I managed to spit out a few of them.

'Did you ever meet Melvin?'

'No,' Felonious said, sounding deeply regretful. 'His crime spree here ended just before I took the job. I moved here from Toledo, Ohio, if you'll remember.'

'I didn't think there was another Toledo,' I said, 'except for in Spain. Anyway, Melvin is a dead ringer for a praying mantis. A giant version, of course. He has a tiny head, huge eyes that swivel in all directions and his limbs are toothpick thin. The only part of the analogy that doesn't hold up to this image is that no giant female praying mantis could stand to eat Melvin Stoltzfus.'

The black Persian kittens on the sheriff's forehead leapt in unison. 'So what you're really saying is that you can't stand your brother—'

'*Half*-brother!' I said vehemently.

8

'But brother-in-law as well, correct?'

'Yes, I was adopted. Susannah is not related to that scum— Forgive me, it is not in my nature to call someone names.'

'Well, I just wanted to give you a heads-up that he'd been spotted,' Sheriff Felonious Stodgewiggle said as he rose stiffly to his feet. 'And now I can be certain that you won't be aiding and abetting this fellow in the event that he does show up in these parts.'

'Likewise, I'm sure. Correct?'

'*I beg your pardon?*' he said.

'If you had done any homework, you would have discovered that the name Magdalena Yoder is synonymous with law and order here in Hernia. Our village could not afford a police department were it not for my largesse. My reputation as sleuth has spread even beyond the borders of our county – I dare say even beyond the borders of our fair state, given that I once solved a crime in the dairy industry in the State of Ohio. There was no use crying over spilled milk when I was done with that.'

Sheriff Felonious Stodgewiggle denied me the satisfaction of even a sarcastic response. Without further ado he turned and barrelled down my steps like a man who had somehow been deeply offended. But by what? I wondered. Oh, well, it presently being summer, I closed my mouth in order to limit the number of flies that sought entry and went back to shelling peas.

9

Two

I much prefer to visit with my friends face-to-face, as the Good Lord intended, *not* Facebook to Facebook. Ergo, because I am the mother of two and run a bed and breakfast, my best friend Agnes Miller and I make it a point of having tea and conversation together at her house once a week if at all possible. Although I truly enjoy Agnes's company, and profit from it emotionally, my visits to her are intended to bring her comfort and succour.

You see, Agnes recently married my oldest friend, Doc Shafer. At the time of their nuptials, Agnes was forty-nine and Doc was eighty-six. Fortunately for one of the newlyweds, and unfortunately for the other, old Doc was as randy as a billy goat. He also owned a billy goat, as he lived on a farm. At any rate, Agnes's extremely short marriage was one during which she never had a good hair day, and to see her walk, you might have thought she was a cowgirl – if you get my drift. Old Doc died of natural causes just ten days after saying 'I do,' but he died an extremely happy man.

Everyone thought that Agnes would be devastated after Doc's death and possibly even remain in seclusion, but as long as we good citizens of Hernia kept her busy by allowing her to meddle in our affairs, Agnes was as content as a cat on a warm window seat, and such was her mental state the day this saga begins. I had taken my toddler, Little Jacob, to visit his 'Auntie' Agnes, and to give him the opportunity to pet her many inherited animals. These, of course, included the notorious goat, who went by the name of Gruff. It was late afternoon – of a Tuesday – and we were 'taking tea' on one of the large farmhouse's several sweeping verandas.

'The British are coming,' Agnes said, with just the hint of a smile.

'That's what Paul Revere shouted from his horse to warn the American colonialists some 240 years ago. Don't you have any gossip newer than that?'

Agnes's plump little mouth turned down. 'I don't gossip, Magdalena, you know that; I merely deliver facts, which I then sometimes feel free to editorialize on, but only when the individuals are truly deserving.'

'You're quite right, dear. And anyway, it was a good thing that Paul warned us poor hapless colonists that the mighty British were about to attack.'

'Magdalena,' Agnes said with growing impatience, 'let's leave the Revolutionary War behind for a moment. Instead, let us think about culture, for it was the British who invented culture.'

'*Really?*' I said.

'Magdalena,' my best friend said as she poured me a cup of tea, 'as I've said before, it would help me a lot in deciphering your emotions if you darkened your eyebrows and plucked all those stray hairs. As it is, I can't tell if you're being serious, sarcastic or if you're genuinely surprised. Which is it?'

I slowly slathered a piece of golden-brown toast with room temperature butter and then smeared globs of homemade strawberry jam over the surface. Then, of course, being an Ugly American, I took a ginormous bite and washed it down with milky tea before answering. After all, one must never comment on matters of international importance on an empty stomach.

'Can't it be all three emotions?' I said. 'What I mean to say is that I'm seriously surprised that you would restrict credit for the invention of culture to *only* the British. Even just Western Culture owes its roots to—'

'Tut, tut,' Agnes said primly, 'let us not speak of King Tut, the Sumerians or even the Greeks. I mean *manners* as we know them today.' Agnes holds her teacup with her pinkie finger so high, and at such an angle, it has been known to poke her in the forehead.

I crammed the rest of my toast into my mouth, which meant that I had to talk with my mouth full. My fourteen-month-old son was trying to climb out of his high chair and needed to be stopped. Allowing a baby to crack his head open is never good manners.

'Agn*eth*,' I said, spewing bits of bread and jam hither, thither, but not quite yon, 'you've been watching *Downtown Abbey* again, haven't you?'

My buddy sighed. 'Mags, how many times have I told you that it's Down*ton*, not Down*town*?'

'Trust me: enough.'

'Yeah? Well, so what if I'm using that

12

television series as a model? The British personify honour and dignity under great duress. "Keep calm and carry on," as Queen Elizabeth's father said. During Queen Victoria's reign they ruled an empire while drinking tea during the heat of the day, and then dressed to the nines for dinner. You've got to admire that.'

'I *do*?' I said. That's all I had time to say as I plunked my squirming male child back into his seat, strapped him in tighter and cut a slice of buttered toast into teensy-weensy bites for him.

'Since you're being enigmatic today, I will ignore your last comment,' Agnes said. 'I invited you to tea today for a specific reason.'

'Oh?'

'Stop it, Mags.'

'Huh?'

'Stop being so darn taciturn. Usually you're as garrulous as a gaggle of old men, but today you're hardly paying attention.'

I licked my greasy fingers before wiping them on my napkin. 'I'm sorry, dear; I didn't get any sleep last night. The guests I have now are probably the loudest bunch yet. They communicate by shouting, and one couple shouts to each other in the hallway as if they're on opposite ends of a field.'

'Typical Americans,' Agnes muttered. Now that she'd become an Anglophile, she was beginning to find her own people objectionable.

I sighed. 'Just stop it, dear. There *are* some good Americans – like you, for instance. I can't see you causing me any trouble if you were to be a guest at the PennDutch Inn.'

Agnes smiled. 'And that,' she said, 'is because I have a little something called class.'

'Don't forget modesty,' I said.

'Oh, no, Mags, that's *your* department,' she said.

'You're quite right,' I said. 'I've always been proud of my humility. It comes with being a Mennonite of Amish descent.'

Agnes selected a variety of shortbread biscuits and arrayed them fan-shaped on her plate before chowing down on them. She has been my best friend since infancy, so what I am about to say, I say lovingly. The fact that Agnes is shaped like a beach ball atop a pair of shoes has less to do with her genes than what she puts into her jeans. For the record, our family trees are so intertwined that they resemble thickets rather than trees, which is to say that the two of us probably share more genes than a pair of conjoined twins.

'Magdalena,' she said at last, 'after your parents died and you first turned your family's farm into the PennDutch, I have to confess that I was a bit worried. After all, it's Lancaster, Pennsylvania that is known for its Amish community, even though it is small potatoes in size compared to Ohio's Holmes County. But Hernia, Pennsylvania? We're a nothing place.'

I happen to be the mayor of our village – population, 2,168 and a half (Joyce Millhouse is just under five months' pregnant) – so I may have bristled at that comment. I bade my hair to stand down so that the rest of me might better relax as well.

'And your point *is*?' I said.

14

Her claim to classiness aside, my rotund friend stuffed her mouth with goodies and chomped as she spoke. 'Thanks to your insistence on giving your guests a genuine Amish experience – you know, making them work hard while they are at the PennDutch – it has become a huge success with the chattering class.'

'Excuse me?'

'The certain people who think that they're special and feel compelled to remind everyone in the world just how special they are every moment of the day. I bet that you haven't had to advertise for eons.'

'Actually not since the first murder happened at the inn,' I said.

'Tell me, Magdalena – do you still enjoy being an innkeeper?'

I wiped Little Jacob's face for the umpteenth time and dumped a handful of seedless raisins on his tray. 'Sometimes. Occasionally I'll have a guest who is both exceptionally interesting and compliant.'

Agnes crammed the better half of a blueberry muffin into her mouth. As it was already full she had to store everything in her cheeks, much like a squirrel, before she could speak. 'By "compliant," you mean someone who will follow your ridiculously strict rules or else risk having to pay monetary penalties.'

'Well,' I said, 'they know what they are getting into from the get-go. I make all my guests sign contracts and disclaimers. The PennDutch is, after all, the only inn that I know of where guests have the opportunity to pay for the privilege of working

15

their fingers to the bone while viewing it as a cultural experience.'

'*Those* are your American guests,' Agnes said. 'Am I right? Europeans are either too canny or too lazy to be bossed around by a farmwoman in a bonnet.'

'It's not a bonnet, for Pete's sake; it's a prayer covering. You know that.'

Agnes started to pop in the second half of the muffin, but I stopped her by gently grabbing her wrist. 'Swallow first, dear. I love you like a sister, but I don't fancy doing mouth-to-mouth resuscitation.'

Obediently, she swallowed. After chugging a litre of milk, my friend was ready to shift gears with renewed energy. 'Well, here is the gist of my idea: you jettison that old business formula and you begin catering to an altogether new clientele. These new folks would never dream of working so you'll have to soak them upfront, *but* playing hostess to this group who really are the mostest – well, that should put a whole lot of fun back into the game. Face it, Magdalena, you already have all the money that you will ever need. What you need now is something to stimulate that excessive accumulation of grey cells that you possess.'

'I see,' I said, although I didn't. 'What is this group? Is it some sort of high IQ society?'

Agnes had the temerity to laugh. 'Hardly! No, I believe I have come up with a new vision for your PennDutch Inn.'

'Please, dear, tell me all about it.' Fortunately sarcasm contains very few calories, or I would have swelled on the spot to twice my size.

16

Agnes formed fists with her sticky hands and pumped them up and down like an ecstatic little schoolgirl. 'It makes me so happy that you're even willing to listen to my idea,' she said. 'Now, it's your inn, so feel free to make changes, but I am envisioning the PennDutch as a place where European nobility might come to lay their silken curls upon your homespun pillow cases while japing and jeering at our backwards ways.'

'*What?*' Had I been wearing dentures, they would surely have landed on Agnes's plate, and she might well have shoved them into her mouth and thence choked to death.

'Oh, come on,' Agnes said. 'They all think that we're nothing but yokels and rubes. Even the English think that, and some of them live in houses with thatch roofs, for goodness' sakes. We're never going to change their opinion of us. I read somewhere that the English objected more to the fact that Wallis Simpson was an American than that she was a twice-divorced woman of somewhat ambiguous gender. So, I say that we play to that strength. Let us be the dumbest, crudest, most culture-deprived Americans that we can be, and still be good, decent Christians.'

'But Agnes,' I wailed, 'you know that I don't belong to that political party!'

'Leave politics out of it, Mags. You know that Obama is spying on you with those NRA whatchamacallits.'

'That would be NSA, dear. Nonetheless, how do you propose that we reach this blue-blood, "to the manor born" clientele?'

'Ha! *You* don't reach them; *I* do, and I already have.'

'*Excuse* me?'

'I'll excuse you just as soon as you say that you'd love to be the grossest hostess, far from having the mostest, to a genuine English earl and his wife, and an equally genuine countess.'

'Would that be Earl Grey and his wife, the Countess Tea?'

'I'm serious, Mags; he is the Earl of Grimsley-Snodgrass.'

'Pardon my layperson's curiosity, pal, but if he is an earl then why is she a countess? Why isn't she an *earl*ess?'

'Because that title would apply only to those women who've been the victims of *really* incompetent plastic surgeons.'

'I see.'

'Besides, Magdalena, and I didn't really want this to be a factor in your decision, but assisting you with a project like this might help divert my mind from constantly thinking about my doc.'

There it was at last; she was playing the widow's card. I should have seen it coming. Over the years Agnes had tried many times to improve my 'shtick' with her 'helpful' suggestions. Most of them involved her buying into the business as an equal partner *but* with creative control. Agnes had studied advertising for two years at the University of Pittsburgh, and she was convinced that I needed to 'jazz' up my approach to marketing. She wanted me to wear Amish clothing, even though I am Mennonite – not Amish. If that wasn't a big enough deception,

18

she wanted my Jewish husband to grow a beard and pose as an Amish man. *Oy gevalt!*

I am not claiming to be able to judge the depth of someone's grief, or their genuine desire to set their minds on other things, but my best friend might consider that I would also be missing her husband of only a few months. After all, I had loved the old geezer far more than Agnes ever could have. Despite the fact that he'd never been able to breech the fortress that was my sturdy Christian underwear, Doc and I had been extremely close ever since his wife died some twenty years prior, and we'd talked about everything – including his relationship with Agnes. Yes, I shall say it unequivocally: I loved the old goat more than Agnes loved him.

I, however, had *turned down* a myriad of proposals from Doc. Therefore, in the eyes of the world, my grief couldn't hold a candle to the spinster Agnes, who had answered in the affirmative only once. No, siree, and Bob's your uncle, if I had wanted to, *I* could be the 'Widder Woman Shafer' with a billy goat named Gruff to share my bed. Believe me, if our situations were reversed, I would do a far better sight of mourning. I would roll around in the dirt like some primitive tribeswoman I'd read about in a novel. And of course I'd do a fair amount of wailing and carrying on – just plain screeching too – since I'm already pretty good at that.

Sad to say, in the eyes of the public, I was *not* bereaved. In their eyes, I had no excuse for rolling around in the dirt while sounding like a rock star with a beehive stuck on her head. Now here was my best friend, trying to blackmail me with *her* grief. Her aim was to get me to take *my* inn into a whole new direction. I'm telling you, Agnes's *chutzpah* had me so hot under the collar that the heat that was generated threatened to melt two of the silver fillings in my teeth.

The only way that I could think of, wherein I would not feel taken advantage of, was if I bested her at her own game. If dear, sweet Agnes was intent on getting all loosy-goosy with the la-dee-dah crowd, then I was more than happy to goose her right back. Perhaps that doesn't sound very Christian of me, but if I lead an exemplary life *all* of the time, then, pray tell, how can I be an inspiration to those folks who need to be shown that one *can* recover from a spiritual stumble by repenting and seeking God's forgiveness?

'So, what do you think about my idea?' Agnes said. 'Mags, you have to admit that it's rather brilliant. The Brits – especially the aristocracy – are essentially clueless about our Pennsylvania Dutch culture, so we can get away with just about anything, and charge them just about any amount of money as well. Heck, what's that famous saying of yours?'

'A tourist will pay any amount of money, and overlook any amount of abuse, just as long as he – or she – can view it as a cultural experience.'

'That's the one. You are so clever, Mags. I have no doubt that you will have these highfalutin, high-born folk eating out of your hand like they were pigeons in a park.'

Alas, that is when I caved and gave in to the Devil and his minions. This is not to say that

Agnes had anything to do with the Fallen Angel's presence. Lucifer, like the Lord Himself, is always hanging around, but in the case of the former, I could almost hear Him coaxing me to puff up with pride.

'Come on, Magdalena,' he hissed with his split tongue (like bad writers would have it, the Devil and his underlings can hiss in dialogue without an 's'). 'First you play hostess to an earl, next to a duke, then finally you offer your bed to a king!'

'Yeth, yeth, yeth!' his minions chorused. 'Your bed to a king!'

My bourgeoisie blood began to burble with excitement. Perhaps I'd had it wrong all along. Could it be that I was destined to host greatness? Well, not that inheriting a title from some undoubtedly ruthless forbear made one great, but it certainly gave one a leg up – so to speak. Perhaps it was the Devil whispering in my ear, but it did occur to me that not *everyone* has the stomach to rise through the ranks by suppressing the peasants, nor can just *anyone* dispatch enough of the enemy to earn themselves a coronet. And once on the throne, it takes a calm head to order other heads to roll. Could it be that the genes that allowed this class of folk to emerge trium- phant while trampling on the backs of their brethren have produced a superior breed of mankind in their descendants? Perhaps today's crop of the titled *were* entitled to the privileges that they enjoyed through no fault of their own.

Silly, sinful, Magdalena Portulacca Yoder Rosen! That was a moot question I'd just asked

21

myself. There is no such thing as evolution. And even if there was, that was a racist, elitist thought. We are all equal in God's sight. The Bible says that God is our only king.

'I can read your mind,' Agnes said as her eyes began loading up with tears. She has the ability to manufacture them as needed to advance her agenda, so it is hard to take them seriously. 'As a woman of deep faith,' Agnes continued, 'you have a hard time getting behind the idea of there even being an aristocracy. The Bible says that we are all equal and God is our only king. Am I right?'

'Stop reading my mind!' I cried. 'The Bible also says that we should kill witches!'

'Mags, since you obviously know the Bible from cover to cover, then you are aware that your favourite book in the Bible was written by King David.'

'She's quite right,' said the Devil, for He also knows the scriptures, and He is not averse to using them for His nefarious means.

'Yeth, thath true,' said Satan's minions.

'Yeth!' I finally cried out, for Agnes's edification.

'Magdalena,' Agnes said quickly, 'it appeared to me that you were having some sort of spiritual crisis over this. You need to remember that we're not really going to be going gaga over these guests; we're going to do this because it will be fun. Think of it as a play in which you and I get to write our own starring roles.'

'OK,' I said, and just like that, all my inner turmoil ceased.

'Fabulous! Now obviously, you're the hostess. I, by the way, am your personal assistant.'

'All right. Let loose the pure-bred hounds.'

I meant that metaphorically, mind you. The hounds, in this case, referred to the aforementioned English aristocrats, *not* the hounds of Hell. Unfortunately, those few times when my words turn out to be prophetic are always when my choice of words leaves something to be desired.

Three

In full disclosure, I have never been on Facebook, nor have I ever taken a 'selfie.' This is just as well, because I have a face that could *sink* a thousand ships. Any resemblance between my visage and that of a horse is purely coincidental, although Mama was particularly fond of a certain thoroughbred and was known to have spent a great deal of time alone in the barn with him. I'm just saying. The facts are that I have a long, narrow face and I tend to snort when I laugh. If you slapped a saddle on my back and hollered 'giddy-yap' I'd break into a full gallop. Indeed, one tourist from England even mistook me for Camilla, the Duchess of Cornwall. Surely by now you get the point: I am no raving beauty.

I am a simple Mennonite woman of Amish heritage, and I live in the village of Hernia, in the south-western corner of the Commonwealth of Pennsylvania, USA. Both the Mennonites and the Amish are Christian denominations that had their origins in Europe around five hundred years ago. Both groups are opposed to infant baptism and they emphasize peace and nonviolence. The Amish are more recognizable because of their distinctive, old-fashioned dress, and the fact that they use horses and buggies for transportation. The Amish also forbid the use of electricity in their homes.

My grandparents were Amish and my parents were Amish, but I am a Mennonite woman of Amish *ancestry*. There are other Mennonites who do *not* descend from the Amish, but that is another category. I am also what is known as an Old Order Mennonite – that is to say my denomination is very conservative, just not as conservative as the Amish.

I am beginning to wonder if I should switch from being an Old Order Mennonite and join one of the more progressive Mennonite churches. Perhaps I feel this way because I married a Jewish doctor, one who is not only a humanist but who also happens to be a member of the Democratic Party. Don't get me wrong – I am still a devout believer, with my heels dug deeply in, but if I keep sliding down this slippery slope of modernity and rationality I am afraid that someday I might find myself twerking shamelessly at some fundraiser for Hillary Clinton. That would indeed be calamitous, given that we Mennonites aren't even permitted to have sex in a standing position, lest it lead to dancing.

My best friend Agnes is also a Mennonite of Amish derivation, but she belongs to a modern-day branch of the church. She's practically indistinguishable from the Baptists in Hernia, except that Agnes doesn't drink. She is also extremely bright. Why, just look at the advertisement that she eventually placed in a British tabloid, and also on the website that she set up on the internet. I, on the other hand, am a bit of a twit, and a dressmaker's dummy, when compared to my friend, and I must confess that I didn't see her advertisement until it had garnered results. More's the pity.

FOR PEERS ONLY. You are herewith invited to spend your holiday at The Heiristocracy Haven, in Hernia, Pennsylvania, USA. It is a place where lords and ladies of gentle birth may loll about and lollygag to their hearts desires, far from the prying eyes of telescopic cameras. In fact, toe-sucking is mandatory every Sunday before tea! Hunt to the sound of the hounds – even at night! (This is the land of bear and moose.) If it's more thrills that you desire, then ride the area's longest zip line and still be back in time for high jinks, Pennsylvania style. Details upon request.

The clever and demonstratively worldly woman that she is, it wasn't long until Agnes managed to snag the Earl of Grimsley-Snodgrass and his wife, Countess Aubrey of Grimsley-Snodgrass, and their three almost grown-up children: Lady Celia and the identical twins, Viscount Rupert and Mr Sebastian. Given that our game plan was to be our ordinary, lackadaisical, overly familiar American selves, Agnes sent them information about how to hire a motor car in either Harrisburg or Pittsburgh and drive themselves down to Hernia and the PennDutch.

'It's only a two-hour drive,' she wrote, 'through the bucolic Pennsylvania countryside. What better way to see the USA?' She neglected to mention that both cities experience major rush-hour traffic situations, and that the Pennsylvania Turnpike, which connects Hernia to either city, is so rough in places that tyres have been known to burst upon hitting the so-called 'potholes.' One family of visiting Canadians managed to launch their teensy foreign car into the abyss of a pothole and, according to that one news channel that Agnes favours, they surfaced again in Harbin, in the far north of China.

Another challenge that motoring tourists would have to face (which Agnes did *not* mention) was the Allegheny Tunnel. This is where my parents were killed almost thirty years ago, squished to death between a tank truck carrying milk and a semi-trailer loaded to the gills with state-of-the-art running shoes. This tunnel is so long that it is rumoured to have given birth to the Chunnel.

What came as a total surprise was that the sleek black sedan carrying the party of bluebloods sported *Maryland* plates. Maryland is the state directly to the south of us, the state which is shaped like an open-mouthed, bushytailed rat that is fighting off a winged squirrel. Since one has to use one's imagination to picture this in the first place, one should then flip the image over on its head to see what I mean. At any rate, it seemed that Agnes's 'nobs' (as she called them) had minds of their own, and had found a better rate flying into Washington, D.C., which is to our southeast. Who could blame the dears?

'Talk about cheeky,' Agnes muttered as the black stretch limousine rolled to a stop. 'I even sent them my American Automobile Association maps and highlighted the worthwhile overlooks, and noted which rest areas maintained clean lavatories.'

'Not now, Agnes,' I said. 'I forget what you

told me. Do I curtsy to the daughter as well, or just the mother?'

'Neither,' Agnes said. 'They aren't royalty, for heaven's sake, and even if they were, we are not obliged to curtsy because they are not *our* royalty – not anymore, and *more's the pity.*'

'Agnes,' I hissed, and properly at that. 'You're not only an anglophile; you're a monarchist!'

'I am not.'

Nonetheless, Agnes's eyes fairly bulged as she watched my noble guests emerge into the bright sunshine of a perfect Pennsylvania afternoon. Also in attendance were my elderly Amish cook, Freni Hostetler, my hunky husband, Gabe the Babester, and our fourteen-year-old daughter, Alison. Yes, and let me not forget my sweet Little Jacob, although he didn't give a rodent's rear end if our guests were aristocrats.

Thank heavens for the Babester, who had grown up in New York City, and thus was comparatively cosmopolitan. George Clooney looks like my husband on a good day (George's good day, not the other way around), and immediately the two noble women began to swoon over my hunk of burning love (not my words, mind you). In fact, the young man who scrambled out close on their heels seemed to swoon over Gabe as well.

As for the older man, whom I took to be the earl, he could have stepped right out of the pages of a badly written novel. He was wearing an Oscar de la Renta suit, but one that had seen a good deal of wear. He had a long, pale neck, which brought to mind an ostrich, and his grey moustache was so much in need of a trim that it obscured not only his lips but hid his receding chin like overhanging shrubbery. His hair – or was it a hair*piece* – brought to mind our very own Donald Trump, the brash billionaire running for President of these United States. I would say, however, that the *pièce de résistance* was his monocle, a piece of glass as thick as my index finger, which he held in place with the aid of a jewel-encrusted stick.

'Hello,' my Jewish prince said, extending his strong George Clooney hand. 'Welcome to the PennDutch Inn.'

'Yes, very well old chap, tend to the bags,' the man with the monocle muttered.

'Excuse me, old chap,' the Babester said. 'Tend to your own bags, or else have your chauffeur get them.' Gabe kept walking and then, scooping up the hand of the Countess of Grimsley-Snodgrass, brought it swiftly, and smoothly, to his lips. 'Welcome, Aubrey.'

'My, but you Americans are a charming lot,' the Countess of Grimsley-Snodgrass cooed. 'But please, you may call me Lady Grimsley-Snodgrass.'

'Well then, *Lady* Grimsley-Snodgrass,' Gabe said, and flashed a smile that revealed twenty thousand dollars' worth of American dental care. Then he turned to the daughter. 'Welcome, Lady Celia,' he said.

The cheeky girl gave my hunky husband the 'once-over' and made a spontaneous decision to go the familiar route with him. 'It's Cee-Cee,' she said. 'That's spelled with four "e"s, and with a hyphen. You do have hyphens in America, yes?'

I saw that as my cue to jump into the 'meet and greet.' 'Indeed, dear, we do,' I said. 'We have hyphens *and* siphons, and since the last hurricane, both of those species have been breeding with pythons down in the Everglades Swamp in Florida. The pythons, you see, were pets that escaped from their owners. Anyway, the hybrids then conjugated with a few verbs, not to mention alligators, and just last week a tour boat was capsized by a sixteen foot hypesiphopythogator.'

'Ach,' Freni squawked, and fled back into the kitchen.

'Don't mind my mom,' Alison said. 'She's nuts, but you'll get used ta her.'

Lady Celia rolled her eyes. 'I hardly think so.'

'Well, I find your mother to be positively amusing,' Lady Grimsley-Snodgrass said to Alison, and then offered me her fingertips.

I suppose that I should have been flattered by Lady Grimsley-Snodgrass's gesture and kind words, but I was not about to smooch any part of her that might have recently come into contact with any *other* part of her that needed a good scrubbing with soap and water before being allowed at my dinner table. It was time to think fast; in other words, *squeak now, or forever hold my grease*.

I leaned forward and pretended to inspect her nails closely, but I did not touch. 'You may call me *Princess* Magdalena Portulacca Yoder Rosen, if you please,' I said. 'And my, what a beautiful French manicure you have. I must say that of the hundreds of women who have been my guests over the years, your hands rank among the most beautiful.'

Poor Agnes; I had promised to be good and not embarrass her, but I just couldn't help myself. We are supposed to be an egalitarian country – although money always pulls rank, and there are certain family names that are synonymous with 'old money' and 'good breeding.' The truth is, however, that it is human nature to have a higher opinion of oneself than of one's neighbour.

'What Magdalena means,' Agnes said, her face the colour of a cardinal's breast, is that she is descended from a Delaware Indian Princess.'

'Really?' Lady Aubrey said. 'So you have a title then?'

'Indeed. I do have a title, Your Ladyship,' I said. 'I keep it with my insurance policy in the glove compartment of my car.'

'How charming,' Lady Grimsley-Snodgrass said. She was an attractive woman in her mid-forties, who'd maintained a semblance of her girlish figure, and her short, sassy hair was just starting to grey at her left temple. Although I know nothing about fashion or expensive clothing, still, I could tell that Lady Grimsley-Snodgrass's skirt and blouse ensemble was not something I could purchase at the chain stores anywhere within a hundred miles of my rural community.

I flushed. 'OK, so maybe what's in the glove compartment is the title to my car, but I might well have royal Native American ancestors – uh, so to speak. One of my forbears, a little boy named Joseph, was captured by the Delaware

Indians, and after displaying an act of uncommon bravery he was formally adopted into that tribe. Unfortunately, I don't know the lineage of his Indian family.'

'Nonetheless, how fascinating,' Lady Grimsley-Snodgrass said pleasantly.

'If ya think *that's* fascinating,' Alison said, 'then ya oughta get a load of this: Auntie Agnes there, and Auntie Freni – she's the old lady who ran back inside – they're both some kind of double and triple cousins ta my mom. And me too, of course. My mom even says that our family tree is so tangled that she's her own cousin, and that I'm her mother.'

Dear sweet Alison, bless her heart, began snorting with laughter at her own joke, thereby inadvertently proving that we were related.

I would have died of embarrassment then, but I didn't have my funeral hymns picked out yet. And anyway, everyone burst out laughing, except for Lady Celia.

'Oh, Mother,' she said, 'that silly child is putting you on.'

'There, there, Celia,' the moustachioed Lord Grimsley-Snodgrass muttered, 'be a good girl, will you, and rouse your other brother from his laborious slumbers.'

'Other brother?' the Babester asked, and craned his neck in a futile attempt at peering into the darkened windows.

'My twin,' said the first young man. He thrust a cluster of fingers at me, forcing them upon me. The ding-dang things felt, and smelled, like over-boiled asparagus. 'I am merely *Mr* Sebastian, but

32

the spoiled one still in the motor car, drooling upon the soft leather seat is my older brother by two minutes. *That* one is Lord Rupert, the Viscount Swithamiens.'

'Wait a minute,' the Babester said, 'if your father is an earl, how come your brother is a viscount?'

'Oh, father, this is *sooo* tedious,' said Lady Celia, who still hadn't budged an inch to retrieve her sleeping brother. 'Must we explain everything to these – well, to these Americans? You know that they will never understand.'

'I think we must, dear,' Lady Grimsley-Snodgrass said. 'The least we can do is be polite, and frankly, I don't think most Brits understand the peerage rankings either.'

Lady Celia let loose with a sigh that could blow the spots off a Dalmatian. I have often read that music is the international language; that statement, of course, became a falsehood with that gobbledygook called 'rap.' I submit that the true international language is the insouciant sounds and gestures of petulant adolescents, even ones who are in their early adolescence.

'Mind your mother, dear,' I said in a fair imitation of Lady Grimsley-Snodgrass's delightful accent. 'We haven't got all day. Soon it will be teatime, and then dinner, and after that your first big hunt.'

But it was too late; Lady Celia had planted her heels into my gravel walkway and crossed her arms defiantly. Her lower lip was stuck out so far that a near-sighted pigeon might have mistaken it for a perch.

'*You* can't tell me what to do,' she said. 'You're only an innkeeper.'

'And you, dear,' I said evenly, 'don't get to tell me what it is that I *can't* do; you're only a child.'

'Bravo,' said Lady Grimsley-Snodgrass.

'Mother!' Lady Celia said as she stomped a ridiculous excuse for a shoe. It was something Julius Caesar might have worn home from a battle.

Unfortunately, I ran with what I thought was parental encouragement. 'Besides,' I said, 'you're a foreigner.'

My guests gasped in unison, but given that they were English, and aristocrats in particular, their combined sound was scarcely more audible than a bee's burp. To my surprise, it was Lord Grimsley-Snodgrass who seemed the most put out by my accusation.

'Why, that's practically racist,' he roared. 'An Englishman *cannot* be a foreigner; that is simply impossible.'

I tried to scoff softly, but *that* was simply impossible. Instead I whinnied like a mare in heat. 'Oh, come on,' I said. 'Surely you jest.'

'Lord Grimsley-Snodgrass jests with no one,' His Pomposity had the nerve to say. 'Least of all a tavern maid.'

Moi? A tavern maid? The maid part was pure flattery, given that I was thirty, now that thirty was supposed to be the new fifty – or was it the other way around? Never mind; the thing is I have never in all my born days put as much as one toe over the line that is the threshold of a bar, pub, tavern, 'watering hole,' or any other place that might serve alcoholic beverages.

We Mennonites believe that drinking alcohol leads to sin. I have a personal reason for not imbibing. To quote the Bible, '*wine is a mocker.*' Believe me, anyone who was born with a face that looks like that of a Kentucky Derby Winner has been mocked enough without having some fermented grapes adding to the torment. Now where was I? Oh, yes, I was about to remind the snobbish nobs which side of the pond they were on.

First, I inflated my scrawny chest as far as it would go. 'Look here, Lord Such-and-Such. You lost the Revolutionary War, the one that we began in seventeen seventy-six. We celebrate our independence from Britain every July the fourth. That makes *you* people the foreigners – we share a special kinship, to be sure, but *you* are still on *foreign* soil. Get it? And by the way, this is an inn, not a tavern. We don't serve booze. The strongest drink you'll get is buttermilk.'

'Stuff and nonsense,' Lord Grimsley-Snodgrass huffed. 'An Englishman is *never* foreign, no matter where he is. He is *English*, for heaven's sake. It is the *rest* of the world that is foreign. Don't *you* get it?'

'I dare say that Americans have a right to feel at home in their own country,' Lady Grimsley-Snodgrass said, smiling wanly. 'Now then, please have someone show us to our suite of rooms so that we might have a little rest before it is time to dress for dinner.'

I returned her wan smile with a sweet one.

'*Garçon,*' I said and snapped my fingers. '*Allez, Pierre!*' When nothing happened, I shook my head and shrugged my shoulders. 'It is so hard to get good help these days, isn't it?'

Somehow the earl, who sounded quite bored, managed to focus both his eyes behind his monocle. 'Rally, my dear,' he said, 'your quips aren't in the least bit amusing. Perhaps they lose something in translation.'

My daughter Alison poked me. 'Mom, are we going to have a rally like he says? What kind of rally, and how come no one told me?'

'He can't pronounce the word "really," dear.'

'And another thing, Mom. How come Lord Grimsley-Snotgrass is wearing a Donald Trump wig? He ain't allowed to vote, is he?'

'That is *Snod*grass with a "*d*,"' His Lordship said through teeth clenched so tightly that he might well have been able to bite a steel cable in two – had he just happened to have one in his mouth at the moment. This, of course, was something that rarely happened.

'Ya sure about the "d"?' Alison said. 'Because, if ya are, then it don't make no sense. Like, what is Snodgrass supposed ta mean?'

'You are a very rude child,' Lord Grimsley-Snodgrass said.

'Hey, I ain't no child,' Alison said. 'I'm a rising eighth-grader at Hernia Junior High. And it ain't none of your business, but I'm officially a woman now, so there!'

'*You?* A woman?'

'Yes, *me* a woman. Lots of girls in my grade had visits from Mrs Monthly over the summer.'

36

'Bother,' said Lord Grimsley-Snodgrass, 'we must have a translator who speaks this colonial gibberish. Where is Viscount Rupert? Didn't he once date an American harlot?'

Lady Grimsley-Snodgrass placed a gloved hand gently on her husband's arm. 'She was a *starlet*, not a *harlot*, darling.'

'Oh, a rose by any other name,' he sniffed. 'Somebody get the viscount,' he ordered.

'*I'll* get His Lordship,' said Mr Sebastian, and practically stomped back to the limousine.

'Don't trip on your lower lip, Sebastian,' his father called after him.

'And tell your chauffeur to start unloading,' the Babester added.

'We don't have a chauffeur,' said Lord Grimsley-Snodgrass. 'One would have thought that one came with the car, but apparently that is not the way it works when you hire an automobile in this country. Upon signing the rental agreement, all one gets are the keys and a useless map.'

'Why was the map useless?' Gabe asked. 'Wasn't it for the State of Pennsylvania?'

'Well I suppose it was, but what good is that when the map unfolds to just under a meter, and your damn state is so big. The distances here are simply outrageous. Why, I wager that Pennsylvania alone is as large as England.'

I am ashamed to say that I felt my pigeon chest puff with pride. 'Almost. Actually, Pennsylvania is smaller, but only by ten percent.'

Lord Grimsley-Snodgrass wagged a finger at each of us in turn. 'What utter hubris you

Americans possess. Grabbing great fistfuls of land like greedy pups at their mother's teats—'

'Ahem,' I said. 'For one thing, there are children present; for another thing, it was you English who initially did the grabbing in your mixed metaphor.'

Agnes, who had hitherto been as silent a partner to me as the Colossus of Rhodes, and every bit as useful, sputtered to life like a long-neglected tractor. 'Perhaps we should begin our tour of this *genuine* reproduction of an eighteenth-century Amish farmhouse. *Condor Nest Travel* magazine calls it "an experience you won't forget, at a price you can't afford."'

'Indeed,' said Lady Grimsley-Snodgrass, 'it was that last bit that caught my eye. People in our set never inquire about prices. We find it so terribly gauche, don't you think?'

'Oh, teh-blee,' I said.

Agnes shot me a look that could have devilled raw eggs. 'Tally ho, pip pip and all that sort of rot,' she chirped, drawing on her knowledge of old Hollywood depictions of Briticisms. She even made the shocking mistake of grabbing Lord Touch-Me-Not's elbow. His Lordship recoiled like cellophane placed next to a candle.

'I am not an invalid,' he growled. 'I lost one eye during the war but everything else works as it should. By this time tomorrow I'll be showing *you* around this place. Then all your secrets will be revealed.'

'Goody,' Alison cried. 'Then finally I'll get to see what's in the elevator.'

'Oh, Peregrine,' Lady Grimsley-Snodgrass said

38

with a purr and a wink, 'you're too much.' Then she turned to Alison. 'Whatever do you mean, dear?'

'Well, lady,' Alison said, 'it's like this: a long time ago this tourist from Tokyo got stuck in our rinky-dinky elevator, like halfway between the floors, but nobody noticed for like three days on account of some holiday or somethin' going on, and then there was this terrible smell – kinda like a dead rat in the wall, only a whole lot worse, so these men came in with power tools, cut through the bottom of the elevator, and do you know what they found?'

'What?' Aubrey said breathlessly.

'Nothing! Leastways there was nobody in it – only a lady's purse.'

'No way!' Lady Celia said, but her eyes were as big as basketball hoops.

'Oh, it's true,' I said. 'Go on, Alison, tell her the rest of the story.'

Alison beamed. 'Well, the police – even the FBI – searched everywhere for this lady. They lifted dogs up into the elevator, they looked *everywhere*, but they never did find her. But sometimes when you're going down them impossibly steep stairs that wind around the elevator, ya can hear pounding coming from the wall and a woman crying.'

'Darling, did you hear that?' Lady Grimsley-Snodgrass said to her husband.

There followed a muffled response, and I got the feeling that Her Ladyship might have erred by voicing an endearment in front of us commoners. She turned quickly to me, her

English skin already the colour of an uncooked brisket.

'We Brits do love our ghosts,' she hastened to assure me. 'Every castle and manor house in the realm is haunted. In our own home, Gloomsburythorpe, we have three documented and named ghosts, and two in the "quite possible" category.'

Now this was a woman after my own heart. Clearly we were simpatico. Had she been a sensible American, I could pinpoint this as the day that a lifelong friendship had taken root.

'I have a friend,' I confessed, 'who refers to ghosts as *Apparition* Americans.'

Lady Grimsley-Snodgrass threw back her well-bred head and laughed graciously. 'Charming! You Americans have such a way with words.'

'*Rally?*'

Startled, I looked over to see an exact copy of Mr Sebastian sauntering towards us from the limousine. That is to say, his features and build were the same but he was wearing a grey flannel sports jacket, a navy ascot and a red leather driving cap pulled cockily down over one eye as one might see in a magazine ad. Perhaps they had a chauffeur after all.

'Swithamiens,' said Lady Grimsley-Snodgrass to the newcomer, 'I see that you have roused yourself, but now, where is your brother?'

'He saw a bright yellow bird, Mother, and went charging after the poor creature. You know how he is about birds.'

'Forgive me,' Lady Grimsley-Snodgrass said, acknowledging all of us with a slight dip of her noble head. 'I'd like to introduce my firstborn by two minutes, Rupert, the Viscount Swithamiens.' For the record what she actually said was 'Vee-cun Swify,' in that curious British tradition of omitting half the sounds in one's surname and then throwing in a couple of new ones, just to throw off the Devil, lest He be nosing around one's genealogical record in hopes of stealing one's errant progeny.

'How delightful,' I said. 'I just love irony, don't you? Well then, let us all troop into my miniscule office and register. You sure don't want to lose your places for the hunt tonight.'

I would have thought that as a good Christian woman, Agnes would keep her fingernails trimmed to a modest length, but *au contraire*, she maintained the claws of a heathen. As my guests began to file past, Agnes pinched an inch of subcutaneous fat above my hip and kept pinching until her two poisonous blades of keratin practically met.

'Mags,' she hissed, 'why are you speaking so loud? They may be foreigners but they speak *English*.'

'Maybe,' I conceded, 'but they speak *British* English, not regular, *real* English like God intended.'

'Pshaw,' Agnes said. 'Why, that's just the silliest thing that I ever heard.'

'I think *pshaw* is the silliest thing that I ever heard, except maybe for *psalm*, which should be pronounced *p-salm*, and nobody seems to know why it's not. Look, Agnes, you're the worldly woman who watches television all the time. Think

41

back to your favourite TV program when you were a girl. What was it?'

'*I Love Lucy.*'

'Was it in British or in proper English?'

'Point taken,' Agnes said, and so we filed into the PennDutch on the heels of a heap of trouble.

Four

Our blue-blooded guests were surprisingly coop-
erative and signed up for every available activity,
including church. While we were still in my
miniscule office, however, concluding our business, Lady Celia and Alison wandered off into
the sitting room. Upon entering they immediately
began screaming bloody murder.

Blue blood and bumpkin alike, we raced to the
rescue, and whereas the others were most certainly
confused by what they saw, I understood the
situation at once. For there, in her favourite,
century-old, straight-back rocking chair, sat the
rigid figure of my long-dead Granny Yoder. It
was obvious to me that Lady Celia could see
Granny, and Granny could see the girl. Alison,
on the other hand, has had to take Granny's ghost,
along with germs and Santa Claus, all on good
faith.

Thank heavens I got to Lady Celia first. 'She's
harmless,' I said quickly.

'Boogers, I am,' Granny said.

'You see,' I said. 'She can't even swear right
in British.'

'But I saw her walk through that wall. She's a
ghost, I'm telling you; a *real* ghost.'

'But I was under the impression that you had
ghosts at Gloomandoombucktoothonthemoors,
dear.'

'Yes, but – but this one is *real*. Look!' In her hysteria, Lady Celia sounded almost as though she were an American.

Music will do that too, you know – that is, make one sound like an American. Of course, that doesn't surprise me; I should think it would be difficult to sing whilst shaping one's mouth to fit the strange sounds of those British brogues. Why, even the Beatles sang in American. I am told that Adele does too. And as for hymns – you can take Granny Yoder's word for it – the angels sing in American English. So of that I have no doubt.

Now, where was I? Oh, yes, the littler Lady had seen a ghost. She really had; Granny Yoder is a real, live, Apparition American – except that she's *dead*. However, until Lady Celia had screamed like a Highland banshee, no one else had ever been able to see her. Not even my sister's mangy mongrel, Shnookums, had ever sensed the presence of another spirit at the PennDutch. This revelation, then, was so exciting to me that I may have gotten a little carried away.

'Granny,' I cried, 'you mind your manners and say "hello." This young lady – and I mean Lady with a capital "L," has come all the way over from the motherland for a visit.'

'Stuff and nonsense,' said Granny. 'It isn't *my* motherland. I was born right here, in this very room. And *our* people came from Switzerland – every last one of them.'

'Actually, you weren't born in this *very* room, Granny, because the original farmhouse was blown to smithereens by a tornado and I had to rebuild it. Remember?'

'Don't be silly, child,' Granny said. 'I was already dead by then. How could I remember?

'Because the tornado picked me up, carried me out into the north pasture and planted me face down in a cow pie. I had to sleep in my barn that night. You paid me a visit and told me that I'd never looked prettier than I did then with cow dung on my face.'

'What the devil is a cow pie?' said my new best friend, the Lady Grimsley-Snodgrass.

The parlour was not built to host a crowd and it was now filled to capacity. Therefore I was understandably annoyed when Agnes piped up with what was to be *my* clever retort.

'Magdalena keeps two Holstein cows, Matilda and Gertrude, which she will give you the privilege of milking for the small fee of only one hundred American dollars. Anyway, her cows are grass-fed, which is why they produce such high quality, hormone-free milk. But as you all know, what goes in . . . Well, let's just say that the *end* product is cow pies.'

Believe me when I say that I am not judging harshly, merely stating the facts when I relate that the Viscount Swithamiens had a laugh that would have appealed to a female donkey in heat. Why, in that small, crowded and overheated room, even I, who was just beginning 'the change' and prone to strange mood swings, felt something akin to a primal urge to jump the young man's bones. I say 'akin,' lest one infer from the word 'primal' that I believe in evolution, which I cannot, alas.

'Stop with that bloody braying,' I hollered above the din.

45

Not only did the braying stop immediately, the Brits stopped breathing.

'Now you've done it,' Agnes said. 'I warned you about *that* word.'

'What's wrong with the word "blood"?' Alison said. 'We all have it. I got a nosebleed at camp when it got hit by a tennis ball. And that's how Daddy likes his steaks, isn't it? Bloody.'

'He likes them *rare*, dear.'

'You see, darling girl,' Agnes said, 'it's a cultural thing.' Sweet woman that she is, Agnes possesses a tin ear. She'd adopted an accent so affected and so supposedly posh that even palace officials wouldn't recognize her words as belonging to an Indo-European language. For all they knew, she could have been speaking a dialect from the highlands of Papua New Guinea while chewing on a mouthful of betel nuts.

'Mom, what did she say?' Alison asked, proving my point.

I crossed my fingers so as not to tell a lie. 'She said that there are free refreshments in the dining room – but for the next half hour only. After that the guests should collect their keys and start toting their luggage up my impossibly steep stairs. That's good for at least two hours, which will take them all the way up to dinnertime.'

'That's not what she said,' Alison whined.

'Well, that's what she *should* have said. Also, folks, don't be counting on any help from us: Agnes, bless her heart, is too portly to be a porter, Alison is still growing her girl parts and my husband is susceptible to hernias. As for *moi*, have you ever seen such long and gangly limbs on a primate that is neither a gibbon nor an orangutan? Not that we're remotely related, mind you, for the Good Lord spoke them into being out of nothing, whereas we humans were created out of clay.'

'Does that make us dirt bags, then?' the impudent viscount said.

'Well I never!' Agnes said. 'Magdalena,' she whispered, 'I am beside myself with embarrassment.'

There wasn't enough space in that crowded room for a woman her size to be beside herself in embarrassment.

'That's all right, Agnes,' I said. 'I can handle this. You, sir,' I said to the viscount, 'undoubtedly find it strange that we Americans are so religious, given that you Europeans have all but abandoned organized religion. I have heard that your churches are empty. I assure you, though, that on that glorious day when the trumpet of the Lord shall sound and time shall be no more, you will be singing a different tune. And don't you be shaking your noble noggin, and snickering like that, because when the fires of Hell—'

'Mags,' the Babester said gently, 'can you move it along, please?'

Now Granny Yoder snickered. 'A woman who has been through the "curse" is a woman with a cause,' she quipped. Maybe she had something there. After all, Margaret Thatcher, Hillary Clinton, Angela Merkel . . . they all seemed to be women beyond their days of child-bearing.

I shook my head to clear it of cobwebs. 'Now, where was I?'

47

'You were giving him hell,' Alison said.

I smiled wanly at her double entendre. 'That too. But I was enjoining all to adjourn to the dining room, or else to check in. Mr and Mrs Grimsley-Snodgrass, I am assigning you rooms three and four, on account of Agnes tells me that even you *pseudo*-royals prefer separate quarters. These rooms have an adjoining door, should you desire to exercise your base needs, Mr Grimsley-Snodgrass—'

'*Lord* Grimsley-Snodgrass to you, Mrs—' said Lord Grimsley-Snodgrass.

'No can do, *Mister* Grimsley-Snodgrass,' I said. 'There is only one *Lord*, and his name is Jesus Christ. That is *not* the name printed in your passport.'

'Cheeky woman,' Lord Grimsley-Snodgrass muttered into his moustache.

'Do you know what?' Lady Grimsley-Snodgrass said. 'I have changed my mind again. I have decided that you may call me by my Christian name after all.'

'Fabulous,' I said, beaming. 'What is it?'

'Aubrey, of course. *That's* in my passport.'

'Aubrey is a *biblical* name?'

Her Ladyship's delicate English skin dimpled as she contemplated my question. 'I'm afraid I don't see how your question is relevant,' she said at last.

'Well, you know,' I said, 'the Bible – Christian – in some circles the two words kind of go together.'

'*Oh*,' she said. 'Like that. I've often wondered why it was called a christening gown. Well, in that case I'm sure that Aubrey was the name of a saint. Yes, I remember now, Saint Aubrey: she was the patron saint of girls with invalid mothers. My mother had polio, you see.'

'How awful,' I said.

'Mother,' said the viscount, 'does her Bible forbid lying as well?'

'Forsooth, you impudent youth,' I said, and gave him a righteous scowl. Perhaps it wasn't my place to chastise him, but he was *in* my place, and one of the big Ten Commandments is that one should honour one's parents. My house; my rules.

Aubrey's aristocratic features turned a lovely shade of pink, quite reminiscent of a pregnant sheep's udder. 'I was only trying to be polite by playing along. Rally, Rupert, why must you always correct Mother?' She turned to me. 'I never paid attention in church school and haven't the foggiest knowledge of saints – although we sometimes spend Christmas in St Tropez – and my mother is perfectly healthy.'

'Ta da!' said Rupert.

'Listen, dear,' I said, 'if you were *my* son—'

'Which he is *not*,' the Babester said.

Rupert twisted his lips into a smirk which even Satan could envy. Mercifully – for him – he said nothing.

'But he taxes my Christian soul,' I wailed.

I don't know what I would have done had not my dear, dear Jewish husband, Dr Gabriel Rosen, aka the Babester, put his arm firmly around my shoulder and whispered his wintergreen-scented breath in my ear. It was better than being held in my mother's arms, as hers were bony, her bosom non-existent and her mood slightly more pleasant than a disturbed hornet's nest.

'Remember that they're your guests,' he said so softly that even my guardian angel had to strain in order to hear. 'And they're foreigners to boot. It's not *their* fault that they're *heathens* and that they can't speak proper English. Just be grateful if they turn out to be housebroken. You did put that on your questionnaire, didn't you?'

'I beg your pardon, sir,' the earl growled. 'We are Englishmen, *not* French! I may have just one good eye but my ears have compensated for my visual impairment. You would be well-advised to remember that.'

My hero squared his broad shoulders. 'Then perhaps you should inform your son that in this house we show our elders respect.'

'Harrumph,' the earl said.

'Hooray,' I said. 'Now where were we – before we got side-tracked by all this unnecessary unpleasantness? Oh, yes, we were working out the matter of names.' I turned to the youngest and fairest of us all. 'So, what do you wish to be called, Miss Grimsley-Snodgrass?'

'If we *have* to go common,' Lady Celia said with a sigh and a slump, 'then remember to call me Cee-Cee.'

'Will do, dear. By the way, you get room six, which has the best view. If you lean way out the window – but take care to hang on to the shutter super tight, so that you don't fall – you can see Stucky Ridge. Not only that, but the part that

50

you can see is Lover's Leap, where legend has it that an Indian maiden leaped to her death along with her white colonial boyfriend. Their love was, of course, forbidden in the year 1768. The settler was my great, great, great, great, great-grandfather, Elias Yoder.'

'Say what?' *Mister* Grimsley-Snodgrass said. 'He was probably some stowaway vagrant from the sewers of London.'

'He was a Swiss farmer,' I said. 'His Christian name was actually Christian, unlike yours, which is Peregrine. Nevertheless, in the spirit of Christian charity, I believe that I shall call you just plain Peregrine. After all, if you were to fall down my impossibly steep stairs, and I needed to call for outside help, it would be much quicker to say: "Help, Peregrine has fallen and he can't get up," than it would be to explain that you were an English nobleman who has taken for himself a title that belongs only to the Lord God Himself, for you see, dear, everyone on our volunteer rescue squad is either a devout Christian or recently descended from one, and will have no truck with such highfalutin ways, although they all own trucks, so go figure.'

'Magdalena,' said Aubrey softly, calling me by name for the first time, 'do they teach grammar in American schools?'

'Of course!'

'Hmm. But do they teach one how to diagram sentences?' Aubrey said.

'Man, them English schools must be somethin' else!' Alison said. 'We learnt about them diagrams in sex education class, but we didn't learn nothin'

51

about putting them into sentences. You sure that you got them facts right, Auntie Aubrey?'

There were snickers all around, and not the delicious American kind, which is a brand of candy bar. A good deal of exception was taken, along with some umbrage.

'My mother is *not* your auntie!' The viscount was obviously quite vexed by my presumptive daughter's claim to kinship.

Aubrey reached out and pulled Alison into a motherly embrace which, I must admit, I thought very American of her. 'You must forgive my son, dear,' she said. 'He is a bit full of himself, I'm afraid. On account of his rude behaviour, I am giving all of you permission – seeing as we are on American soil, anyway – to call my first born by his Christian name: Rupert. And I am quite sure that Rupert comes straight out of the Bible.'

Oy vay! If only Alison would learn when to put a sock in it – I mean that metaphorically, of course.

'No way, Auntie Aubrey,' she said. 'Did you know that Adam was the very first man to have sex?'

God Save the Queen, and God bless Aubrey, who turned the colour of raw chicken livers. But just as any true Brit would under those circumstances, she remained calm and carried on. Is it any wonder that we Americans are such Anglophiles?

'Well then,' she said, 'I suppose we should all be glad, because that is how we got here. So, be a dear and show me to the dining room. Then after I've taken my tea, you can lead me up your mother's impossibly steep stairs. But remember, you're not to tote any of my bags on account of you're still growing your important lady parts; I shall carry my bags by myself, rather like a Sherpa climbing Mount Everest.'

'It's a deal,' Alison said.

'The dead woman is at the top of the elevator car,' Cee-Cee said.

The room was instantly so silent that I could hear dust motes settling on drapes three yards away. '*Excuse* me?' I said. 'Say that again.'

'Your Granny Yoder just told me what happened to that missing Japanese tourist. She is on top of the lift car.'

Every hair on my body stood on end, which was rather indecent of them, if you ask me. At least the hair on my head behaved, thanks to the five pounds of hairpins I use to keep my coiled braids in place.

'That is just plain ridiculous!' I said. 'There is only a two-inch gap – at most – between the elevator car and the ceiling. Even a very shallow person, such as your brother, couldn't possibly fit between the two. Yoko-san was a petite woman but she wasn't two-dimensional.'

Cee-Cee could still see Granny Yoder's withered lips, whereas by then I had already stepped out of the parlour. 'Ma'am, your granny says to tell you that when the elevator was halfway between floors, somebody stopped it, forced open the upper doors and then pushed the Japanese lady out on to the roof of the elevator car.'

I don't mind sharing that this information stunned me. It sounded so true that I could *feel*

53

it in my DNA. This phenomenon has only happened to me a couple of times, like when I've read certain scripture verses, or once years ago when Agnes forced me to watch an *Oprah* show with her. My point is that I needed no more convincing; what I needed was a game plan for how to proceed. That's me, your typical Magdalena Yoder Rosen, lurching from crisis to crisis but never waiting for as much as a minute before casting about for Plan B or Plans C and D.

Alison was the first to break the stunned silence. 'Ya mean there's been a rotting dead lady in there all this time and I ain't had a chance ta see her? Man, how is that fair? All the kids at school can talk about is zombies, and here I got me a real live one but it don't do me no good!'

Cee-Cee gave Alison a light, playful push. 'You Americans are a fun lot; a real *live* zombie! Jolly good, that.'

'Yeah?' my daughter said. 'Because I'm thinking how cool it woulda been if we'd got to her in time to watch her eyeballs fall out, like in that insurance commercial on TV. Then we coulda sold the video to YouTube or someplace like that and made us, like, a gazillion bucks. I know that you're already super rich and everything, being a novelty and all, but I read someplace that ya can't be too rich or too single.'

'Cheers,' Rupert said. 'I'll drink to that.'

'The actual quote is too rich or too *thin*,' Agnes said through pursed lips, 'and if you ask me, one certainly *can* be too thin. If you don't believe me, just page through any beauty magazine the next time you get your hair done. All the models shown are one lettuce leaf away from utter starvation. Someone with murder on his mind wouldn't have any trouble stuffing one of them through the gap between your elevator doors, Magdalena.'

'Was that comment necessary?' the Babester said in my defence.

Bless my husband's heart. I did, however, understand where Agnes was coming from. The truth is that the last time the poor dear tried to ride in my rickety contraption she couldn't squeeze through the elevator doors and had to take my impossibly steep stairs. My friend was barely able to clear the stairwell, and the journey of eighteen steps took her over an hour, but due to the circular nature of both friend and stairs, had she fallen she would not have travelled far before becoming safely wedged by one of my attractively painted walls.

'Well, dears,' I said generously, 'let us bid haste, for we have much to do before tonight's fun and games begin.'

'Ah, yes, hunting for the fearsome Hernia *snipe*,' sniped Rupert as he rubbed his smooth aristocratic hands in mock anticipation.

Alison, a veteran snipe hunter, chortled in sheer delight, but I quickly stifled her with a gentle nudge on her behind by one of my bony knees.

I had to hand it to Agnes; so far it was a lot more fun dealing with five foreign fops than any number of 'ugly' Americans. Truth be told, they really weren't that foppish, except for the matter of toting their titles across the border, but fortunately lovely Aubrey had made short shrift of that. The one to watch closely was the uppity Rupert, who was reluctant to close the door on being a nob – even just for a few days.

As for the other twin, Sebastian, the hormone half of the identical duo – he would either show up in time for the evening's escapade or he wouldn't. Frankly, when one has lived through as much of life's ups and downs as I have, and solved case after case of murder and mayhem, whether or not someone else's adult son stays out all night is very low on one's list of priorities.

Just as long as no one died on tonight's hunt, that would be fine with me.

Five

HOW TO MAKE THE PERFECT CUP OF TEA

When boiling the kettle, always use freshly drawn cold water. This helps the flavour develop.

Warm the teapot in advance by swirling a small amount of boiled water in it before discarding.

Insert one teaspoon of loose tea per person, and one extra teaspoonful for the pot.

Allow the tea to brew in the teapot for six minutes before serving.

Ideally, the tea should be drunk from a porcelain teacup. (Just as fine wine may not live up to its full potential when drunk from a mug, the same can be said of fine teas.)

Always pour in the tea before the milk.

Six

Agnes stayed over for 'tea' and Saturday night supper. In addition to the two cows, we at the PennDutch are home to an old grey mare named Becky, fifteen laying hens, a rooster named Chanticleer, a flock of rock doves, eight Indian runners (a breed of duck), six guinea fowl, four Chinese geese and a pot-belly pig named Cindy. In addition to those we have a multitude of bass, bluegill and turtles in our newly built pond. Many of these critters we acquired at the urging of spouse and eldest child, both of whom require a bit of care themselves. Simply put, we no longer serve fancy-schmancy dinners anymore.

It was Agnes's intent to give our English visitors a bit of a culture shock, or, as she put it so eloquently: 'a slice of ordinary American life.' Therefore supper was hot dogs and buns (along with condiments), baked beans (without toast!), tossed salad (choice of three dressings), crisps, and for the pudding, homemade peach ice cream using milk from my very own cows.

I don't permit alcoholic beverages on my farm, and state this clearly in my advertisements. Nonetheless, I was exceedingly grateful that the issue was never raised. My guests had to quench their thirst with 'sky juice' (water), 'cow juice' (milk), or orange juice (juice from oranges, in case one needed to ask).

58

Agnes had warned me to anticipate some resistance, not only to my ban on alcohol, but to the fact that I assigned seating and said grace before the meal. The truth is these supposedly well-bred folks were, for the most part, really well-behaved table guests. Perhaps food was their motivation, but I didn't really care. What mattered to me were the results. Even when I fell short of my goal, they didn't seem to mind.

'Ach,' I said at one point, 'I forgot to make toast.'

'Why do we need toast, Magdalena,' lovely Aubrey said, 'when you've supplied these wonderful buns?'

'To put your beans on, dear,' I said.

Alison dropped her fork with a clatter. 'Beans, beans,' she intoned, 'the magical fruit. The more you eat, the more you toot.'

There followed a moment of awkward silence, and then Sebastian, who had shown up at dinner, instead of his rather arrogant brother, clapped vigorously with his strong, manly hands. 'Jolly good performance,' he said. 'How heart-warming it is to hear that flatulence is practiced on both sides of the Atlantic.'

'How disgusting,' Agnes sniffed. 'Shame on you, Alison. You may excuse yourself from the table.'

'Huh?' Gabe said. In his defence, he was busy feeding his male offspring. It is a job that he thoroughly enjoys, and which occupies much of his attention. The Little Bruiser, aka Little Jacob, is a miniature version of his father. As I've stated before, I *don't* believe in evolution, or genetics, but *if* I did, I would venture to say that one of

59

the reasons parents love their children so much is because they are loving little versions of themselves. This is evolution's way of perpetuating the human race.

'Hold your horses, missy,' I hissed, wagging my finger like the tail of a happy dog – except that I wasn't happy, and I was wagging it at Agnes and not my Alison. '*You*, best friend though you are, have no right to discipline *my* daughter.'

Alison, who had been rightly embarrassed by Agnes's chastisement of her, was now smirking. I knew that my daughter was thrilled that I was taking her side 'for a change,' and in front of all of Auntie Agnes's 'fancy guests.' 'Take *that*, Auntie Agnes,' is probably what Alison *wanted* to say, instead of just smirking, but even at her young age, she has begun to learn the art of compromise. *Remember your goal* – three words to live by that Gabe had been trying to drill through her thick, but still somewhat permeable, skull. In this case, Alison's goal was undoubtedly not to get grounded.

'As for you, young lady,' I said to Alison, 'since you are so fond of poetry, you would be wise to remember the following ditty: "There's nothing like smirking to bring on the irking."'

There followed another awkward silence. Thank heavens my sweetheart, the Babester, my Gabe, took a break from baby-feeding long enough to start the conversation going again. This time he directed a question to Sebastian.

'Tell me, young man,' he said but in an awful imitation English accent, 'how you *rally* feel

60

about being born without a title? I mean, your twin *brothah* is *lahd* such and such now, but when your *fathah* dies, than he will become the next *oil*. Doesn't it *bothah* you that you will always be just plain Mr Sebastian?'

At that the young man's noble father, the '*oil*' in question, cleared his throat in a not-so-genteel way. It was obvious that he wished to formally interject an opinion. In the old days, I suspect, he might have had someone, such as a footman, blow a bugle before such a forthcoming announcement.

'I shouldn't suppose it bothers Sebastian at all,' he said. 'This is how it has always been done, so this is how it is; we don't question such things. Why, we scarcely give these silly matters a thought at all.'

'Bravo, Papa,' Cee-Cee said.

'Actually, Papa, I *do* mind, rather,' Sebastian said. He looked down at his plate. 'After all, that silly fool is only two minutes' older than me, and that is only because he is the one whom the surgeon removed from Mother's tummy first. Isn't that right, Mother?'

'Yes, well, it was my womb, to be precise,' Aubrey said.

Sebastian looked at me as if asking for *my* support. 'Miss Yoder, my brother and I were delivered by Caesarean section, you see. He was taken out first because he was the smallest and the weakest, and therefore the one most at risk. Do you know that he didn't even show up on the ultrasound because his heart was positioned directly under mine?'

61

'That is quite true,' Aubrey said. 'That has happened more often than you might think. We went to hospital expecting one infant and came home with twins.'

'So anyway,' Sebastian said, 'the entire time that mother was pregnant, it was *my* heart that was seen beating on the ultrasound screen. *I* was the heir whom they both named and planned for. It was only when some wretched surgeon reached into my mother's belly—'

'Sebastian!' Peregrine snapped behind his moustache, 'that will be quite enough.'

'But Papa—'

Peregrine looked at me accusingly. 'Do you see what that husband of yours has started with that ridiculous and irrelevant question of his?'

I puckered my brow as I shook my head. 'No. Frankly, dear, I can't see that far, given that it was such a small thing, and he is all the way down at the other end of the table. Perhaps you'd care to ask *him*.'

'Ooh,' Cee-Cee cautioned as she sucked up half the room's oxygen – or enough, at least, to cause the drapes to sway.

Peregrine stood abruptly, pushing his chair over backwards as he rose. 'What I would like is for you to bring my supper up to my room on a tray.'

'What a lovely idea,' I said, clasping my hands together. 'Too bad it's against the rules.'

'The *rules*?' Peregrine roared. 'Madam, surely you jest!'

'Jest not, lest it lead to jousting,' I said solemnly. 'Be forewarned that I never joke about any of my rules. While I am a pacifist, born and bred, there have been times when a rolling pin, or a broom handle, has found its way into my hands with me fully intending to use it.' It would have been self-defeating to point out that those were the times that I intended to either roll out a pie crust or to sweep the floor. However, once, while daydreaming, I may even have swept the floor with a pie crust dangling from the end of my broom handle. There should be limits to self-disclosure, don't you think?

'*What* rules?' Lord Huff and Puff was getting quite impatient with me.

I arranged my lips in what approximated, or so I hoped, a placid smile. 'I don't allow food to be taken upstairs. You see, here in the colonies we are plagued by all manner of vermin, such as have been long since eradicated on your side of the pond. Just the other day I saw a cockroach as large as a Volkswagen Beetle. It was trying to wrestle a mattress out of room six, on account of some woman tourist had sneaked a bag of chocolate bars into her room and then accidently sat on one, thereby mashing it into the bed.'

All traces of belligerence melted from Peregrine's face. It was like watching a soufflé fall when the oven door has been slammed. Unfortunately, this caused his moustache to droop further, making it even more difficult to understand his hoity-toity accent. Can I then be blamed for tuning out a lot of what he said? Based on what the Babester filled me in on later, what follows is a somewhat faithful rendition – I say only 'somewhat,' because, alas, I don't always pay strict attention when the Babester is speaking either. One might say that I have a short attention span.

'Frankly,' he said, 'you are one fine specimen of a woman: good teeth, long limbs, strong withers. I take my membership in the House of Lords quite seriously, you know; I believe in the principle of *Noblesse Oblige*. In all honestly, it has been a *long* time since I've been privileged to encounter a spokeswoman both as articulate and – dare I say – imaginative as you in either chamber of government. You, madam, are an honour to your sex.' With the last remark he doffed an imaginary top hat.

I had nothing that I wished to doff. *Au contraire*, I donned my serviette by draping it over my heaving yet oddly concave chest. There are times – perhaps such as this – when I might do well to listen carefully to the other person rather than jump to conclusions based on one or two key words.

'Why you cheeky, uh, bowl of bouillabaisse,' I said. 'My sex life is none of your business.' I *attempted* a one-eyed wink at the Babester. 'And although it is off limits,' I continued, 'in the spirit of the special relationship our two countries share, I will throw out the following statistics: once on Mondays, twice on Tuesdays, thrice on Wednesdays, etc., but never on Sundays, because that's my day of rest.'

The Babester winked back.

'Huh?' Alison said. 'What's going on?'

'Brava!' Aubrey whispered.

'No fair,' Agnes managed to hiss without any 's's.

'Remember that I've only recently been widowed.'

'Jolly good,' Sebastian said. 'Not about you being a widow,' he hastened to assure Agnes, 'but the other thing.'

Cee-Cee gazed at the Babester adoringly. Trust me, I could read the large print in her late adolescent brain. Not only was this handsome American her father's age, he was both fertile and virile. These qualities alone were enough to drive her parents crazy. But the fact that Gabe was a doting father – well, there is nothing sexier to any woman than the sight of a man caring for a baby. Even cool, calm and collected Aubrey salivated every time the Babester scooped up Little Jacob and smothered him with kisses.

'Harrumph,' Peregrine probably said, although strictly speaking it sounded more like 'hump-a-lump' to my ears.

'Now, dears,' I said, as much to change the subject as to inform, 'Agnes shall forthwith serve dessert, known to you in your quaint version of our common language as the *pudding*, and since this is cake, it is certainly *not* pudding, although there *is* real American pudding in the cake mix, in order to keep the cake moist. But I must have been a pudding-head to even have brought this up, when I should, instead, be explaining to you the rules and regulations of tonight's hunt.'

Oh my stars, you should have seen the way all four of the guests sat up in their chairs. It wasn't the mention of sweets that did it, either, but when I dropped the 'h' word. Even Agnes, who had started to get up in order to serve the pudding-cake for the 'pudding' that wasn't

65

pudding, plopped back on her seat with a soft thud. I also thought that I heard the back of her chair groan a bit too loudly, as per everyday wear and tear, but I resolved not to mind. After all, the snipe hunt had been Agnes's idea, and she had put it all together from start to finish. By rights, it was *she* who should do the explaining.

I cleared my throat of any residual disappointment. 'I must apologize for what will be a slight delay in receiving your pudding course. You see, Agnes is also the mistress of the hunt.'

'Who?' Agnes said. Behind her horn-rimmed glasses she looked and sounded uncannily like a barn owl.

'Don't tease us, Agnes,' I said. 'Although I must admit that you do an excellent job of imitating Timothy, our resident owl. Now, be a dear and explain the rules.'

Agnes reached into her cavernous handbag, which sat on the floor, and whipped out a notepad and felt-tip pen. 'Snipes,' she read, 'are plump, North American game fowl, about the size of small barnyard hens. That is to say, they are similar in size to chickens. Are your Royal Highnesses familiar with the word "chickens"?'

'Lord love a duck,' my Babester groaned, 'they're neither Royal Highnesses nor are they blithering idiots, Agnes. They're simply Brits whose ancestors either bought a title or else bashed enough heads in, in order to get one.'

'Ha,' Peregrine said, 'you can be sure that my family had no need to buy its titles; we rose through the ranks of the aristocracy by bashing

66

heads, as you so quaintly put it. Lots and lots of Norman heads.'

'*Tempus fugit*,' I said. 'Carry on, Agnes, with the snipe-hunting spiel.'

'I'll thank you not to swear,' Peregrine said, scowling at me. 'But indeed, do carry on with this tiresome lecture.'

Agnes flushed. 'Uh, because the birds – I mean, the snipes – live in heavily forested areas, they possess small wings, and therefore are poor fliers, preferring to run along the ground when frightened or pursued. Snipes live in small flocks of about a dozen related individuals. Their diet is similar to that of quail. Both sexes are brown with black herringbone checks fading to buff on their undersides, but the males have a startlingly green, iridescent circle around each eye.'

The above description was total hogwash. It was something that Agnes had written just for that night's entertainment. Nonetheless, I was a freckle's thickness away from being a believer. After all, it sounded like something that *could* be true, and since it was in black and white that meant it had to be right – except that it didn't. I mean, both the Book of Mormon and the Koran were also in black and white and I didn't believe them. And Gabe didn't believe in the New Testament – *or* the Old Testament, for that matter.

Anyway, now that Agnes had everyone's attention, she licked her lips seductively. 'Snipe meat is moist and tender, and far more flavourful than even the most expensive free-range chicken. Fresh snipe meat, like that which we are about to catch tonight, is considered to be one of the most sought-after delicacies in the world.'

'Balderdash,' Peregrine said.

'I beg your pardon?' Agnes said through a mouth that had shrunk to the size of a Cheerio.

Peregrine emitted a moustache-ruffling snort. 'If that claptrap about tripe meat were the case, then I dare say that I would have heard about it before this. The chef at my club in London is up on all the latest trends and he's never mentioned tripe.'

'That would be *snipe*, dear,' I said. So he's half deaf, as well as blind, I noted to myself.

Before continuing, poor Agnes shot Alison a warning look. My fourteen-year-old was about to explode with pent-up mirth. A snipe hunt is a practical joke; a fool's errand. In a few minutes we would lead the eager hunters out across my moonlit pastures to the distant woods, each armed with a battery-powered torch and a cotton pillow case. Then Agnes would station the four unknowing nobles about thirty meters apart along the edge of the woods. The Grimsley-Snodgrasses would be directed to stand quietly and wait for the rest of us to fan out into the woods and flush the snipes.

The clueless aristocrats would wait, and wait, and wait, until finally one of them caught on that it was only a game and that they had been played. If they were good sports – which they would be, given that all Englishmen were jolly, good-natured folk – they would at last come trudging back to the inn wearing sheepish grins and making plans for holding their own snipe hunts once they returned to their native soil. The only time a snipe hunt backfired on me was when I foolishly attempted to play the trick on a party of Germans. They stayed out *all* night, refusing to consider the notion that the proprietor of such a reputable establishment as mine would pull such a stunt on unsuspecting foreigners.

Of course, that was then and this was now, as Alison was wont to say. Then there were a few Germans goose-stepping over my grave, but now, curiously, when all should have been fun and games, I felt as if there were a gaggle of greylag geese rehearsing the rumba in my tummy.

'Abort mission!' something, or someone, screamed in my brain. Was it my guardian angel or was it my overactive imagination? Not that it mattered, however, for as usual, my rational nature took over and I followed the course of least resistance: I stuck with the status quo.

Seven

I honestly believe that if all the Redcoats had
been as good sports as Aubrey, and even Celia,
we colonialists might not have been turncoats
and declared our independence from that 'Looney
Tunes' King George III. The two Grimsley-
Snodgrass womenfolk came traipsing back to the
PennDutch in high spirits. They were laughing
and carrying on as only a mother and daughter
could – just not my mother and me.

This lack of gaiety in us Yoder gals wasn't our
fault, mind you. The Bible states quite clearly
that one must fear God, and so my people had
– for hundreds of generations. All that fear was
bound to produce a few sourpusses. Yes, I know
that just stating this sounds like I'm espousing
genetics and evolution in some weird, twisted,
theological way – which I'm not. As for those
who wish to set me straight with a purely scientific point of view, my answer is simple: don't
confuse me with facts. Enough said.

I was beginning to think that Sebastian might
have inherited a God-fearing gene or two as well,
because he returned to the inn rather rankled.
First he stomped on the outside steps like a wine-
making peasant, next he slammed the kitchen
door, and when no one ran to greet him he
slammed it again.

'Where is everyone?' he shouted. Woe was me;

70

I could feel it in the marrow of my bones. That gaggle of gabbling, grave-galumphing geese had finally come home to roost in the mixed metaphor of my overactive imagination.

I took a deep breath and prayed for a calm spirit so that I might carry on properly and not shame my fellow countrymen. Instead, my pulse pounded even faster and my thoughts chased each other so fast that they blurred into butter. At that point I could choose to lie down and accept defeat, or, like a tigress, go down fighting all the way. I decided on the latter.

'Coming, dear,' I trilled and sallied forth into the adjoining kitchen through the swinging saloon-style doors. Between forefinger and thumb I held aloft a saucer-sized chocolate chip biscuit, of the American variety: soft, chewy, full of short-ening and a hundred million calories, and of course a gazillion chocolate chips. It is the kind of snack that you can feed to an enemy and then watch his, or her, hips literally swell in front of your eyes with each bite that is swallowed. In fact, I once wrote to President Obama that there was no need for drone strikes. All he needed to do was drop large bags of cookies down to each ISIL operative and watch them explode from within. My hopes of being appointed Ambassador to the Court of St James, on account of my service to my country, were dashed when I received a brief note telling me that I was not only naïve, but that the cookies had been confiscated by the Secret Service and demolished by explosives for his protection.

Thank heavens that Sebastian wasn't as cautious

as all that. 'Give me one of those,' he said, '*after* you explain to me why it is that you played such a nasty trick on us.'

I waved the fragrant biscuit under his nose and led him through the swinging doors and into my spacious, formal dining room where everyone else sat waiting. That is to say, everyone was there except for Peregrine, who had yet to return from the fields. The remainder of us were drinking tea or cocoa and were eating a variety of home-made treats. One could say that we were having a 'jolly good time.'

'Oh, Sebastian, do give it a rest,' his mother said and took a sip of her chamomile tea. 'Celia and I had a lovely time.' She turned to her daughter. 'Didn't we, dear?'

Celia sprung from her chair as if she'd been fired from a gun. 'Yeah, Sebastian. And you're not going to believe this, but after Mother and I walked down from where you and Papa were standing, we each caught three of them. *Three*, Sebastian!'

'Aren't you special,' Sebastian said, contorting his mouth with every syllable.

'Sebastian,' said Aubrey, 'please cut back on your sarcasm. Whatever will the Americans think?'

'That I intend to immigrate?' he said.

'That's rude,' Celia said, thereby forever putting herself in my good graces, which for a teenager is a pretty ding-dong hard thing to do.

'You go, girl,' I mouthed.

Poor Aubrey looked desperate. 'Please, darlings, mightn't we all just get along? For the sake of

72

England?' She began softly humming 'The White Cliffs of Dover,' which never fails to bring tears to my eyes.

Celia gave her poor mother half a nod, which, I suppose, is better than no nod at all. I have been a teenage girl, but never one with a brother to best. However, I am quite sure that, had I been in Celia's expensive English shoes, I would have done exactly the same thing.

'Nice plump ones they were too,' she said. 'Mother said that they looked to be every bit as succulent as those French capons that cook got her hands on this spring. Magdalena agreed that they looked to be young, tender snipes. She put the snipes in with her chickens for safe keeping until morning. Gentle as lambs, they were – walked right into the pillow slips.'

'You're putting me on, you are!' Sebastian grabbed one of my fabulous chocolate-chip biscuits and began tearing into it like a lion into its prey. 'There isn't any such thing as a snipe.'

'Strictly speaking, dear, there is,' I said as I dabbed at my eyes with a plain white cotton handkerchief.

'Maybe so,' he said, 'but it's not what you describe. In the meantime, my papa is missing.'

'Missing?' Aubrey said. 'What do you mean? I just saw him.'

'Yeah?' Sebastian said. 'Was that before or after you and Celia caught these plump, succulent game birds?'

The Babester, ever my handsome hero, stood and handed his son off to Alison. 'Hey,' he said to Sebastian, 'enough with the attitude. I don't

73

care if you are our guest; in this house, people respect their mothers.'

Of course, there was stunned silence all around. Alison was the first to speak.

'You go, Dad!'

'Thanks, and the same thing applies to the peanut gallery,' Gabe said with a wink.

'I ain't no peanut gallery!'

'Shh,' I said, 'you're going to wake Little Jacob, dear. How about doing me a big favour and putting him to bed tonight? Then you can watch TV in our room.' Mind you, that was an *enormous* privilege, so the favour aspect was really all stacked in her direction.

'Ah, do I hafta?'

'Yes,' said her father firmly. 'You must.'

'Man, this ain't fair! Yinz are so mean, ya know that?'

I don't believe in reincarnation, but if I did, at one point I must have been a fish that took the first baited hook that it encountered. Perhaps it's because I try my hardest to be the best mother that I can that when Alison tosses out these 'wiggly worm' accusations I swim right up to her boat.

'I am *so* fair – I mean, life isn't fair. No, that's not right, either. It's all in God's hands, and we don't know His plans. Enough of that. We definitely aren't mean; we just have grown-up things to discuss. You should be happy that I'm even letting you watch TV, which, as you know, I consider to be an instrument of the Devil, except for *I Love Lucy* and *Are You Being Served?* Although, personally, I think that given the state

74

of the world today there should be a show titled *Are You Being Saved?* Of course, finding a good Christian actress is a bit of an oxymoron, isn't it? Too bad that Aubrey here is Church of England and not a proper Protestant, as the Good Lord intended, because she does have a lovely bone structure—'

'Ahem,' Aubrey said, 'I, and my lovely bones, are sitting right here and my husband is still missing. Do you mind if we talk about *him*?'

'Well,' I said, feeling my ears turn red, 'you don't have to tell *me* twice on which side of the toast to spread the marmite. I suppose that I do carry on from time—'

'Mags,' Gabe said sternly, making a zipping motion across his mouth. 'Alison,' he said just as sternly, and pointed towards our bedroom.

Meanwhile, Agnes sat with her hands primly folded on the table, her features arranged in the same manner favoured by Queen Victoria in the many long years of her widowhood. I don't believe in the transmigration of souls either, but if I did, I would swear (something else that I don't do) that my best friend had fled for parts unknown on holiday, and that the 'Mother of Kings' was her temporary replacement.

Call me old fashioned, but *sometimes* I don't mind it when Gabe pulls back on my reigns, especially when I've been making a fool of myself. As for Alison, it looked as if Buckingham Palace was weighing down her lower lip, but she managed to stomp off without another word, and miraculously without waking up Little Jacob.

'Now then, *people*,' Gabe said, giving Sebastian

75

and Celia stern looks as well, 'I am going to give you back your torches – only we call them *flashlights* here in the States – and we shall all return to the scene of the crime. Oops, bad choice of words. We'll go to where this young man says that Perry disappeared.'

'His name is *Peregrine*,' Sebastian said, and practically without hissing too. Believe me, there is no man quite as virile as an Englishman.

'Shouldn't you call the constable, so that he can organize a search party?' Aubrey said.

That's when Agnes came to life and began to wring her plump, although perhaps not tender, little hands. 'Unfortunately, the search party would be Magdalena's bailiwick.'

'Et tu, Brutus?' I said. 'Why "unfortunately"?'

Quite fortunately, the Babester stepped in again. 'Hernia is a small village, mostly populated by Mennonites and surrounded by Amish farmers. Both sects are extremely peaceful and law-abiding. For instance, in their religion it is forbidden to take a human life, even in self-defence. It is also a rather poor community, and whereas it once had a two-person police force, it is currently down to just one person, whom Magdalena pays out of her own pocket. Incidentally, Magdalena is the mayor, for which she receives no salary, and she is also the captain of the all-volunteer Hernia Search and Rescue Squad – again, without compensation. If it wasn't for my wife's largesse, this community would be without most of its vital services. As for what Agnes might mean by her remark, I have absolutely no idea.'

'Yeah?' Sebastian sneered. 'Is that so? Well, I remember reading about several murders happening right here at this very inn. They were written up in that brochure Mother received in the post.'

At that dear Aubrey came around the table and lightly touched my shoulder in what I was to later learn was the English equivalent of a full-body embrace. In all honesty, had the Good Lord created me with other proclivities, and had Aubrey *actually* embraced me – well, who knows just how many sins that kettle of fish might have contained.

After all, just because God made you a certain way, that doesn't mean that you get to act that way. *Au contraire*: clearly the Almighty wishes homosexuals to suffer, or else he wouldn't punish them by all His prohibitions against what He calls 'abdominal' behaviour. Someday when I get to Heaven I shall ask the Dear Lord why he bothered to create these painful hurdles for these dear folks to begin with. After all, it isn't *their* fault that they were born with these urges.

My word, there are times when I do digress! 'Yes,' sweet Aubrey said, 'it is true. On the internet there are numerous articles about the murders that have taken place here. Frankly, that is the reason why I chose your charming inn, Magdalena.'

'You don't say!' I said.

'Ah, but I do say. It was Chambers – she's my secretary – who discovered your advert in the back of the beauty magazine. Frankly, it wasn't the Amish angle, or the little bit of history that you Americans have that attracted us, but the uncanny number of murders that have happened under the watch of one woman. Magdalena, your life really is stranger than fiction.'

Well, that got my knickers in a knot – pardon my French. I slowly and quite obviously brushed my shoulder where Aubrey's shapely fingertips had momentarily rested.

'You would think it even stranger, dear,' I said, 'if you could have read my mind a minute ago.'

'I beg your pardon?'

'Never mind. But since you have brought the matter up, most of these murders were solved by yours truly, and were it not for them I would not be the wealthy woman that I am today.'

'Wealthy and generous,' my loyal husband said. 'She single-handedly supports all the public services in the village. She even brings in a doctor once a week to hold a clinic in the jail.'

'Saint Magdalena,' Sebastian sneered.

'Shut up,' Celia said. 'I don't suppose you need to be rude all the time, do you?'

'That's telling him, isn't it?' said Aubrey. She turned back to me. 'I loved how the press gave each of the murders a title, almost as if they were books. *Too Many Crooks Spoil the Broth*, *Parsley, Sage, Rosemary and Crime* – the list is endless, and each one more clever than the last.'

'What did the papers call the last one again?' Celia asked. 'Mother particularly liked that one.'

'*The Death of Pie*,' Sebastian interjected just to be mean.

'Listen, dear, you needn't worry about any murders taking place while you're here on holiday. Nobody here knows you, therefore nobody dislikes the admittedly unlikable personality of one of you notable nobles, so the only motive could possibly be to keep you from talking after an armed robbery, seeing as how you're filthy rich, but an armed robbery is simply out of the question because first your presence in Hernia and environs has got to even make it on our radar screen – so to speak. So far I haven't told a soul about you titled la-dee-dahs or your valises bulging with tiaras, coronets, ermine capes or what have you – well, except for the two hundred and forty-three members of my church; the eighteen ladies of the Mennonite Women's Sewing Circle; my double first-cousin once removed, Sam Yoder, who owns Yoder's Corner Market; the cashiers at Miller's feed store; and possibly my banker up in Bedford whom everyone calls Mr Busy Lips.'

Although Agnes is a kind, Christian woman and my best friend, that didn't stop her from giving me the evil eye. 'Magdalena, how could you!'

'It's actually fairly easy,' I said. 'Although all that talking did get me a little bit hoarse, but, oh my dear, it certainly is satisfying. At the moment, I am the envy of virtually everyone in the county.'

Agnes made ripping motions above her head, which was not a good sign. Not every woman is blessed by good hair after a certain age, and Agnes, I hate to say, falls into that category. Heaven forefend that the dear girl hastens the day when, like her nudist uncles, she fails to sport any hair at all. I am not gossiping, mind you, merely reporting the facts: given the rather odd shape of Agnes's head, and her peculiar colouring when aroused by food, there was a good possibility that Agnes, while at a church potluck supper, would have her head mistaken for a peeled cantaloupe by myopic Irma Berkey, who would then attempt to stab it with a plastic fork.

Again, the Babester, the 'big' man in my life, came to my rescue. 'What about you, Miss Goody Two Shoes? How many people did you brag to? We wouldn't have royalty staying here if it wasn't for you, so I'd bet that half the county knows. I'm surprised there wasn't a news crew here to film their arrival, or do you have them scheduled to do a morning talk show in Pittsburgh?'

Agnes dropped her hands and slapped her cheeks; she probably wanted to slap Gabe's cheeks for being so cheeky. 'How many times do I have to explain to you, Gabe, that the Grimsley-Snodgrass family are not royalty, they are merely aristocrats?'

'Whatever you say,' the Babester said, and slipped into the kitchen to answer his cell phone.

Aubrey surprised me by raising her slim pale hand like a tentative schoolgirl. 'You are correct, Agnes; however, I dare say that both Peregrine and I have more *English* royal blood flowing through our veins than our beloved reigning monarch, Queen Elizabeth the Second does.'

'Harrumph,' Agnes said, proving that she is, if anything, a quick learner.

'Never mind the bloodlines,' I said somewhat impatiently. 'You're not horses. Agnes, how many people have *you* blabbed to?'

'Harrumph,' Agnes said again, 'a bump and a horse's rump. I did all the work arranging this visit, so why shouldn't I brag? And yes, I did brag: I bragged on my blog, I tweeted, I wrote about it in my church newsletter, and you *can* expect *Good Morning Pittsburgh, Special Edition* to show up here tomorrow at ten.'

'Jolly good,' Sebastian said with a grin. 'I've never been on the telly before.'

'Mother,' Celia said, 'will you help me fix my hair? That adapter for my hairdryer better bloody well work, or – or—'

'Or what, dear?' Aubrey asked sweetly.

'Or else!'

Aubrey turned her gentle gaze on me. 'Magdalena, just in case, do you have a hairdryer that we might borrow? They don't seem to come with the rooms.'

I smiled, eager to help. 'Yes and no. I don't have any fancy-schmancy electric hairdyers, if that's what you need, but since you are here to experience the old-fashioned ways, why not use the Amish hairdryer?'

'I beg your pardon?' Aubrey said.

'She means the sun,' Agnes snapped.

'*Tres amusant*,' Sebastian said.

'Sarcasm does not become you, dear,' I said graciously. 'And I wasn't being facetious about using the sun to dry your hair. Just slather on sunscreen and then take a folding chair out into the driveway about nine in the morning. Your hair will be dry in twenty minutes. That will leave you plenty of time to finish getting dressed, Celia, especially if you wise up and leave all that other

81

gunk off your face. Too much black around your eyes makes you look like a raccoon – either that or a nineteenth-century bank robber.'

'I say there!' Celia said, rearing back like a startled colt.

Aubrey's laugh brought to mind tiny crystal bells. 'Magdalena, you are so refreshing – in that American sort of way.'

'She means "rude,"' Agnes said.

'Nonsense,' Aubrey said. 'But rally, shouldn't we be putting more thought into searching for Peregrine? According to the research that I did before coming here, there are bears in these woods, and animals called coyotes. No offense to you Americans, but it seems as if everyone here has a gun, and if someone looks at someone else just a wee bit wonky . . . Well, I'm just saying that Peregrine wandering around the woods late at night might well appear to be threatening.'

'It's that d— monocle,' Sebastian said. 'He won't listen to reason and get a proper pair of specs.' Sebastian actually said a four letter word, which I refuse to repeat!

At that moment my hero burst through the swinging kitchen doors like the sheriff in an old-timey saloon. 'No need to stress yourselves further, folks. *Missing* Peregrine is no longer missing! He is safe, if not sound of mind, and shall return here momentarily.'

Then, lo and behold, the doorbell rang.

Eight

'No proselytising here,' I said when I saw who was standing on my veranda. I started to close the door.

For the record, I knew ding-dong well that the waist-high woman in a nun's habit was Gabe's Jewish mother. Standing next to her, looking a bit chagrined, was the heretofore missing Peregrine. For the record, Gabe's mother's birth name was Ida, but her spiritual name was Mother Malaise. She was the founder and self-appointed head of a made-up religion called the Sisters of Apathy. These so-called nuns were cloistered in a convent that had been converted from a farm-house that was located directly across the road from the PennDutch.

Although she has vehemently denied it on many occasions, Mother Malaise had created her cult for the sole purpose of causing her Jewish son to feel guilty for having taken a Christian wife. It began as a way of showing her son how broken-hearted she was that he had abandoned four thousand years of tradition to marry a *shikse* – which is a not very nice way of say 'a gentile woman.' However, Gabe has never felt guilty about anything, and since he couldn't even bring himself to *act* guilty, things quickly went down-hill from there.

Soon Ida, aka Mother Malaise, invented the

bizarre theology of disparagement. This consists of one religious tenet broken into three parts: despair in all things; despair at all times; despair everywhere. The adherents to this whackadoodle concept have the chutzpah to refer to themselves as Trinitarians, although clearly three sandwiches shy of a picnic hamper is what they really are.

'Shtop!' Mother Malaise barked. 'Eets me, your mudder-in-law und a duck of some kind.'

'I am an earl,' Peregrine said, 'not a duke, and most certainly *not* a duck.'

'Yah? Und I'm zee Queen of Sheba.' Mother Malaise laughed; something which certainly wasn't in her favour. That woman has been the bane of my existence, starting with the day that Gabriel told her that we were engaged. There was room for only one Mrs Rosen in her world, a fact which she soon made very clear by sending her son a one-way airline ticket from Pittsburgh – our nearest airport – back to New York City, where she lived at the time.

When Gabriel returned the ticket, unused of course, his precious 'mama-leh' moved to Hernia; lock, stock and barrel. Hernia is not New York City; it has no public lodgings. Guess who had to move in with *me* for a while, because you-know-who couldn't bear the embarrassment of being a bachelor living with his mom? So what if it was the other way around? Many was the time I'd find them both in their pyjamas, and she happily cutting his toenails, or combing his hair like he was a little kid, which I guess makes perfect sense, since she still cuts his meat for

84

him! And him a heart surgeon! Oh, well, who am I to tell tales out of school?

I have learned from my younger sister Susannah and my daughter Alison how to emit world-class sighs. That said, I gave birth to the mother of all sighs, one that raised the tides along the coasts of Cornwall and Devon.

'All right then, come in if you must,' I said, stepping aside. 'But not you, dear.' I meant, of course, that 'none dressed as a nun' should enter my inn at that late hour. In the event that she did, it would raise my hackles so high that I would have to sleep clinging to the ceiling in order to keep my blood pressure company.

'Vhat you say?'

Trust me; Mother Malaise was anything but apathetic.

'I want you to go home, Ida. Go back to your misguided Sisters of Apoplexy or whatever you call yourselves. There is no more room at this inn.'

I could smell my sweetheart's earthy manliness before I heard his voice. 'Hey, what's going on here?'

'Your vife!' his mother said. 'Like alvays, yah?'

'Peregrine!' my darling husband said, for once ignoring his mother. 'There you are.'

And for once, as he eschews public scenes, the man who shares my bed dared to slip his arm around an *English-English*man's shoulders, as if he were a regular person, and lead him to the dining room. This left his precious 'host womb' in the most hostile of moods. Ida Rosen, aka Mother Malaise, may be built like a badger on

85

steroids with a gym addiction, but when properly riled she is virtually unstoppable. Or, as she would say: 'unshtoppable.'

'Out of my vay!' she roared, sounding like a jet engine.

The next thing that I remember I was lying flat on my back. I could hear Ida's Yiddish-Russian-Ukrainian, and sometimes just plain what-have-you accent, assaulting my ears all the way from *my* dining room.

Perhaps I should explain that when the Good Lord created me, he implanted within my brain a fertile imagination. I have always threatened to write a book one day, but as anyone who has ever said that knows, who on earth has the time to actually sit down and do that? Oh, and don't give me that hogwash about discipline and talent. Writing skills can be taught in any number of venues, and as for discipline, that wouldn't be an issue for me, just as long as I had the time.

My point is: my fertile imagination sometimes leads me to think up scenarios that are more likely to take place on the so-called silver screen than within my beloved family. Then again, having only been to see one movie in my entire life – *The Sound of Music* – what do I know about movies? I had to drag Mama to see that show all the way up in Pittsburgh where nobody knew us, but she was so scandalized by the scene in the gazebo where two teenagers kissed that she dragged me out of the theatre and wouldn't stop shaking until we got home two hours later.

So what scenario might I create for Ida Rosen,

a reasonable person might ask? My answer, of course, is reasonable as well: Ida Rosen, aka Mother Malaise, Mother Superior to a convent of forty-four habit-wearing nuns, would be the head of a drug cartel. *That* is not farfetched. No siree, and Bob's your uncle! Hers is not a religious order, mind you. These women – four of them are men – do not don the long grey robes and wimples for reasons of modesty. If that were the case, then they wouldn't hold an annual Run Through Hernia Nude Day, which, thank God, has been rained off two out of the three years since its inception.

I ask you, what better place to hide drugs than in the folds of yards and yards of loosely hanging cloth? And who is going to suspect people with names like Sister Dispirited and Sister Disenchanted of being 'players?' With the exception of my combative and excessively jealous mother-in-hate, every time I run into one of those folks I have a strong urge to lie down and take a nap.

And yes, it has even occurred to me that the old biddy packs heat. In layperson's terms, that means that she carries a firearm – a gun. Given that she is only four feet and two inches, it would have to be a very small hand gun, but then again, her bosoms enter a room a full two seconds before she does, so it could be a Colt 45. Any rate, after being run over and having gathered my wits, I staggered to my feet, took a few cautious steps and then flew like the witch that I supposedly am into the next room.

I can tell you that Ida was genuinely surprised.

Perhaps she thought that she'd at last been successful in grinding me into chopped liver.

'*Nu?*' she said calmly. 'Vhat took you so long? Vee vas having a family meeting.'

'Oh, is that so, dear? With all my cousins in attendance?'

'Vhat? Da duck, and da duckess, dey are your cousins?'

Gabe groaned. 'Come on, Mags, I know that Ma can be a pain in the *tuchas*, but she's an old lady for crying out loud.'

'*Oy*,' Ida cried as she struck a surprisingly large fist against her gigantic bosom. 'So now your own mudder, who gave you life, is a pain in the *tuchas*? It vasn't my *tuchas* dat hoit so much da day vhat you vas born – und for tearty-tree hours. Alle dis because you haffe such a beeg head. Like a ten-gallon vater bottle da doctor tell me. So, he has to make wiz de surgery—'

'Well,' said Agnes, 'that does it for me for tonight. Remember, Your Noblenesses, we meet down here tomorrow morning at ten for the interview. They requested bright colours – something that would pop on TV. Maybe a vivid red or a royal blue. *Royal* blue, ha, ha. Get the joke?'

'Not really,' Peregrine said. I could tell that he was seeing red because even behind his monocle his blue eye looked cold enough to set a gelatine salad.

It had been a long day for Agnes, and she looked crestfallen.

'American humour – now that's an oxymoron,' he said.

I decided to come to my friend's aid. 'Another

definition for oxymoron: a castrated bull that is connected by a Spanish conjunction to France's favourite comedian.'

No one laughed.

'Ox – y – Jerry Lewis,' I said. 'Get it?'

Again, no one laughed. No one offered up as much as a courtesy snicker.

The Bible says that Satan will use *anything* that He can to trip us up, and that we are to be ever diligent on that account. I was well aware from experience that Satan loved using my low self-esteem and my propensity for acting punitively. It had never occurred to me, however, that Satan might put it in mind to invite my guests to church!

'Postpone that interview until Monday, Agnes. Tomorrow is Sunday, remember? A traditional Mennonite church experience is what is scheduled.'

'Oh, how exciting,' Aubrey said, pressing her sculpted fingertips together in breathless anticipation.

'Rally?' said Sebastian. 'Have you quite forgotten that we're Church of England? I don't suppose you have one of those in this godforsaken place. Also, I'm afraid we're frightfully Low Church; Papa doesn't go in for the smells and bells – too Papist, ha, ha. Small joke there, in case you missed it, what with your frontier sense of humour.'

'How dare you!' Gabriel said, ever the loyal husband. 'As long as my soul mate is here, God has not forsaken this place.'

'Tank you, son,' Ida said. 'Und I love you too.'

'He was talking about me, Mama *dearest*,' I said so sweetly that I later lost a molar on that account. 'As for the rest of you, I have decided that the best way for you to experience Mennonite culture is to attend Magdalena Yoder's traditional Old Order Mennonite Church. By the way, this will be followed by a potluck luncheon, which is supplied by the ladies of that church. This will offer you a tremendous opportunity to socialize with the locals; it is something to which other tourists are not privy. In the afternoon you are free do what the Lord hath commanded you to do, which is to rest – i.e. nap, stroll about the farm or take buggy rides about the countryside.'

My attention was drawn to what sounded like a snorting ox. I was somewhat relieved to see that the real creature of my concern wasn't quite as dangerous, given that it was only Agnes, and that Mr Lewis was not in sight. Nonetheless, Agnes was pawing the floor of my dining room with her remarkably petite and overburdened feet, and her remarkably plump fists were held stiffly out at her sides (given her shape, a forty-five-degree angle was the best she could achieve).

'Magdalena,' she said through gritted teeth, 'I am literally beside myself with frustration.'

I glanced to her right, and then her left. 'No, you're not.'

'Don't you tell me how I feel,' she hissed, managing to hiss without that pesky 's.'

'I'm not telling you how to feel,' I said. 'All I am saying is that you aren't beside yourself *literally*. Although, who knows, maybe those

90

award-winning mystery writers might start using that word incorrectly as well.'

'Aargh! You know what I meant. Anyway, tomorrow is the only day that the film crew from Pittsburgh has the time to come out and film.'

'Tomorrow is the *Lord's* Day,' I said. 'Read your Bible if you've forgotten.'

'Actually,' Gabe said, 'if you could read it in the original Hebrew, as I can, you would know that today, Saturday, is the Lord's Day.'

'Yah, dat is so,' chimed in So-and-So, much to my everlasting irritation.

'You no longer practice Judaism, dear,' I said. 'You worship the Goddess Apathia, and her lover, Entropy, which makes you a heathen and subject to stoning.'

'Oh, my, now this rally is exciting,' Aubrey said. 'I must say, you Americans are frightfully entertaining. We haven't seen a good stoning in ages.'

'We can be frightful all right,' I said, perhaps a wee bit annoyed that she obviously found Ida's shenanigans more appealing than a proper church service. 'Agnes, as tour director, I will expect you at eight tomorrow morning to help us enjoy a hearty Pennsylvania Dutch farm breakfast. Then at half past nine we will load up and depart for the church.'

'Actually,' Peregrine said as he lightly stroked the left tip of his moustache, 'I shall defer on the pleasures of the Lord tomorrow and pay more attention to rest. After all, if memory serves me right, there is nothing in that passage about church.'

'That's not *fair*,' I wailed. 'The Ten Commandments were given in the desert, when the ancient Israelites were just a wandering tribe; churches didn't even exist then.'

'Say what?' Celia said. Who knew she was even still listening, given that she had a sixteen-year-old brain, which is compelled by biology to shut down after just six words uttered by ignorant adults.

'What?' I said.

'What I *mean*,' she said, 'is why did God give the Ten Commandments to *those* people and not us?'

'Well—'

'And since God didn't give them to *us*, why do *we* have to follow them? Answer me that. I'm just asking, mind. But rally, God didn't tell the English not to steal, did He? So suppose I was in Harrods and saw this jumper that I rally liked—'

'Celia!' Aubrey said with surprising sharpness. Now *that* really endeared the woman to me. It is one thing to raise our daughters to be strong and independent thinkers, speaking their minds under the right circumstances, but it is quite another thing to permit sacrilegious ideas to percolate through their brains like water through coffee grounds. The end result of that is anything but a stimulating beverage – it's unadulterated swill!

The teenager obediently zipped her lip, but she rolled her eyes exactly like an American teenager. If you ask me, it isn't music that's the international language; it's body language.

'Ladies,' said Peregrine, looking at me perhaps a wee bit reproachfully, 'it has been a long, tiring day. If you will excuse me, I think that I shall retire to what passes for accommodation overhead.'

'This *accommodation*,' I said, 'passed very well for our past three presidents, as well as our current Head of State.'

'You're joking?' Peregrine said.

'I never joke about business,' I said. 'This inn has also hosted many movie stars and people in the music industry, including Babs.'

I was met by blank stares all around except for the grin on the Babester's face. 'Babs,' I said again. 'That's what I call her. You might know her as Barbra. She sang *Mammeries*!'

'She means "Memory,"' Agnes said drily.

'Oh, *that* Barbra,' they all chorused.

'My wife doesn't listen to secular music,' Gabriel said loyally.

'Und I dun't leestin to sexy music eider,' Ida said.

'Before you go, Peregrine,' I said, 'we'd all like to learn what happened to you?'

'Nothing happened to me, dear lady! I merely stepped into the woods for a moment to, er, water the undergrowth, when I became slightly disoriented. *Slightly*, I say. It's not as if I thought I was back on the grounds of our estate or hunting with Prince Charles up in Balmoral. At any rate, I saw a light – not *the* light – and headed straight for it, as per my military training, and it led me to this so-called convent. That is where I encountered the, ahem, Mother Disjointed here.'

'Jolly good!' I said, for he had given me a remarkably straightforward account of his whereabouts while he was missing. Not only that, but he had come up with a ding-dang good name for me to add to my list of appellations for the Queen of Apathy. The erstwhile missing earl was beginning to rise on my barometer of likability.

'Now that the mystery is solved,' Sebastian said, 'I'm out of here then as well.' He stood, and then in the unabashed way of which only the truly young and naïve are capable of acting, he stretched his arms to their limit, straight up into the air. Normally I don't pay close attentive to such matters, but Sebastian boasted an exceptionally long torso, and by adopting this stance the youth's shirttails pulled loose from his waistband. The result was that I couldn't help but be assaulted by an expanse of what the kids today refer to as a 'six-pack.' You know, tight, rippled muscles. In this case the six-pack was deeply tanned and separated into two equally erotic halves by a line of curly black hair.

'Get behind me, Satan!' I cried softly, surely too softly for anyone of corporal form to hear.

I am not superstitious, but Sebastian must have had the ears of a demon – I'm just saying. 'What the heck do you mean by *that*?' he said. 'Is stretching against your religion too?'

'Not stretching zee truce,' Ida said.

'She means "truth,"' Gabe translated loyally. Despite the content of his marriage vows, and his many promises to the contrary, if Ida and I had both slipped off the deck of a ship and neither of us could swim, the first person Gabriel would try to save would be his precious Mama. *That* might not even bother me, if I believed that he intended to raise our son Little Jacob to put *his* mama before everyone else. Alas, I believe that there is a fifty–fifty chance that my son will grow up having been brainwashed into plucking the plucky Ida from the briny deep and not yours truly.

That's when dear, sweet Aubrey jumped to my defence. 'Well I, for one, find Magdalena utterly delightful,' she said, 'and I say that there is absolutely nothing wrong with embroidering one's words in order to facilitate the conversation. I should imagine that Magdalena would have fit quite well into the salon set, don't you, dear?' She turned to Peregrine.

'Oh, Mother, must you be so ridiculous?' Celia said and left the room, although it was not she to whom the question had even been addressed.

'Quite right, dear,' Peregrine said, and acknowledged his wife with a glinting tilt of his monocle.

'Well, I'm off then,' said Sebastian, and out he strode, all nine stones of him, with his broad shoulders, washboard abs and narrow cowboy hips.

That left me with the two As: Agnes and Aubrey, current BFF and possible *new* BFF, knowing how fickle I can be. I'm just being honest. I *am*, after all, only human. What I mean is that if Agnes continued to thwart me and Aubrey continued to charm and delight me – well, I'm just saying, that's all. Of course, it goes *without* saying that both Rosens remained.

I breathed a prayer for strength. 'Agnes, would

you be so kind as to give Ma a ride back to the Convent of Perpetual Pity?'

'Da name eez *Apathy*,' Ida said. 'Und since vhen vas I your ma?'

'I stand corrected. Agnes, could you please give Apathy a ride back to the convent for us?'

'Mags,' Gabe said, 'enough with the teasing. She's a helpless old lady, for gosh sakes.'

'Helpless my *As*-ton Martin,' Aubrey whispered just loud enough for everyone, except Ida, to hear. Even Gabe smiled.

Heaven help me, but I was one 's' away from falling in love and becoming a lesbian, which, of course, I never would. But like I said before, I'm just saying.

Nine

Freni Hostetler, who is both my elderly cook and kinswoman, normally doesn't work on Sundays. On this particular Lord's Day, however, she refused to have it any other way.

'If you promised them "Dutchy" food,' she said, 'then I will make them for to eat real Dutchy and not the pretend Dutchy, like over Lancaster way. These English-English will eat the *real* thing.' By that, Freni meant that she would serve food cooked according to the recipes handed down from her mother, who got them from her mother, etc. These recipes dated back hundreds of years.

An Amish farm breakfast is a hearty meal, although not all of it is to my taste. For instance, I'm not a big fan of scrapple – or head cheese – and I didn't suppose that our British guests would care for it either, until Agnes clued me in on haggis.

'Just make sure to serve baked beans,' she said. 'The Brits have to eat baked beans with every meal.'

'Are you *sure*?' I said. I simply couldn't imagine anyone wanting to eat beans for breakfast, especially when planning to share a church pew in due order.

'I am positive,' Agnes said. 'And ideally the beans must come from a tin, not from a can, and they must not be made from scratch.'

Freni scratched her head on that one. 'Yah, but how is a tin different from a can?'

'Semantics,' I said softly, for her ears alone.

'No, it's not,' Agnes said.

'Harrumph,' I said. 'It looks like Agnes is anti-semantic.'

'Ach!' said Freni, genuinely horrified. 'Gabe, Little Jacob, maybe Alison too – they are semantic, yah?'

'You mean Semitic,' Agnes said.

'Yes, but you can bet your couscous, cousin,' I said, 'that these British-style breakfasts can get really out of hand, even when served from a tin, instead of a can – I hope you don't mind my speaking in rhyme.'

'I do, actually,' said Agnes, who looked as if she'd been sucking on a pickle.

'Harrumph,' I said again. 'At any rate, the British will expect marmite, vegemite and marmalade for their toast, which, by the way, can be no darker than the inside of my wrist. It is common knowledge that when Brits see our toast, all they see is a plate covered with ashes. Ah, yes, both their toast and their bacon have to be served in a weird little device called a rasher.'

'Ach!' squawked Freni. 'Uncle!' That was the secular American way of saying 'I give up' during physical competitions when I was a girl. Where on earth Freni picked up this phrase is beyond me, but the older I get, the more I've come to understand just how strange this world is, and that its mysteries are constantly unfolding.

For the most part we needn't have worried about our breakfast selection. I served it buffet

98

style, and the sideboard fairly groaned under the weight of the many platters and bowls it supported. I heard many appreciative 'ahs' and 'ohs' in the serving line, and when folks started eating, the compliments coming out of their mouths gave stiff competition to the food going in.

There was only one fly in the oatmeal – er, ointment. Rupert, the oldest son by two minutes, had deigned to lift his silken locks off my guest pillows and make that terrible trek downstairs to the dining room. I know, sarcasm does not become me, and I have heard it said that women are incapable of it, so I have had to check beneath my sturdy Christian underwear *twice*, in the telling of this, to be sure of my gender, but that young man's arrogant behaviour really steamed my bonnet.

After all the work that my seventy-six-year-old cousin did that morning to prepare a feast fit for a king, much less a viscount, Rupert should have at least had enough good manners to say *nothing* rather than something hurtful. Instead, with Freni standing there at one end of the buffet, Rupert screwed up his face as if he'd also been sucking on a pickle and said: 'I say there, have you ever seen such a disgusting display of rubbish all in one place?'

Both the Amish and we Mennonites are known for our pacifism. Many's the time that we have been martyred for our faith. We are a humble people, even proud of our humility, and may the Good Lord forgive me but I cannot help feeling defensive when it comes to my family. Perhaps I am a closet Baptist and I don't know it. After all, as a teenager I caught myself inadvertently wiggling my patooty to Little Richard's *Tooty Fruity*, that time when I heard the tune coming from a shop doorway. That night I confessed this sin to Mama, who then gave my offending behind ten whacks with the backside of her hairbrush.

Now, where was I? Oh, yeah, as Alison would say, no one, but *no one*, hurts dear old Freni. Even Babs couldn't get away with a statement like Rupert's. The only thing that prevented me from tackling the ungrateful tourist was that Agnes stood between us with her Sumo wrestler's girth.

'You take that back, buster!' I roared. 'Take it back right now or it's off to the Tower with you!'

'I beg your pardon?' Rupert chirped.

'It's not *my* pardon for which you should be asking,' I growled, 'but Freni's. How can you say such a hurtful thing to an old lady? Don't you have a grandmother?'

At that Agnes manoeuvred a turn between the table and the sideboard so that she faced me. 'Magdalena, what are you carrying on about? I don't see how Freni enters into my private conversation with Rupert. He was showing me a picture of the garbage strike in Naples on his smartphone. It really *is* disgusting.'

When I used to complain about having big feet, Papa always said that God made them that way so I could think fast on them. I tried putting them to good use that morning.

'Oh *that*,' I said. 'I must have been thinking aloud. It had to do with the dialogue I'm writing for the Christmas pantomime – you know, the one I'll be directing for the Sunday school.'

For the record, I abhor fabrication and eschew embroidering with words, if they are meant to deceive, and/or take advantage of someone. However, I believe it is quite different *if* one follows through and actually performs a task that has been alluded to. That, of course, meant that I would have to set pencil to paper and prepare a script for puerile pubescent players – or else be guilty of telling a whopper on the Lord's Day.

'I always enjoyed acting in pantomimes,' Rupert said. The young man was irritatingly agreeable. If it hadn't been for his lavender shirt and his unmistakable use of rouge on his cheeks, he could well have passed for your average red-blooded American male – well, almost. Although it wasn't any of my business, I can't help but state that the coral shade of lipstick he was wearing not only didn't suit his skin tone, it would have set him apart from other local youth his age.

'Well, there is no doubt in my mind that you have movie star good looks,' Agnes said.

'Just what Mother always says,' Rupert said without a trace of humility.

Gore blimey and gag me with a spoon! That was my deepest, darkest thought, and I've already made no secret of the fact that I am a sinful woman, in need of salvation. So anyway, I'm telling it like I felt it.

'Yes, my boy is the greatest,' Aubrey said. 'Freni, what do you call these divine little cakes?'

'Pancakes, ma'am,' Freni said.

'Indeed,' Aubrey said. 'They look very much like crepes, except that they're rather stouter, don't you think?'

Poor Freni, my stout cousin, looked as put upon as a sheep asked to solve a maths problem. 'Yah, I think,' she finally said.

Much to my astonishment, it was Rupert who attempted to swoop in and rescue Freni. 'My dear woman,' he said, 'would you by any chance happen to have a box of muesli lying around? I'm not complaining, mind you. This rally is a splendid layout, but I'm afraid that travel has a way of – should we say – tying things up for a while, if you get my drift. A bit of muesli to sprinkle on my porridge would be first rate – or, as you Americans are so fond of saying: "da bomb."'

Freni wears glasses, which have lenses thicker than my cell phone. Her mouth opened and closed, but it was clear that everything Rupert had just said might as well have been delivered in Vietnamese.

'Certainly we have muesli,' Agnes said, and much to Gabe and my mutual astonishment she reached into an enormous handbag that was resting on a dining-room chair beside her and extracted a box of that enigmatic European cereal. I refer to it as that because privately the Babester and I call it "sticks and twigs," and we joke that if we left a bowl of it out on the deck in early spring, the birds would make short shrift of stealing it for the purpose of building their nests.

Truthfully, if the Good Lord wanted us to suffer at mealtimes, then He would forbid us to eat

Cinnabons, which are those enormous cinnamon rolls that are served warm, with cream cheese icing, in airport kiosks. God wouldn't torture us by making us think that adding kindling material to our breakfasts makes us any healthier – not when we already have Kellogg's Raisin Bran, the kind with two scoops in every box. Of course, who am *I* to judge? Unlike my Jewish husband, I blithely stuff my face with bacon and pork sausages, even though God said quite clearly that these pig products were not allowed, and never, ever would be on account of His commandments being everlasting – *l'olam va'ed*.

Yes, I know, the Apostle Peter had a dream that overturned this commandment, but I ask you, who trumps whom in this case? Who is the Big Kahuna, so to speak, the Great Almighty whose word is Eternal, or a Galilean fisherman whose dream conveniently allows millions of Gentiles to convert because now they can keep on eating their BLTs? Those are *not* my words, by the way, but Gabriel's! I happen to find Gabe's statement absolutely shocking and sacrilegious.

Once more I have digressed as, sadly, is my wont. Needless to say, our English guests were terribly impressed and Ida, who had invited herself to breakfast, was terribly perplexed, so that anyway you chose to slice the massive wheel of locally made cheddar, most of us were quite pleased. But as nine o'clock drew near and bellies grew round, I clapped my hands. This was much to Agnes's annoyance, I'm afraid.

It's not that I'm a controlling person, mind you; I am merely an organized person who abhors last-minute chaos. A little 'Magdalena oil,' albeit as unpleasant as castor oil, might be just what is called for in situations where people mill about like sheep in front of a corral without any dogs to herd them in.

Had I a pleasant singing voice, I might have chanced breaking into song to get everyone's attention. However, in all honesty, the kindest thing that can be said about my attempts to sing soprano is that I sound remarkably like a screech owl that has been caught in a snare by the neck and is being slowly strangled. In my church everyone is given the opportunity to participate in the choir if that is what they so desire, but the year that I decided to join nobody else did; the word was that no one wanted to be associated with my adenoidal abominations. Ha! I showed them; every Sunday I bravely stood up and sang a solo of some cherished Mennonite hymn, and every Sunday a pack of salivating male blood-hounds would greet me at the side door of the church. Don't get me wrong, I am not complaining – merely stating a fact. A fan club, regardless of its members' species, is still composed of fans.

On this particular morning, however, I clapped my hands loudly. 'People,' I blurted in what I am told is my Oprah Winfrey voice (oh, your UK libel laws drive me crazy!). 'May I have your attention, please? In order to make it to the church on time, we must all move smartly. Peregrine, dear, you have enough crumbs in your "stash" to feed a flock of starlings, and you, Celia, darling, will need to put on an actual shirt, or blouse, over that bit of an undergarment you young folks call a "camisole." As for you, Rupert and Aubrey, I dare say that you two pass muster, although Rupert, your lavender shirt might garner its fair share of snickers, so be forewarned.'

'Ahem,' Peregrine said, ignoring his crumb-laden moustache. 'I told you last night that I was taking a walk; that is still my plan.'

Celia pointed a bare shoulder at me defiantly. 'Papa, may I go with you?'

'Certainly, dear. Although, rally, I suppose you should ask your mother.'

'Oh, mummy, please, do say yes! I'll be ever so good for the remainder of the holiday. I promise that I will. I'll even buff the dry skin off your heels between your visits to the pedicurist – you know, like you've been begging me to do.'

Poor Aubrey turned a sinner's shade of red on Judgement Day. 'I only asked you to do that once, dear. Please don't give these people the wrong impression. Yes, you may accompany your father, but stay with him until I return. Remember that you're in a foreign country and we don't even speak the language.'

'Why I never!' I said, for the first time taking umbrage with any words that fell from Aubrey's bow-shaped lips. 'Of course we speak the same language. Can't you understand what I am saying now?'

Aubrey winked in a way so that I could see it, but not Celia. 'Slow down, Magdalena, and speak a bit louder. Then perhaps I might understand a word here and there.'

'Blimey,' Celia said. 'You two are bonkers.'

105

'Hey, vait a meenut,' my mother-in-law said – she who is truly bonkers. 'Vhy dun't youse all cum to da coinvent wiz me? Vee vill dunce nekkid und zing prazez to da Goddess Apattee.'

'Ma!' Gabe moaned.

'Did I hear correctly?' Peregrine said. 'Did she just reference dancing in the nude?'

'Gross,' Alison said. 'Trust me, youse guys, ya don't want to see that; they're all old women and, like, so old that their boobies hang down to their knees. Except I forgot to mention Auntie Agnes's brothers – sorry, Auntie Agnes, but ya really don't want to see them either, on account of they're like a million, gazillion years old and *their* winky-dinks—'

'I say there,' Rupert said, 'although I was rather looking forward to the traditional Mennonite service at Magdalena's church, singing praises to the Goddess Apathy while dancing about in one's birthday suit rally does have its appeal – hanging winky-dink body parts and all. Yes, jolly good then, count me in for praises with the geezers.'

'That settles it for me,' Peregrine said. 'What is sauce for this gosling is sauce for this goose.'

'More sauce for another gosling,' Celia said. 'Please, mummy, dearest, *please*. I promise not to sass you for an entire week.'

Aubrey gave me a look of quiet desperation that can only be understood by one who has cared for a teenage girl. As a good Christian, I believe in the power of *caramel* just as much as I do in karma. However, what we call the Golden Rule is, in effect, behaving as if we believe in karma.

The difference is that we don't *expect* to be rewarded for our good behaviour. I nodded to give her the go ahead; in fact, I didn't stop there.

'Why don't we all go?' I said.

'Rally?' said Celia.

'Rally,' I said. 'Gosh, it is a lot more satisfying to one's mouth to say "rally," than it is to say "really" – rally it is.'

'Mags,' said the Babester, 'are you feeling OK?'

'I'm fine and dandy. It's just that it's a beautiful day out. Why waste it inside, in a stuffy, musty building, listening to a boring sermon that might possibly elevate us spiritually when instead we can observe octogenarians dance with apathy.' I turned to the others. 'Did any of you happen to pack inflatable haemorrhoid cushions? The courtyard is ringed by benches but they're all concrete. Also, if you want to join in the dancing, I suggest that you wear sunscreen because the rays in this part of the world are especially brutal – not at all like up in the UK. Total nudity is an absolute requirement for that, isn't it, Ida, *dear*?'

Aubrey flashed each of her family members a warning look. 'We are going only as cultural observers. Magdalena, do you mind terribly if we bring our bed pillows to put on the benches?'

I'd been afraid of that question because the truth was that I did mind. I'm not a complete dunce: I know that my guests engage in the reproductive act and other icky things in my rooms. In the old days when I couldn't afford to hire someone to gather the linens each morning, in my mind I would sing 'la-la-la-la-la.' That was

107

then, and this is now, and I don't want my pillows plopped anywhere that apathetic postulates might have plonked their pathetic pink patooties.

'What a droll idea,' I said. 'One of Britain's most noble families toting a motley collection of pillows – ranging from silk filled with eiderdown to burlap filled with straw – into a make-believe convent filled with naked, despairing women. Now that's a sight for sore eyes, as we say in America, and also a sight guaranteed to make English eyes sore. I will be sure to record this and put it on YouTube. It will undoubtedly go viral.'

Poor Rupert; his was the burlap pillow with the straw stuffing, which undoubtedly still had a certain *eau d'rodent* about it. I almost felt sorry for the lad, but my most expensive room package: The Settler's Experience, had been a special gift to him from his parents for not being arrested for drunk driving for the last three months. It wasn't my fault that he'd had to lay his noble noggin on a pillow that I'd made using the torso of one of my scarecrows. At least I'd taken care to evict the family of mice that had taken up residence in it, and not being quite the heartless innkeeper some folks on Facebook have made me out to be, I first found new quarters for this rather large family of rodents.

'Oh dear,' Aubrey said, pulling a long face, 'how positively middle class! Imagine that, Peregrine? The Earl and Countess of Grimsley-Snodgrass toting their motley assortment of pillows! Don't you just love it? Magdalena, I can't think of anything more delightful. And I suppose there will be a surcharge on the toting – yes? Oh, *do* say, "yes"! Make it a hefty fine.'

'Yes, hefty,' said Peregrine. 'Nothing could please me more than hefty.'

'Ach,' Freni cried, throwing her stubby arms heavenward (of course not literally). 'I do not understand these English and their riddles.'

Young Celia recoiled in umbrage. 'What riddles?'

'She finds you to be enigmatic,' I said. 'Chronologically she is two generations older than you but culturally it is more in the neighbourhood of five.'

I glanced at my watch. 'Well, *tempus fugit*, folks. And though we will not be attending a proper house of worship as the Good Lord intends, but will instead be watching a den of deviant nudes, clad only in wrinkles and age spots, dancing indecorously about to scratchy pirated tunes from the nineties – not the best decade for music—'

'No offense, Magdalena,' Rupert said, 'but how would a Mennonite farmwoman like you know what constitutes good music?'

'Uh, be careful son,' Gabe said. 'My wife knows just about everything. Don't ask me how; just trust me on that.'

'Rally? Is that so?'

'Rally, you rascally rabbit,' I said, to show him just how worldly I had become over the years, having once even watched a cartoon or two with my son at a friend's house. 'Now get upstairs, all of you, except for Freni. Brush your teeth and put on some slumming clothes – but do not bring

109

down your pillows. It's either sore bums on concrete or its church.'

'What about me?' Agnes said. 'Where should I wait while everyone is getting ready?'

'Well, dear,' I said, 'you can either be a sweetheart and help Freni clear the table, or else you can wait in the parlour with Granny Yoder's ghost.'

'I'm helping Freni!' Agnes declared without a second's hesitation. Although she's never actually seen my ancestor's 'Apparition American,' she *has* heard Granny's voice on numerous occasions, and oft times Granny has been rather critical of my best friend. Frankly, I chalk this animosity up to jealousy. Granny Yoder was a bitter old woman when I knew her, and in my humble, respectful opinion, death does not become her.

As for the rest of the breakfast bunch, stumbling, mumbling and grumbling, they all obediently pushed and pulled each other up my impossibly steep stairs. In fact, one too many folks attempted the arduous, dizzying ascent.

Ten

BANANA NUT BREAD

1 cup liquid shortening
1 cup dark brown sugar
1 cup white sugar
4 eggs
6 ripe bananas (mashed)
1 tbsp lemon juice
½ cup melted butter (or margarine)

Beat above ingredients together until well blended. Add following dry ingredients that have been mixed together:

2 tsp baking soda
2 tsp baking powder
½ tsp salt
2 cups whole wheat flour
1 cup chopped pecans

Mix well; pour into three greased and floured loaf pans. Bake at 250 degrees for one and a half hours. Cool on rack for ten minutes before taking out of pan.

Eleven

The master bedroom is downstairs, below Alison's room. That way I can keep track of her comings and goings, as a proper mother ought to do, without being literally in her face. At any rate, I'd scarcely enough time to retire to my boudoir to attend to last-minute personal details when what was surely the world's loudest bellow was emitted from somewhere on the second story of my very respectable inn. Believe me when I say that the following description is just barely an exaggeration.

Only once before have I heard a bellow of such magnitude, and that was when Willard Bontrager brought his prize-winning bull, Clarence, over to breed my two dairy cows. Despite her readiness for male companionship, Daisy did not find Clarence attractive and repeatedly rebuffed his advances. Finally, when Clarence wouldn't take a hint, Daisy let loose with a bellow that was heard for miles around.

Emma Hershberger, who owns a catering business over in Bedford, told me that this deluge of mega-decibels caused all ten of her chocolate soufflés to instantly deflate while still in the oven. Reverend Watt Seeno, pastor of the church with thirty-two names up by the interstate highway, declared to his congregation that Daisy's bellow was, in fact, the premiere sounding of Gabriel's horn, soon to be followed by another, and that the rapture was imminent. Perhaps the most momentous consequence of Daisy's peeved outburst was that a planeload of immigrants from the United Kingdom flying into Pittsburgh encountered unexpected turbulence created by the soundwaves. As it happened, the jet had been chartered by a group of authors fleeing the excessively strict libel laws of the United Kingdom. These poor underpaid men and women were so terrified by the intensity of this experience that they each, to a person, ascribed it to an outraged Divinity bent on punishing anyone so arrogant as to think that they might escape the most ridiculous statutes on the face of the globe.

Now where was I? Oh, yes, the bellow that I heard coming from upstairs on that Sunday when my English guests were supposed to be readying themselves for church was not bovine in nature, but emanated from an adult male of the Homo sapiens species. As we are responsible for the welfare of our guests, and not merely overly inquisitive – er, nosy-hosts, we dropped what we were doing (in Gabe's case, his trousers), and hoofed it up my impossibly steep stairs. Having grown up with this staircase gave me an advantage so that I quickly caught up with him, slipped past him on the landing and appeared as if by magic at the top. I'll also have it be known that I wasn't even breathing hard.

When I observed my guests gathered in a tight knot in front of the door of my tiny elevator, I suddenly began to have problems with my respiratory system. My strange symptoms suggested

113

that the oxygen supply had somehow become depleted in the upper story of my now-world-famous inn.

'W-what's going on?' I gasped.

'Oh Magdalena, it's dreadful,' Aubrey said. 'Peregrine discovered – well, you tell her, dear.'

Peregrine waved a flashlight in my face. The Brits, who are far more refined than we, their boorish American cousins, call this item a *torch*! And to think that we poor, pathetic troglodytes reserve the word 'torch' for flames emanating from the end of a pole.

'I had my passport with me,' Peregrine said, 'just in case that nudist colony gets raided by the police – you know how hung up you Americans are on the subject of nudity.'

'And with good reason, dear. If prancing around naked was all right, God Almighty wouldn't have personally tailored tunics out of animal hides for Adam and Eve. Genesis, chapter three, verse twenty-one.'

'I dare say that the pair of them were created naked to begin with,' Rupert said.

'Darest thou?' I said, allowing my dander to rise. 'Do *you*, a lapsed Anglican, actually believe that?'

'No, I can't say that I do—'

'Then butt out, dear.'

'Good on yer, mate,' Aubrey said, sounding incongruously like an Australian. Then again, with this bunch of notable nobles, it seemed like, as the old saying goes: anything goes.

'Well, I won't butt out,' Peregrine boomed in a voice almost as loud as his bellowing. 'What

114

happened next is that I accidently dropped my passport and somehow it slipped down there, between the bloody lift and the floor, so I pushed the "down button" just to move it a bit and guess what I discovered laying across the roof of your miniscule lift?'

'Hmm, well it wasn't America, because Christopher Columbus did that – although actually the Vikings got here long before he did, but they didn't stay, and they didn't enslave entire cultures. And the Good Lord only knows that you English helped the Spanish decimate the native populations of the New World, what with your smallpox and your many Indian wars. And if you want to get really technical, the Indians – many folks call them Native Americans these days – arrived on this continent well over ten thousand years ago, which is four thousand years earlier than the Bible says that the earth was created. Now there is a brainteaser for you, one which you could be asking my preacher, the good Reverend Diffledorf, *if* you decided to accompany me to God's house today instead of shaking your booties with the naked heathens in that Gateway to Hell across the road.'

'Does she *ever* shut up?' Aubrey whispered. Boy, did I feel betrayed.

'Rarely,' said Gabe, just as disloyally. He had, by the way, pulled his trousers up by then. 'But she might now, if just for a minute.' His eyes were as big as cinnamon buns, and he was pointing past Peregrine in the direction of the elevator.

'*What?*' I said. Just to prove my critics wrong,

115

I closed my mouth. And anyway, a closed mouth allows me more energy with which to open my eyes even wider. I didn't, however, like what I saw.

'Holy guacamole!' I screeched. 'What *is* that thing?'

'What does it *look* like?' Peregrine said. At that point he was standing off to the side of the elevator and his demeanour was calm – strangely calm, if you ask me.

'Gabe,' I cried, 'you're a physician! What do *you* think? What I'm looking at doesn't make any sense – but man does it ever stink!'

'It's a mummy of some kind,' Peregrine said.

'Magdalena,' Rupert said, 'if you don't mind me saying so, now that's what I call some first-rate entertainment.'

'Rupert!' his mother said with surprising sharpness. Aubrey turned to me. 'It *is* very realistic, Magdalena, and I'm so glad that you arranged to have Peregrine find it.'

'I most certainly did *not* arrange to have him find this – this, whatever it is!'

'It's a preserved body,' Peregrine said with the equanimity that only a Brit could muster under such horrific conditions. 'When discovered in Egypt and Peru, we called them mummies. Given that this is a Mennonite establishment, shouldn't this be called a "memmy"?' Then he laughed, and to put it frankly, he sounded just like a jackass. '"*mem*" – instead of "mummy,"' he finally said. 'Don't you see?'

'Jolly good joke, that,' Rupert said, and did his own imitation of a braying donkey.

'It's about as funny as a toothache, dears,' I said.

'I'd better call Toy,' Gabe said.

'Yes, Toy,' I said. The reality of what it meant to find a corpse on the roof of my defunct elevator was beginning to hit home and I was beginning to shake.

'Rally?' Aubrey said, for now she had totally turned on me. 'Shouldn't you be calling the police instead of blathering on about toys?'

'Toy *is* the name of our Chief of Police,' Gabriel said as he slipped his arm around my shoulder. 'He's from Charlotte, North Carolina, which, despite its name, is one of our Southern states. And Toy is just like one of those pot-bellied, Southern sheriffs from an old black and white movie that is set in the nineteen sixties: he has a chip on his shoulder as large as the Rock of Gibraltar. He is particularly xenophobic. He can't stand anyone who can't speak English. Good old A*mur*ican English.'

'Say what?' Peregrine said. '*We* speak English. We speak the King's English.'

'That would be the Queen's English,' Aubrey said.

'Not to Toy's ears,' I said to Peregrine as Gabe dialled Toy. 'You speak British. Aubrey speaks a few words of English – Rupert, you seem to have a facility for languages, don't you, dear?'

The lad smiled. 'Rally? You think so?'

'Of course, dear,' I said. Divide and conquer: that was the name of the game, even for a pacifist, and one who had to resort to manipulation in order to win her battles. 'Rupert, repeat the

117

following phrase after me, making sure to rhyme the similarly spelled words with "gain": *the rain in Spain runs down the drain in vain.*'

'I beg your pardon?' Rupert said and shuddered dramatically. Perhaps he was genuinely horrified at the way we Americans torture our diphthongs, or he had never heard the actual lyrics from *My Fair Lady.* Then again, he might have been just a young smart aleck having fun at an old biddy's expense.

'Well, dear,' I said, peevishly, 'we simply must take care not to break the UK's ridiculously strict libel laws, mustn't we? At any rate, practice saying the phrase I gave you – about a thousand times a day – and you'll soon be speaking English as well as Arnold.'

'Arnold? Arnold who?'

'I can't say,' I said. 'It's those pesky libel laws again.'

'Toy's on his way,' Gabe said and gave me a supportive squeeze.

Alas, Toy did not make it there in time.

Twelve

Perhaps I should be more forthcoming; it was, after all, my elevator – but it was not my 'lift', as the Grimsley-Snodgrasses insisted on calling it. 'Lifts' are pads that short men put in the heels of their shoes to make them appear taller, or sometimes the word is used to describe a short ride in one's automobile given as a favour – all right; this is a difficult subject for me to broach. I had been very fond of the young Japanese girl who went missing from my inn, and the second that I laid eyes on this desiccated corpse I knew it was her. Compounding my problem was the fact that Cee-Cee had arrived at the same conclusion.

'Copulating excrement!' she shrieked. 'It's her! Mummy, it's that Japanese tourist, Yoko-san.'

To be sure, those were not the young lady's exact words, nor was she being a proper lady for saying them. Nonetheless, I felt the thumping of webbed feet and heard the familiar honking as a gaggle of geese tromped over my grave – and me not yet buried. How on God's green earth did the cheeky, chai-sipping Cee-Cee know that the young Japanese woman had been named Yoko?

Yes, Yoko is a common enough name in Japan, and virtually everyone on the planet must have heard of Yoko Ono, given that I already had. But Cee-Cee wasn't *everyone*: Cee-Cee was a

119

teenager. Besides, I had raised my sister, Susannah, who was a master manipulator, and who should have been awarded a doctorate in hysteria. I knew when someone was faking it. Believe me, Cee-Cee was not putting us on.

I grabbed Gabe's arm for support. 'My dear,' I said to Cee-Cee, 'how do you know her name?'

By then Cee-Cee's face had turned the colour of feta cheese, a look which did not become her aristocratic features. 'She told me.'

'*Granny Yoder?*' I asked incredulously. The small landing was packed with bodies, now that Agnes and Freni had huffed and puffed their way up my impossibly steep stairs to investigate the hullabaloo.

'Don't be daft,' Cee-Cee said. 'You don't see that old lady anywhere, do you?'

'No, but—'

'Yoko-san told me herself.'

'Now hold your horses, young lady,' the Babester said. 'First off, don't you be calling my wife daft. You *will* respect her. And second, are you saying that a dried-up, desiccated corpse spoke to you?'

English eyes roll with American accents – or is it vice versa? If Cee-Cee had been my child I would have confined her to her room, what with all the eye-rolling, sighing, lower-lip protrusion that kid produced during her stay with me. Why, one day when she was pouting, a family of eight could have dined al fresco on her bottom lip, it stuck out so far.

Now where was I? Oh, yes, when Gabe demanded that aristocrat brat with the attitude treat me with respect, she actually did – for at least a little while.

'Yes,' Cee-Cee said emphatically, but without a trace of nastiness. 'Yoko-san told me her name, and she is speaking now.' The pretty girl, dressed in a Sunday frock, edged closer to the open shaft and cupped a dainty hand behind her right ear. 'What is that you say, Yoko-san? No, I reckon that they won't believe me, but I'll tell them anything that you want me to.'

Of course, I wouldn't believe her, but that didn't stop me from edging closer to the elevator shaft and admonishing everyone to 'shush,' so that Cee-Cee could hear every word. After several minutes, during which Cee-Cee alternated between making comforting noises and asking questions of the corpse, she finally turned away from the shaft whilst covering her face with her sleeve. I'm sure that Cee-Cee did so in order to hide the fact that she'd been weeping, for the Brits abhor any public display of emotion. One tear too many and there goes the starch from a stiff upper lip!

Therefore I allowed the poor child sufficient time to regain her composure by ushering everyone back downstairs and into the dining room. Once there, I made them take their proper places at my expansive table (built by my ancestor Jacob the Strong). The expression 'it was like trying to herd cats' was far too generous to use in describing the effort required to manoeuvre this group, despite the fact that my impossibly steep staircase is rather narrow and thus does not allow many escape options. I would, instead, compare the act of getting this motley crew downstairs in a timely manner to that of trying to dress a six-legged cat in a pair of four-legged tights – not that I've had much experience with the latter, mind you. At any rate, when Cee-Cee did begin to speak on behalf of the dead woman, the others had grown so silent that one could have heard a frog fart from as far away as my neighbour's farm pond.

'Yoko-san has been dreadfully lonely,' Cee-Cee said. 'It's been three years since that awful lift pinned her up against the ceiling, pressing her there like a flower that has been placed between the pages of a book to dry. She says that not once have you paid her a visit. It's not like she would have blamed you, even though the accident was your fault – what with the terrible state of repair your lift was in. And when her weak cries for assistance went unanswered – for she didn't die immediately – well, she was even willing to overlook that. But when you began complaining of the stench from her decomposing body, blaming it on a family of mice that had died behind the wallboard – that was just too much for her to bear.'

'Ahem,' Gabriel said, 'corpses do not have emotions – ergo, they cannot be said to find things unbearable.'

'Ahem, yourself,' Agnes said. 'This is far better than *Downton Abbey*! This will be excellent for business, Magdalena, because zombies are really big right now – which is, of course, how we'll explain our so-called talking corpse. You don't suppose that we could laminate her and keep her where she is, do you?'

'What in Satan's Home?' Gabe roared. He actually said a much worse word, which I will not repeat. 'The "*her*" to which you are referring, Agnes, happens to be a girl. She is not your driver's licence!'

'Honestly, Gabe,' my bestie said, her lower lip quivering, 'you don't have to be so rude.'

I am quite certain that Cee-Cee gave my Beloved and I each a smug look before opening her big yap again. 'Poor Yoko-san. She says that the big hairy *gaijin* roars like a drunken sumo wrestler, and this prevents her passing from being a peaceful one. Mrs – uh – Maga – Mrs Yoder—'

'You may call me Magdalena, dear, although normally one has to be older than my sturdy Christian underwear in order to do that.'

'Well then, Magdalena,' said Rupert in his leering, aristocratic drawl, 'you've been holding back on us, have you? Do tell us everything about your *dirty* Christian underwear.'

'I said *sturdy*, not dirty, you id— I mean, dear. You see, a proper Christian wears thick, hefty undergarments that cover all the shameful parts. A really good Christian woman – and I'm not judging here, mind you – always wears a skirt, and a nice full petticoat, and of course her unmentionables, which should have enough white cotton fabric in them to supply a schooner with sails.'

'Puh-*leez*, Mom,' groaned Alison, 'ya ain't gonna bore us with that story again, are ya, just when Cee-Cee's about to tell us more about what the dead lady said?'

'Forsooth, I am,' I said. 'It happened up there on Stucky Ridge, that very mountain over yonder.'

I waved a gangly arm. 'I was doing detective work, as is my wont from time to time, and on this particular occasion I came to the startling conclusion that the murderer was, in fact, our very own police chief, Melvin Stoltzfus. I confronted him with my theory and it was all downhill from there for me – literally. The chief, who was the meanest, craziest cretin that ever walked the face of the earth, immediately pushed me off a sheer cliff. As I plunged hundreds of feet to my death, I asked the Good Lord to forgive not only my sins but the sins of that nut job as well.' I took a deep breath and paused for dramatic effect.

'Und den vhat?' Mother Malaise demanded. 'Did you live?'

Ding, dang, dong! To my credit, I kept my swear words to myself. But really, how could I be blamed for thinking them? My diminutive but top-heavy nemesis had somehow managed to dodge the occasional horse that clops along Hertzler Road and infiltrate my perfect example of an English breakfast. For the record, I know that it was perfect because it was all Agnes's bailiwick. When that gal gets a bee in her bonnet, even the Kremlin puts in orders for honey.

'Und did you live?' Ida persisted.

I smiled broadly. 'Yes! I lived, and all because of my sturdy Christian underwear. My petticoat caught the breeze, opened up like a parachute and lowered me gently into the outstretched arms of a giant oak tree. Then, since my God-given life was still at stake, I threw both caution and modesty to the wind, slipped out of my enormous white cotton bloomers and hung them from two branches. There my unmentionables flapped in the breeze rather like an enormous flag. In all honesty, that breeze felt pretty good you-know-where.'

'You go girl!' Mother Malaise cried triumphantly.

'Rally, Magdalena,' Peregrine said with surprising gentleness, 'as interesting as your tales are, I do think that your daughter has a point: it would be disrespectful *not* to listen to what the young Japanese woman has to say. While it is true that she does not have eyes, ears, and a mouth in the traditional sense, she has crossed over a threshold that separates the omniscient from the merely aware. Since the creature has given my daughter the ability to communicate with those who have passed ahead, as she has put it so eloquently, it would be an affront to Him not to avail ourselves of this opportunity.'

'*I* said all that?' Alison asked. 'About a *front* and a *veil*, and all that kinda stuff?'

Gabe winked. 'All my women say deep things.'

Mother Malaise blushed with pride and patted her wimple. 'Ya, Gabeleh, und even me?'

'Yes, Ma.'

My mother-in-law lacks a neck. This is only conjecture, mind you, as I have not yet attempted to wring it. Whatever the case may be, Ida Rosen, aka Mother Malaise, can swivel her head 360 degrees and with the speed of a ceiling fan set on high when she feels threatened.

'Ha, Magdalena,' she said. 'Und you said dat I vas only as deep as my shadow. Mebbe you aren't such a schmarty pants after all. Who knows, mebbe I'm schmarter den you!'

Just as a tart retort was forming on the launching pad that is my tongue, I spied our Chief of Police, Toy Graham, standing in the doorway to the lobby. Heaven only knows how long he'd been there. If he'd only just arrived, perhaps I still stood a chance of giving him the impression that I was somewhat in control.

I smiled benevolently at Ida. 'Yes, Mother Mayonnaise, whatever you say.' I turned to Cee-Cee. 'Carry on, dear.'

Cee-Cee didn't waste a second. 'Yoko-san wants to go home,' she said.

'*Home?*' Aubrey said. 'You mean, to England?'

That was too much even for a rabid anglophile like Agnes. 'Not *everyone* stranded on foreign shores identifies with England as home,' she said rather curtly.

Aubrey coloured slightly but nonetheless stood her ground. 'Yes, but I've heard that many people amongst the second, and even third generations of Australians, New Zealanders and South Africans of English descent, speak fondly of England as "home." We were once a mighty power, you know, and our strong moral compass and impeccable manners were the gifts of civilization that we so generously spread throughout the heathen world.'

'Along with venereal disease and a God who punishes his victims for all eternity,' Gabriel said.

'I beg your pardon!' Peregrine boomed. 'You, sir, will apologize to the Lady Grimsley-Snodgrass at once.'

126

Knowing that Gabe would not apologize, I jumped in to diffuse the situation. 'Actually, I'm pretty sure that my husband knows what he's talking about, because he's a doctor and he knows that venereal disease was spread by seaman – uh, no pun intended. As for the punishment part, he's pretty accurate about that too. You see, Gabe is Jewish, and in Judaism God's punishments don't last longer than eleven months, but in Christianity – well, if one doesn't accept Christ's free gift of salvation then one suffers forever in the place called Hell.'

'True that,' Alison said. 'Yinz can see why I picked my dad's religion.'

'Stuff and nonsense,' Peregrine said. 'If we're ever going to get to the nude dancing we'd best finish this séance in a timely manner.'

'It's *not* a séance,' Cee-Cee said emphatically. 'It's a *reading*. And what Yoko-san has been so patiently waiting to tell us is that her home is on the Island of Honshu in a city called Kakogawa in Hyogo Prefecture. Although her city is on the coast, it has a steel mill so it isn't very attractive, but the mountains behind the city are beautiful. Yoko-san said that her parents both died in the Kobe earthquake of nineteen ninety-five. But her grandfather is an apple grower on an ancestral plot of land at the back edge of the city towards the mountains. The variety of apples that he grew was known as the sweetest in all of Japan. She wants to return home to him and have a proper Shinto burial ceremony. But first you must cremate her remains.'

Upon finishing this rather lengthy narration,

Cee-Cee closed her eyes and slid down in her chair until she all but disappeared beneath the massive oak table. By all appearances, acting as a medium had left her deeply exhausted.

'Oh, darling,' Aubrey said and patted her daughter's slumped shoulder. This was the English equivalent of Aubrey crying out in alarm and then clasping Cee-Cee tightly to her bosom whilst rocking her to and fro.

Truth be told, I was gobsmacked by what I had just heard and seen. For one thing, Cee-Cee's tone and diction had been much improved during her recitation. It certainly hadn't sounded like a teenager's voice and it wasn't her normal high-falutin accent. Nor was it Yoko-san's voice. But the thing that I found to be the most shocking was that the information it conveyed was all true.

Yoko-san herself had shared the story of her parents' tragic death in Kobe, when a highway overpass collapsed on their car during the earth-quake. Her parents had gone into the big city on a semi-annual shopping trip. I shared with her how my parents were squished to death in a tunnel by a truck carrying running shoes and a tanker filled with milk. My parents were also headed into the big city – Pittsburgh – to shop. After sharing our stories, Yoko-san and I laughed ruefully and called ourselves the 'shopping trip orphans.' I also knew that the young Japanese woman lived with her grandfather near the moun-tains. After all, I had his address down as her home address in my register.

The fact that Cee-Cee really could communi-cate with bones and hair in my house left me feeling spiritually conflicted and a trifle guilty. The Bible makes it very clear that one is not to communicate with the dead, and when King Saul visited the Witch of Endor and had her conjure up the spirit of Samuel, he was punished for it. Endora – now wouldn't that be a fitting name for a witch? Ach, but I keep digressing. What I want to say is that despite this biblical injunction not to chat with the dearly departed, I really have had no choice with Granny Yoder. *That* Apparition-American appeared to me in all her gory – pun intended – the night of my eighth birthday, and has stuck to me like white on rice ever since. The harder that I try to ignore her, the more she intrudes into my life, popping up hither, thither and yon like small, sticky hand-prints when one has a toddler in the house.

'Earth to Magdalena. Come in, Magdalena.'

'Huh?'

'Or do I need to go back to calling you Miss Yoder again to get your attention?'

It is true that I can zone out rather intensely. However, it was quite pleasant to be reined back into the public sphere by the melodious voice of the extraordinarily handsome Toy Graham. On second thought, I might be a menopausal woman but I am not dead, so it may have been his phero-mones and not his voice that pulled me back to consciousness. By the way, please allow me to state emphatically that although they are both Southerners, Toy Graham is not even distantly related to Senator Lindsay Graham!

At any rate, I stood and saluted Toy. 'Magdalena is my name, ask me again and I'll tell you the

129

same.' Then I bowed and with a sweeping gesture acknowledged my guests. 'These are my aristocrats *d'jour*. They don't have royal hinnies so they're not Royal Highnesses. He's only an earl, and for some strange reason she's a countess, and as for the lad, he's a viscount, but the letter 's' in his title doesn't count, and neither do any of their titles, as a matter of fact, since they're over here in the liberated colonies.'

'Even so,' Cee-Cee said, 'you didn't mention that I have a title.'

'You're quite right, dear,' I said. 'This cherubic-faced youngster is the lovely Lady Celia.'

'Oh, blimey,' the girl said. Unlike Agnes, I can't tell the difference between Downstairs and Upstairs speech, but if I had to venture a guess, I'd say that this was the former.

Toy remained as cool as macaroni salad. 'Lovely to meet you,' he said.

'Humph,' I said. 'Now, allow me to introduce you to the rest of the Grimsley-Snodgrass family.'

Toy extended an impeccably groomed hand to Aubrey. 'Welcome to the United States of America, and to Hernia, Mrs Grimsley-Snodgrass.'

Aubrey wilted like an overcooked asparagus spear. 'Charmed, I'm sure,' she chirped in a register I'd yet to hear her use.

Peregrine, on the other hand, was slow to extend *his* hand in return. 'I say there, young fellow, judging by your uniform you are either a bobby or a constable. In either case you are woefully ignorant of the proper protocol exercised upon greeting visiting dignitaries. I am not *Mr*

130

Grimsley-Snodgrass. Since you are a foreigner, I suppose that some allowance should be made. Therefore I am acquiescing to a previous arrangement with the innkeeper: if you *must* address me personally, you may call me by my Christian name: Peregrine.'

Sometimes I just can't help myself: the Devil whispers in my ear and my tongue slips. 'I was mistaken about having no royal visitors,' I said. 'Peregrine is the Prince of Pomposity. He keeps forgetting that *he* is the foreigner here.'

Toy is a consummate Southern gentleman. His ability to placate with prevaricating platitudes is unprecedented in my opinion. Frankly, I don't understand his regionalisms, but when delivered in his charming Southern drawl, even snippets from the telephone directory would soothe this savage beast.

'I beg your pardon, sir,' he said to Peregrine. 'Now take two ducks and rub them together, and when ships pass in the night joy cometh in the morning.' At least that's what it sounded like to me; our Southern dialect of English has many idioms which an idiot like me can be slow to decipher.

'Apology accepted,' Peregrine said with a smile. 'I think that I'm going to like this chap.'

A gal is allowed to change her mind about soothing snippets. This was the first time that I'd seen the earl's lips curl in an upward direction and it irked me to no end. Surely the gobbledegook from *this* goose, meaning *moi*, was just as good as the gobbledegook from a gander named Toy.

'The aubergine wore gabardine and the piglet played Rachmaninoff,' I said, every bit as soothingly.

Peregrine recoiled in disgust, as if I'd dangled a slice of burnt American toast in his face. 'What the bloody blazes does that mean?'

Gabe stood and extended his muscular arms out to me in pity. 'Hon,' he said softly, 'it's been a trying day for you. Perhaps you need to lie down.'

His meddling mother jumped to her feet as well, but given the fact that her legs are the shape and length of upended bowling pins, she gained no height by standing. 'Dat vun,' she said, pointing accusingly at me, 'eez *meshuggeneh*.' She gave each noble noggin a meaningful nod. 'Ya know vhat I mean? Crazy, yah?'

'Ma!' It was barely more than a whine. My handsome hunk of a hubby, the man who adores me, is tied to his mother by apron strings that have the power to regenerate themselves.

Thank heavens that the younger of the room's two hunks came to my rescue. 'Miss Yoder,' Toy said, sounding very professional. 'I need to speak with you alone on a matter of police business. The rest of you may be excused to go about your day.'

'Gut,' Mother Malaise said. 'Now vee vill go und dunce nekkid.'

Thirteen

Neither the Babester nor our daughter wanted to see Ida and her mirthless mob of misanthropes cavort about in the altogether, so they headed into Bedford (an actual town of several thousand people!) to 'catch a movie.' This meant that poor Agnes was stuck chaperoning our guests across the road to the pseudo-convent. There she would be forced to watch the heathens shake their hinnies. The woman was going to be humiliated yet again by her two nude octogenarian uncles. It wasn't simply their nudity that embarrassed Agnes (she grew up living next door to them), it was the total abandonment with which Big Will and Little Will shared their willies with the world (certain attributes being not at all equal between them, if one gets my drift).

Toy, of course, wanted to inspect the corpse, and insisted on climbing out on the roof of the elevator. There he crouched, having donned surgical gloves and a mask, and bearing a torch and magnifying glass. He gave the appearance of a man who actually knew what he was doing. Admittedly, this surprised me a wee bit, as I had hired him fresh out of the police academy down in Charlotte.

However, in what seemed to me to be a some-what cursory investigation, Toy shone the bright beam of his torch on the ceiling of the elevator shaft. Had the shaft been empty at that point, one could have heard a pin hit the bottom if dropped from the second floor.

'You see that?' said Toy. 'There you have an almost perfect imprint of her body left on the ceiling by her bodily fluids – how shall I say this delicately – as she expanded and shrank during the process of decomposition. To put it bluntly, Miss Yoko-san was pressed up into the ceiling, rather like a panini, where she remained stuck for some time. It never occurred to anyone to search for her up there. Then, at some point, which forensics can determine, gravity claimed her desiccated corpse and it came to rest solely in the roof of the elevator.' Without further ado, Toy hopped down and stripped off his gloves.

'Toy,' I said, 'that was very impressive work. But before you go any further with the investigation, it's only fair that I tell you that this corpse is haunted.'

The chief glanced back at where he'd just been. 'Haunted? In what way?'

I leaned in close to him so that I could whisper. He had the heady scent of a virile man in his twenties – one who'd recently showered but who had not covered up his own smell with manufactured odours. I'm not confessing to any sinful thoughts, like a desire to jump his bones or anything like that, but one should be ever vigilant lest the Devil gain entrance through the back door during a sneak attack. I'm just saying.

'Apparently this corpse is able to talk,' I said while maintaining a businesslike tone.

'*What?*'

'Just like Grandma Yoder talked to you,' I said. 'I told you later that I was just playing along with you in order to keep you calm. Of course I did *not* see your great-grandmother's ghost; I don't believe in that nonsense.'

'We Mennonites do not believe that violence solves anything either, but it still exists.'

'Apples and oranges,' he said.

'Perhaps,' I said. 'Anyway, Yoko-san was something of an expert on apples, remember?'

'Yeah,' Toy said. 'Her grandfather was famous for a sweet variety that he grew in the foothills of the Japanese Alps.' He looked at me quizzically. 'What's this apple business all about?'

'Yoko-san mentioned it to my youngest guest – a girl, age seventeen.'

As Toy absorbed this new information, he began to nod. 'Magdalena, you mean that she related this information to your guest several years ago.'

'No. The conversation took place this *morning*.'

Toy backed against the wall. I might as well have told him that I had a new type of plague.

'You're creeping me out, Magdalena.'

'How do you think that I feel?' I wailed.

'But please tell me that you didn't hear the voice as well,' he said.

'No, dear, I'm merely wacky; I'm not a whackadoodle. Cee-Cee, on the other hand, knew everything about Yoko-san's family: about her parents dying in the earthquake, about her living with her grandfather who hybridized apples. Tell me, where would a seventeen-year-old girl, visiting from England, get that information?'

'From your files? Kids own the internet – if you know what I mean.'

I wagged my head in a kindly, motherly fashion. 'You poor, misinformed, *enfant effete*. Why on earth would I risk having my records shared with the world – thanks to some hackist – when a trusty yellow pad of paper and a No. 2 pencil is all that I need? It wouldn't surprise me to learn that the New Testament was written with a No. 2 pencil.'

That wasn't meant as a joke, but Toy laughed anyway. 'Good one,' he said. 'Please don't take offense, however, when I tell you that the correct word is hack*er*, not hack*ist*.'

'Don't be silly, dear; offense was indeed taken. In my day, we wouldn't have dreamed of correcting our elders. Now, where was I? Oh, yes, I was about to divulge the location of my private files. Do I have your solemn word as a gentleman that you will never disclose their whereabouts to anyone else?'

Toy held up one hand as if he were in a courtroom and about to take an oath. 'I solemnly swear,' he said.

'For the record, a simple "yes" would have sufficed, given that the Bible forbids us to swear. But seeing that you are a lapsed Episcopalian, which is merely a transplanted Anglican, and barely one step away from Rome, I shall let it slide – for now. So come on, follow me down my evil – I mean, impossibly steep – stairs. Just don't follow me too closely on account of I'm as scrawny as a half-stuffed scarecrow and my bones break more easily than those of tinned salmon.'

136

'I have an idea,' Toy said bravely. 'I'll go first, and then if you fall you can land across my broad shoulders and feel my rippling back muscles and then my tight buns as they bring you gently, and lovingly, to a stop. However, if I hear you begin to stumble before you start toppling, I shall whip around, catch you in my bulging biceps and pull you in close, to hold you next to my washboard abs.'

Now, to be utterly truthful, I have taken the liberty of paraphrasing Toy's words. Perhaps a good deal. Maybe as much as ninety per cent. Suffice it to say, I followed him down to the main floor and then led him into the parlour, where I proceeded to roll back the corner of a suitably threadbare carpet: that is to say one of sufficient shabbiness as to warrant its place in a pseudo-authentic Pennsylvania Dutch farmhouse that had been converted into an inn. My Amish ancestors would have held that even a pretend Persian was too prideful, insisting that nothing but plain wood floors would do. I, however, am not Amish but Old Order Mennonite, and being on the liberal side of that spectrum, have taken liberties to keep my tootsies warm. Yes, I could have chosen a plain brown or even a fancy grey rug in various shades of that colour.

But God could have chosen to make the peacock brown, or fifty shades of grey – which He most certainly did not! I am convinced that if it was the Creator's wish that we live a life of drabness He would not have given us peacocks, sunsets, flowers and the sapphire blue of the Babester's eyes.

137

'Holy Cannoli!' Toy said upon viewing my cleverly hidden trapdoor. 'To think of all the times that I've been in this room and I never suspected that there was anything under this ratty old rug.'

'I beg your pardon!'

'I meant no offense, Magdalena. I'm sure, just judging by the wear on this relic, that it was that crazy old granny of yours who bought it – when she was *alive*, ha, ha.'

The ambient temperature of the room plummeted even as the temperature under my collar rose. 'I'll have you know that Granny Yoder may have been as tart as a peck of crab apples, but she wasn't crazy. She had a mind like a steel trap and the focus of a falcon at a brush fire. You would do well not to speak ill of her in this room, the very place where she holds court.'

'Oh, phooey,' Toy scoffed. With his false bravado he expelled enough air to raise a disturbingly dense cloud of dust. It is my philosophy that dusting one's house, just like combing one's hair, is a grand waste of time, as it is an activity which will invariably need to be repeated. For the record, I do comb my hair, because I 'must.' Mama drilled this lesson into me on my behind with my hairbrush. This rule, along with brushing my teeth three times a day and making my bed, are what I call the Rules of *Must*erbation. Dusting is an option that I offer to my guests; for fifty extra dollars a day they may dust the room of their choice. Unfortunately, the Grimsley-Snodgrasses had thus far proved to be a lazy bunch and had signed on for very few of my – ahem – admittedly pricey options.

'Phooey yourself,' a somewhat reedy, disembodied voice said. Honestly, it did not emanate from me.

'What the devil!' Toy ejaculated. Of course I mean that in the most genteel sense of the word.

'I will not tolerate swearing in my house!' Granny Yoder said, her voice growing stronger.

'Holy smoke!' Toy turned as white as your average American's teeth, ones that have been brushed three times a day and also periodically subjected to expensive bleach strips.

'Turn around,' I said. 'Now look over there – in the rocking chair. What do you see?'

Without a doubt, the young Chief of Police saw Granny Yoder. If I was a betting woman – which I am not, because gambling is a sin – I would have bet the PennDutch Inn *and* my twenty-five acres of woods and pasture that Hernia's Chief of Police was staring at my resident spectre. Of course, the staring only commenced *after* he'd stepped back into the shoes he'd jumped out of, and had slicked down his hair which had stood on end.

Toy took forever to answer. 'I don't see anything,' he finally said. 'Well, except a ton of dust motes illuminated by those light rays that somehow manage to filter through your filthy curtains. Really, Magdalena, no offense but I'm a better housekeeper, and I'm a bachelor.'

'Yeah? Well, you don't run a business, plus have two little boys and a teenager to care for now, do you?'

139

'You don't either,' Toy said. 'You only have one little boy and that's Little Jacob.'

'Harrumph,' I said. 'Are you forgetting that when I married Gabriel, the famous heart surgeon from New York, his mother still cut his meat for him?'

Toy shivered and managed to laugh at the same time. 'That is pretty ironic: a man who cuts into the body's most vital organ has to have his mama cut his steak for him. At least she doesn't do *that* anymore.'

'That's right, dear,' I said, 'but only because *I* cut his meat for him. The woman who spent thirty-three agonizing hours bringing him into this world – "oy, oy, such pain you wouldn't believe" – was over here Tuesday night and wanted to cut up his ground beef casserole for him.'

'And?'

'I sent her back to the convent with a mashed turnip and turkey liver pie.'

'Yuck,' Toy said. '*You* made that?'

'Bite your tongue, dear. We had a dessert exchange at church and I ended up being the loser for the eighth year in a row. Anyway, make nice with Granny now so we can get on with our business.'

Toy cleared his throat loudly and squared his shoulders. 'Again, Magdalena, I don't see your granny. Frankly, and I don't mean any disrespect, neither do you. Ghosts don't exist; they are just figments of overactive imaginations.'

'Bullfinches!' Granny said.

If Toy hadn't been so startled by the force of

140

Granny Yoder's outburst, I might have jumped into his strong, sinewy arms and have him hold me next to his sculpted body for protection. As it was, I thought the young man was going down for the count, and *I* was going to have to scrape *him* off my cheap facsimile of an Oriental carpet. After that I would clasp him tightly with my stick-like appendages, pressing him against my bony carapace until he got his second wind and demanded that I release him.

'Stop it, Magdalena,' Toy said angrily when he could at last speak. 'Stop it with this ghost nonsense. I don't know how you're managing to pull off these illusions or that bit when you threw your voice just now. This is not the time for parlour tricks – no pun intended.'

My temperature had started to climb but premenopausal hormones had nothing to do with it. 'Don't toy with my temper, Toy. I may exaggerate but I don't fabricate out of whole fabric, not when it's official police business.'

'Listen,' said Toy, 'I'll take your word for it that you keep your files in some hole under your living-room floor—'

'*Hole*, shmole!' I said. '*That* is a proper cellar with head clearance even for yours truly, she who stands five foot ten in her thick cotton stockings. My ancestor who built the original house was one of the Hochstetlers who survived the Northkill Amish massacre. The family managed to survive the night in the cellar of their burning log cabin by splashing cider on the wood ceiling. Although attacks from the Delaware Indians had ceased by the time the family moved here, their memory

141

had not. Think of this as the prototype of a "safe room."'

'Hmm,' said Toy, 'it seems more like a death trap with a trapdoor to me.'

'Ignorance may be bliss for some, but in this case it's a wide miss. *This* cellar has an escape tunnel, which was originally built by my ancestors who had survived massacres in the eastern part of Pennsylvania. But the other trapdoor opens above a so-called "safe-room," which the Babester insisted that we build – never mind, I have said too much. I shouldn't have even mentioned the existence of the second safe room. The fact that one is safer than the other—' I slapped both cheeks. 'For further penance, I shall chew a mouthful of thumb tacks and wear lipstick to church.'

'Hussy,' Granny Yoder hissed. 'Only trollops wear lip rouge.'

'You tell her, Granny,' Toy said with a laugh.

'Aha,' I cried, 'you *can* hear her!'

'What?' Toy said. 'I didn't hear your granny; I heard you threaten to wear lipstick to church. Your kind of Mennonite doesn't wear "war paint," as you have so often, charmingly described it.'

'Give me a break,' I said.

'Puh-leeze,' he said, 'can we finally get back to discussing the matter of the corpse and the countess?' With that he took one of my wrists in one of his impeccably manicured hands and steered me gently back into the dining room.

In my opinion, a man who grooms his fingernails without being coached is such a rarity that he should be given protected minority status. If he keeps his nostrils *and* his ears free of unsightly hair, he deserves public recognition. But woe to the man who dares to eat at any establishment, no matter how humble, in a sleeveless garment locally referred to as a 'wife-beater' T-shirt. 'Armpit hair and *haricot vert* are not compatible,' a winsome wag of the feminine persuasion once wrote.

Now where was I, besides feeling the pleasant warmth of that perfectly cared-for hand? Ah, yes, I was facing off with a very stubborn young man who couldn't be honest with himself.

'Cee-Cee is *not* a countess; she is simply a Lady – with a capital L, because she's not always a lady, if you get my drift.'

'Look,' he said, just to prove my point about being stubborn, 'if your granny really did hang around as a ghost, why don't you have her communicate with Yoko-san directly and have her get the whole gruesome story from start to finish? Or more to the point, why is it that *you* can't communicate with the remains of your Japanese guest and this Cee-Cee girl can?'

'I'll take your questions in order, dear. First of all, Granny doesn't realize that she is dead. If she did, she'd be in Heaven with Grandpa. Now, I know that's not good Christian theology—'

Toy let go of my wrist and planted his tight, round buttocks on the dining-room chair next to me. 'Spare me the sermon, Magdalena. I'm crossing your granny out of the picture for good. But the English girl; that's another story. That one's hard to explain.'

I smiled wryly. 'Impossible is more like it

143

– unless the girl had a chance to peek at the official police report on Yoko-san's disappearance. *That* report is stored in the files at your office.'

Toy is generally a mild-mannered man, but just then he pounded the table so hard that crumbs from the breakfast scones danced. 'You better darn well be joking,' he growled. 'I keep my cabinets under lock and key and nobody else has access to their contents. Even my secretary has to ask for the key when she wants to file something away, and Darla Hipslinger has been with me for eighteen months.'

'It was nineteen as of last Thursday,' I said pleasantly, 'but who is counting? Certainly not Darla. When I interviewed her for that job she thought that a year had just ten months in it. It was you who told her that she had the job before we'd had a chance to confer.'

'That's because she'd be working for me.'

'But *I'd* be paying her salary. I'd also have to be assaulted by the sight of her gigantic bosoms bobbling about in her low-cut blouses every time I stepped foot into the police station, which, by the way, I also maintain.'

Some men emit an off-putting odour when they are angry, reminiscent of a polecat, but not Police Chief Toy. Warm gingerbread pudding with lemon sauce was as close as I could describe his scent, perhaps giving a literal interpretation to the expression 'I could eat him with a spoon.' Yes, I know, according to both Jesus and Jimmy Carter I have already committed adultery in my mind, but I had *not* intended to. I had not set out to lust after a man younger than my oldest set of sturdy Christian underwear. It just happened!

'What's come over you, Magdalena?' Toy said curtly.

'I beg your pardon?'

'You're behaving strangely.'

'Yam I – I mean, *am* I?'

'Yes. If it wasn't so preposterous, one might be tempted to think that you're jealous of poor little Darla.'

When they say that the truth hurts, is that because it stings as if one's face has been slapped?

'*Excuse* me?'

'Forgive me; like I said, it was an asinine thing to say. I mean, what would a gorgeous mature woman like you see in a dud like me?'

I tried responding but my tongue, which had become detached from its base, was roiling around in my mouth in a sea of foam like a giant eel and was threatening to strangle me. I tried swallowing this saliva-covered monster, but that only made things worse.

Toy appeared to observe me warily. 'You're not coming down with the flu, are you?' he asked.

'I beg your pardon?'

'Your eyes are hooded and your face is pale,' he said, not unkindly. 'If you're going to get sick, please turn and face the other way; this is a freshly-laundered uniform.'

I gasped. 'Why I never!'

'These incidents can be hard to predict,' he said matter-of-factly. 'Why, once in Charlotte, at my Auntie Gayle's house for Christmas dinner – or was it at Uncle Rob's, when we were there for Easter brunch—'

'Please spare me the nauseating details,' I hissed. 'Physically, I am quite all right.'

'And emotionally?'

'What is *that* supposed to mean?' There are times when I am sure that my words are capable of slicing through a block of aged, extra sharp Irish cheddar. However, it is rarely my intention to be downright mean. When I was nine years old I purposely leaked India ink from my fountain pen on to Norma Harmon's pink party dress. Granted, this was not a nice thing to do, as my sore bottom reminded me for the next few days. Then again, Norma had unwisely chosen to wear that dress to school just to taunt me, so I wasn't entirely at fault. Anyway, what got me dancing with the Devil cheek to cheek that day was that Norma Harmon had invited every girl in my class to her house after school, except for me. The reason for my exclusion, relayed to me by my mother, was that my feet smelled. Anyway, that's as mean as I ever got.

'Magdalena, you are not superwoman,' Toy said, interrupting my reverie. 'You don't have to keep pretending that you are.' He reached across the table and scooped my twitching hands up in his. 'You're a hard woman to read; perhaps I was way out of line before. If so, I apologize. No, I *do* apologize. Of course, you're just stressed out by the corpse on the roof of your elevator car. I mean, who wouldn't be? Like, duh, right?'

Like duh? Alas, poor Yoko-san, what would William Shakespeare think of his language now?

146

Who knows? He might well embrace it, given that he had a penchant for inventing new words himself.

'Right,' I said to Toy, just to prove that I was hip and not in need of a hip replacement.

With his strong, masculine but well-manicured hands still holding mine, he began to muse out loud. 'What we need now is some sort of game plan. Right?'

'Right, again.'

'Magdalena, you hired me; you know that you got me up here on the cheap because I graduated at the bottom of my class.'

'Shh,' I said. 'The walls have ears. Besides, we agreed never to speak of that again.'

'Yes, but you know that I don't think good under pressure.'

'Well.'

'Excuse me?'

'You don't think *well* under pressure. *Good* is incorrect usage.'

'You see? I can't speak well under pressure, either.'

'Not to worry, dear; I am not the grammar police.' I pulled my hands somewhat reluctantly from the warmth of his. Truth be told, for me there are few pleasures which can trump that of a full-scale murder investigation. 'This is what we'll do,' I said. 'You just follow my lead and in no time at all we'll solve the case of the corpse on my elevator car roof.'

Fourteen

'First,' I said, 'we need to ascertain whether or not Yoko-san's death was murder or an accident.'

Unlike yours truly, Toy is 'married' to electronic gadgetry. Nonetheless, when it comes to investigating crimes he prefers to jot information down by hand in pocket-size notebooks using ballpoint pens. He said this practice comes from years of watching television shows about private investigators.

'Agreed,' Toy said as he scribbled away at the tiny tablet. 'And we can't rule out suicide, either.'

'*What?* I'm not trying to be argumentative, Toy, but who in their right mind would squeeze apart the elevator doors on the upper level, lie atop the roof, and then wait for someone to ride the elevator up and hopefully squish them against the ceiling?'

Toy's eyes scanned me calmly. Kindly. Even lovingly – in the good friend sort of way.

'Magdalena, who in their right mind commits suicide?'

'Touché, Toy,' I said. 'So, how do we proceed from here?'

Toy raked one of his impeccably groomed hands through a head of thick brown hair. 'If this was one of those cosy mystery novels that you ladies are so fond of reading, I would suggest

148

that we begin with a cup of tea – perhaps even a pot – while we rehash the facts and wait for an epiphany.'

'I beg your pardon, dear. What makes you think that *I* read those dreadful mystery novels?' I rolled my eyes in mock dismay. 'I read only nonfiction books; why read fiction, I say? After all, fiction is all made up.'

Even when he grimaces, Toy is devilishly handsome. 'Somehow I think you're not kidding. Well, anyway, here's what we do: we divide the work even-steven. First I'm going to call in a forensics coroner from Harrisburg. I'm thinking of Dorothy Stillbladder. She's said to be the best the state has to offer. What are your thoughts?'

'I think that she is a brave woman not to have changed her name,' I said.

'She did,' Toy said. 'That's her married name. It used to be Jones. But trust me – she is the best at what she does. She's the one who found a pinkie bone in a landfill and correctly identified it as belonging to a left-handed, bisexual, female, vegetarian, octogenarian, Mennonite pole-dancer who was six foot nine inches tall, raised parakeets and was allergic to wool, kale and broccoli.'

'No way!'

Toy smiled coyly. 'That's all true, except for the Mennonite part; she was actually Methodist. Anyway, I also plan to interrogate the other guests who were staying here at the inn the weekend of Miss Yoko-san's demise.'

'No can do,' I said, only half listening. I was trying to wrap my head around that image of a six-foot-and-nine-inch Methodist pole dancer who raised parakeets. Not that I ever wanted to dance around a pole, or with a Pole, but I have always wanted to raise parakeets! Budgies, the Australians call them. Cute little things they are – and so non-judgemental.

'Earth to Magdalena,' Toy said.

'Not again,' I wailed. 'Why does everyone always say that?'

'Because you always look so spaced out. You're not on anything, are you, Magdalena?'

'On anything? Like what?'

'Like drugs. Marijuana, for instance.'

Now *that* hiked my hackles so high that I had to stand up in order to keep them company. 'I am high on the Lord!' I snapped.

'Whoa there, I'm just covering all my bases.'

'Look,' I said, 'I can tell you right now that you won't get anywhere trying to interview the other guests who were here the same week that Yoko-san was.'

Toy frowned, causing me to feel a sinful urge to reach across the table with a long, spindly arm and smooth his troubled brow. 'Don't you be saddling me with *your* limitations,' he said archly. 'I'm a trained interrogator; you're an innkeeper. Hmm, I doubt if you've even trained for that sort of work.'

I brushed some scone crumbs into my hand before rising and then pointed with my chin towards the front door. 'Well, good luck interviewing the dead. You'll find Scott and Lois Robinson in Evergreen Cemetery in Covington, Kentucky. They were killed in an automobile

150

accident. They were on their way back home from holiday when their brakes failed.'

Toy considered this new information for a minute. 'So, were they, and Yoko-san, the only guests that you had that week? Don't you rent out six rooms?'

'"Six en-suites for the spiritually mature who find they are ready to take on the inequities of life,"' I said, quoting from my welcome pamphlet, for which I charge a measly ten dollars (I've been thinking of raising the price to fifteen). 'But to answer your question, yes, there were just the three of them. The others, a party of four from Toronto, cancelled at the last minute because one of them heard an anti-Canadian joke on late-night television. Tell me, Toy, as one who regularly indulges in worldly entertainment, are these anti-Canadian jokes a common occurrence?'

'Eh!' Toy scoffed. 'They're not *anti*-Canadian jokes by any means! We love our Canuck neighbours; some of us down in the Carolinas love them even more than we love you Yankees.'

'Why, I never!'

'Those jokes are all told in good fun, kind of like you'd rib a favourite cousin who was maybe a little—'

'You better stop while you're ahead, dear.'

'Advice taken.' Toy glanced at the functioning replica of a genuine grandfather clock in the far corner of the dining room. 'When will the Sisters of Apathy be finished with their shimmying and shaking?' he asked anxiously.

'Pretty soon, I reckon. They're getting long in

151

the tooth – and I mean that literally, in some cases.'

'Well then, we – I mean, *I* – better hurry up and come to a decision about what to do. Uh – hmm – you know—'

I wasn't born yesterday; I'm pretty sure of that, because I remember yesterday, and I can't remember being born. I have, however, been on the earth long enough to recognize the sounds of a man desperately pleading for help. The Bible exhorts us to love our neighbours as ourselves; therefore, I was obliged to lend the floundering, flustered and fledging chief a helping hand – an *un*-manicured one to be sure, but nonetheless one which was quite shapely. Can I help it, however, if the solution that I was about to share may have involved some methods that a person with more rigid ethics – say a perfect person – might find objectionable? After all, I am but a sinful creature. However, and this is speaking plainly, if I might, I have yet to stoop to the standards of many an elected politician.

'Get behind me, Satan!' I cried. 'What a wicked, wicked thought thou dost tempt me with!'

'Oh, Magdalena,' Toy said, sounding immediately relieved, 'you are a strange bird but you never fail to come through for me. The Devil, indeed! You make Him sound like a *real* person.'

'He *is* a real person, and not to be toyed with, Toy, you Henry VIII heretic. Now, if you suspend your rational thinking – all that intellectual Episcopal, Anglican, twenty-first century, scientific Motherbo-jumbo and just listen to me for a minute, you might learn something.'

'I'm suspended with both ears cocked,' Toy said insouciantly, not to mention nonsensically.

'Hammurabi had a code,' I said.

'Say what?'

'*Oy!*' I said, borrowing from my mother-in-law's lexicon. 'And to think that a simple Mennonite woman, like me, would be better schooled in history than a worldly lad from a city the size of Charlotte.'

The perfect symmetry of Toy's features was ruined by a scowl. 'No lectures, please. Besides, I've had lots of colds – everyone has – big deal.'

'Not that kind of code! Think Morse Code.'

Toy scratched his handsome head and appeared to think; at least that was a start.

'Listen,' I whispered, on the off-off chance that my guardian angel had momentarily tuned out, 'I can't come right out and lie. That's one of the Big Ten. But on the other hand, we've been given tacit permission to lie by people supposedly far more important than us.'

'I beg your pardon?' Toy said.

'Forsooth, 'tis true. Presidents, heads of state, politicians, car salesmen, religious leaders, fiction writers – they lie all the time. I, however, refuse to do so. Nay, I much prefer the word "prevarication," seeing as how it is not to be found in my well-thumbed copy of the King James Bible.'

'But it means the same thing as lie, right?' Toy said.

'Let's not be picky, dear,' I said, my voice unconsciously rising. 'Now about my code, pay attention: as your mayor, I am not going to give you instructions that might brush up against

153

county or state law. But as the owner of a horse and two cows, they each have their own *what* in the barn?'

'Poop.'

'*Excuse* me?'

Toy flushed. 'Well, they *are* live animals, aren't they?'

'The word is *stall*.'

'Stall?' Toy said.

'Exactly,' I said. 'Leave poor Yoko-san right where she is for the meantime. Trust me, she's in no hurry to go anywhere and no one is expecting her anytime soon.'

'But what about the fur inners?' Toy said.

'Huh?'

'*Fur* inners,' said Toy, much louder this time and with some irritation.

Then it clicked. Fur innards! The clean-shaven young man was caught up in that zombie, were-wolf, vampire trash craze that was ruining our young people's minds. This rubbish was tearing them from their Bibles and the teachings of their churches, and setting them on a slippery path of occultism which would eventually funnel them straight into Hell.

I shook my head. 'Oh, not you too, Toy! Please tell me that our very own Chief of Police has not stooped so low as to watch zombie movies and that television program that I hear so much about called *The Walking Head*.'

Toy shook his head in turn. 'For your information, it's called *The Walking Dead* and it's fabulous. Magdalena, forgive me for saying this to you – my elder, my mayor, my employer, and

154

my friend: with a mind as narrow as yours it's a wonder that there is room enough on your face for two eyes. While I do indeed watch many zombie movies and TV shows, I fail to see what my viewing habits have to do with this investigation.'

'Then what's all this nonsense about furry guts?' I wailed. Perhaps what I really did was howl, because from somewhere in the woods behind the house a coyote responded.

Toy's reaction was priceless. He slapped his forehead with the palm of his hand.

'Well, duh,' he said, 'I forgot to speak Pennsylvanian there for a moment. The word I meant to say is *foreigners*. You know, as in your English guests.'

'Ah, foreigners,' I said. 'Well, I would never have guessed it because the context does not apply. The English are never foreigners, you see, because they are – well, *English*. They are the nexus of the universe by Divine Ordinance – or so I've been told. Granted, it's a hard concept to grasp unless you are English, or at least a member of the United Kingdom.'

'Actually, it's not,' Toy said. 'My mother's family is originally from Charleston, South Carolina.'

'Oh,' I said excitedly. 'Does she know Abigail Timberlake?'

'*What?* Who?'

'Never mind, go ahead with *your* diversion.'

'The point of my diversion is that in Charleston there are folks who see no need to travel because they are *already* there. In other words, Charleston is all that anyone should ever desire.'

'Hmm,' I said, 'I shall cogitate on your analogy. In the meantime, let us return to the corpse in my shaft – not to be too coarse about it. I was hoping that we could agree upon a course of action that would be predicated on the status quo, which would give us both plenty of time to do our jobs. I'll do my best to keep the Brits here voluntarily but if they want to leave you must find a way to detain them so that we have time to investigate how Cee-Cee got her information on Yoko-san.'

Toy scratched his handsome head, and for a fleeting moment I had head envy. Down, girl, I told myself. Back off.

'Why didn't you just say all this from the beginning?' Toy said.

'Well, duh,' I said, 'I guess I forgot to speak pseudo-legalese. I mean, aren't you supposed to report all deaths to the state? And isn't a coroner supposed to examine the remains? I was just hoping that we could *stall* things a bit and give ourselves more time before the big boys come in and mess up the crime site.'

'*O ye of little faith*,' the lapsed Episcopalian, not-quite-an-Anglican said, throwing scripture at me with all the alacrity of a Born-Again Mennonite. 'Sorry to burst your bubble, Magdalena, but in this booming metropolis called Hernia, which lacks even one traffic light, your police department – that is to say, *me* – has complete autonomy. *I* decide when, and what, needs reporting. And as far as a coroner goes, at this point, all we need to do is to confirm that the subject of my report is dead.'

Toy can be most annoying at times, and so as not to let me forget, he cupped his hands to his mouth. 'Hello,' he called. 'Hello? Is there a doctor in this house?'

At that very instant, the front door opened with a slam that almost brought the rafters down upon my head. When I saw who the intruder was, I wished that the roof had indeed crashed down upon me, rendering me senseless among the rubble.

Fifteen

FRESH FIG BREAD

Combine and let sit for fifteen minutes:
1½ cups chopped ripe figs
¼ cup cooking sherry

Mix in small bowl:
1⅔ cups flour
½ cup chopped walnuts
1 tsp cinnamon
1 tsp baking soda
½ tsp nutmeg
½ tsp salt

Beat together in large bowl:
1½ cups sugar
½ cup salad oil
2 large eggs

Blend flour mixture into oil mixture; gently fold in figs. Pour batter into well-greased 5 × 9 inch loaf pan. Bake at 350 degrees for 1¼ hours. Cool in pan for 10 minutes; invert on rack to cool. Freezes well.

Sixteen

Pastor Diffledorf is a kindly old man who possesses at least two faults of which I am aware. His most obvious failing is that he insists on retaining a silly-sounding family name that I can't, for the life of me, seem to remember. His only other flaw is that he never had enough ambition to get a *real* paying job. My church pays him, of course, by passing around two much-battered offering plates every Sunday morning. However, even though we have not become godless pagans like the unchurched Brits, our attendance has dropped drastically as our young people flock to the shopping malls, stay home to watch sports on television, or in the case of Elmer Gingerich and Rudy Swinefister, misbehave in the hayloft. The sad truth is that not even a church mouse on the dole could survive on the pittance we pay Pastor Dufflediff.

'Pastor,' I cried in alarm. 'It's not my turn to serve you Sunday dinner is it?'

'No, Magdalena, it is not, but neither is it your turn to skip church.' He looked around with mock astonishment, which in God's eyes is surely just a hair's breadth away from a lie. 'Why, just look at the earthly mansion which you inhabit. It is no wonder that you care naught for your Heavenly abode, which is even now being prepared for you.'

'*This* is a bed and breakfast hotel,' Toy said gallantly, 'not just Magdalena's private residence.' He paused only a millisecond. 'Although, I would wager that she's raking in the loot with both hands and *could* afford to put a mansion down anywhere that she wants – even in Heaven.'

'Toy!' I said while waggling my long, shapely index finger at him. Hernia's young, Episcopalian peace-keeper and my aged clergyman do not see bright blue eye to grey-blue eye. I turned back to Pastor Daffleduff. 'Now that you are here, looking after my soul, who is back at the church, hectoring the flock – I mean, delivering the sermon?'

'My wife.'

'Your *wife*?'

'That would be Daphne Diffledorf, a woman whom you know quite well. Sits in the front right pew every Sunday morning. Black hat, black gloves. Anyway, since she has to listen to me rehearse my sermons all week long, she practically knows them by heart.'

Of course I knew the pastor's wife! I'm the head of the search committee that gave the elderly gent his job. But Daphne Fiffledord didn't just sit in the front right pew, she *filled* it. Once, after a particularly long service on a hot, humid day when Daphne stood up, the pew rose with her. I am not being unkind when I relate this detail, mind you; I am merely fulfilling my duties as a keen observer of the human condition.

'But Pastor Dumblefirth,' I exclaimed, 'is a

160

woman even *allowed* to preach in our denomination?'

The old man nodded. 'With consent of the individual congregation, the answer is "yes." Perhaps I should have checked with you, however, given that you, a *woman*, are the Senior Elder in the church, but then again, you were nowhere to be found – except for here, keeping company in your own *bed* and breakfast hotel with an exceedingly handsome *young* man.'

'I explained everything,' I mumbled miserably. 'But for what it's worth, given that I am already an inadvertent adulteress – having once unknowingly married a bigamist, I mean – my reputation is so tarnished that I sometimes think I should just bid my morals adieu and become the scarlet woman whom I have been made out to be. At least I might have a bit of fun for a change. No, no, I take that all back – I didn't mean it! Living into my reputation would be a terrible sin, of course. I'm just saying that – *oy!* Look, it isn't easy keeping to the straight and narrow path when one is always being judged. Besides, red is really not my colour.'

'I didn't come here to judge you,' Pastor Faddledeaf said. 'And maybe you did already explain things; I'm getting old and my hearing isn't what it used to be. Anyway, where are the royalty? The ladies of the church have prepared a bounteous buffet for the Queen and her entourage.'

It was Toy who snickered then, not me. 'Pastor, dear,' I said kindly, 'Her Majesty is approaching ninety, if she hasn't already achieved it. Therefore

I doubt if she has plans to visit Hernia in this lifetime. My guests this week are merely members of the aristocracy – lords and ladies and, alas, a lad who will not be entitled to a title.'

Dear Pastor Fiddlefuddle looked absolutely befuddled. 'Magdalena, yet again you have managed to communicate naught with your flowery verbiage.'

'Thank you, dear. That is indeed my intention – at least half of the time.'

The wise old gent shook his head sadly. 'I suppose that the rest of the time you babble incessantly without a direction in mind?'

'Oh, woe is me; I've been found out for the charlatan that I am!' I cried as I beat my chest with my fists (lightly, of course, given my lack of natural padding).

Toy snickered again. 'I'm sure that happened a long time ago,' he said.

'Indeed, it did,' Pastor Fiddlesticks said. 'Magdalena, you are aware that the *ladies* of your church, although they do not hold titles of nobility, are going to be beside themselves with disappointment when they learn that your *titled* guests have already returned to their palaces in England. What are they to do with the sumptuous potluck lunch which they have prepared with their old, arthritic, and I am sure, very painful hands that have been damaged by years of hard labour as they toiled side by side with their husbands in the fields?'

'Well, uh—' I was admittedly slow on my boat-size feet.

'They haven't left yet,' Toy blurted. I am sure

162

that he was only trying to help, and I will give him the benefit of the doubt, but only because he is so easy on the eyes.

'*Oh?*' Pastor Fumbleforth said. He had ears like bonnie Prince Charles and was able to rotate them in my direction like a pair of remote-controlled satellite dishes. 'Am I to believe that they are up in their rooms as quiet as palace mice or, perhaps, as still as the young Japanese tourist in yon elevator shaft?'

The hairs on my head stood on end, causing my white organza prayer cap to teeter precariously atop my do. Granted, that statement was hyperbolic, but not by much. Even Toy seemed to be caught off guard.

'What is this about a Japanese tourist?' he said, recovering faster than I did, although his voice was almost an octave higher than usual.

Pastor Fibberblatt had the temerity to hold Toy's steady gaze. 'Forgive my poor choice of words,' he said. 'I forgot that you law enforcement types speak only in certainties and the Japanese girl's final whereabouts were never conclusively determined.'

'Exactly,' I said. 'In fact, one quasi-official party floated the theory that Yoko-san is alive and well in Nebraska, where she owns a noodle shop called Udon Have to Stay Forever. It serves affordable meals to migrant oil pipeline workers.'

'I see,' Pastor Flutterbutt said. 'Is there any chance that this half-baked theory-floater would be you?'

I gasped. 'Mind your tongue, Pastor Patterfelt!

163

I'll have you know that I am *quite* baked – through and through.'

'Oh, come on, Magdalena,' Toy pleaded. 'We may as well come clean for this man of the cloth and tell him where everyone is. He'll find out soon enough, anyway. You know that what's-her-name can't keep a secret.'

'Aha!' The clever clergyman's faded eyes suddenly flickered with an unfamiliar intensity. 'Your mother-in-law has them, doesn't she? I should have known as much; Mother Malaise possesses a silken tongue as persuasive as the serpent that coaxed Eve to eat the apple in the Garden of Eden.'

'Ha,' I said. 'Now it is you, Pastor Piffledaffle, who embroiders the truth!'

'Not hardly,' he said. 'And need I say that should Mother Malaise's words ever fail her, why, that handsome heathen could rely on her looks alone to lead sinners into the gates of Hell.'

'She might *scare* them through the gates,' Toy said, reading my mind and thus earning my undying gratitude for saying what I could not say.

Yes, I know, I should not even have *thought* such a horrible thing about my husband's mother. Jesus taught that if we kill someone in our heart it is the same as if we've done it in real life. Of course, I can't argue with my Lord, or can I? My Jewish husband insists that wrestling with God is precisely what we're meant to do. Well, in my defence, as weak and useless as it might be, I just want to say that Jesus did *not* have a mother-in-law.

164

'Harrumph,' Pastor Pumppump said. 'You are certainly a judgemental young man. If I were not already married, and Ida Rosen, aka Mother Malaise, a Jewess and a Heathen, I would certainly set my cap for her.'

'And you are behind the times, pastor,' I said, not unkindly. 'The term "Jewess" is no longer used by educated folk. The suffix "ess" is added to the names of animal species to indicate the female gender, as in lion*ess* or tig*ress*, but we don't apply it to religious or ethnic groups. For instance, when is the last time you heard someone say Baptist*ess*, or French*ess*?'

Pastor Poopdidoo could be argumentative at times. 'What about baron*ess*? Or marchion*ess*?'

'Stuff and nonsense,' I said. 'While you're splitting hairs, your happy, handsome heathen doth gyre and gimbal in the wabe – and in the altogether too, I might add.'

'Whatever is she jabbering on about?' Pastor Huffandpuff said.

'They are prancing about naked,' I said, admittedly with relish. 'Your second choice for a helpmate is frolicking about without a stitch of clothing on, her sagging body parts heaving here and there. But not only that, by now I'm sure that she has seduced the Brits into shedding their clothes as well. After all, the distance from Anglicanism to apostasy can't be all that far.'

'Again with the judgement!'

'A fact is a fact, dear. So, do you want to do something about it – maybe salvage a meeting between the congregation and our English visitors – or just register a complaint?'

165

'The third option,' Toy said with a wicked glint in his eye, 'is to cross the road to the convent and let it all hang out.'

It appeared to me as if Pastor Diffledorf had just been made an offer that his flesh was having a hard time refusing. It is desire of the flesh, as St Paul was so intent on warning us, that is truly the Devil's most effective bait. It was up to me to tip the scale a wee bit in the other direction, even if it wasn't quite the truth. Sometimes the means does justify the end, especially if it can prevent two ends from coming into contact.

'My dear Pastor Diffledorf,' I said, 'by now you have lived in our community long enough to have heard all the rumours concerning me. You know that I was a virgin until age forty-four, when I was tricked into a bigamous marriage with my second-cousin, Aaron Miller. Thus, you know that I am a pious—'

'Ahem,' Pastor Diddedorf said. 'I also heard that you sat on your washing machine during the spin cycle. That is hardly the act of a pious woman.'

'No woman should deny herself a ride on a three-legged washer with unbalanced load,' I roared. 'That is a God-given right in America. And as for that blazing look of lust in your eye, I was about to say: "Down boy." The Countess Aubrey and her daughter, the Lady Celia, are so hideously deformed that when they emerged from their vehicle a flock of starlings dropped dead from the sky and all the flowers along the front walk immediately wilted.'

166

'Not to mention the sidewalk cracked under their weight,' Toy said.

At last the good pastor saw the light. 'What must I do to save the day?' he asked.

'Hie thee back to thy sacred space,' I said. 'That is to say – *our* church – and have the ladies pack up the food. Then have everyone drive up to the picnic area atop Stucky Ridge. In the meantime, Toy and I will waste no time in getting the errant aristocrats back into some suitable Christian clothes. That done, we will meet you there. Oh, and bring the hymnals. It's about time we subjected those Anglicans to some rousing American hymns.'

'Huh?' said Toy. 'You mean like hymns written in the late nineteenth century, back when God was still in charge of things?'

'Exactly. Tra-la-la-la-la,' I sang in my pleasant but off-key voice as I all but pushed the pastor out the door.

When my thick front door had closed securely behind my clergyman, I turned back to Toy. 'A word before we retrieve any naked nobs.'

'Yes, ma'am.'

'Don't you think it very strange,' I said, 'that he referred to poor Miss Yoko-san being in the elevator shaft?'

'Yes, ma'am, I did,' Toy said. 'And not only that, it sounded like he thought it might be problematic for the others. It was as if he'd just been called with the news of her discovery and he knew that she was still in there.'

'So what do you think that means?' I said. I started to tremble. Ever since I'd started down the road of playing detective – not *my* choice, mind you – it has become ever more apparent that no one is so spiritually evolved that they can be held above suspicion.

Toy scratched his perfectly formed head. 'It means that I'll take care of the body. In the meantime, you attend the picnic and watch the reverend like a hawk.'

Honestly, that was what I intended to do. It really was.

Seventeen

Stucky Ridge is a marvellous place for a summer outing. The highest point in the county, it offers unparalleled views that stretch all the way to the Maryland border. The flat top of the ridge is divided almost equally into three strips: a grassy picnic area on the south side, a copse of birch and pine trees in the middle strip and Settlers' Cemetery on the north side. This way a multi-generational family has its needs met simultaneously. The parents and young children can enjoy a picnic while appreciating the scenery, the teenagers and young adults can engage in questionable activities in the woods and the old folks can visit their friends in the cemetery. This is not to say that I approve of the woods. *Au contraire*; as acting constable, when the Village of Hernia has been between professional officers, it has fallen on me to police that area. One would not believe the depths of depravity that I have encountered there. Sometimes I have had to take a long second look, just to make sure that I had not jumped to any conclusions before I blow my whistle.

On this particular day, when the Brits and the Mennonites picnicked together, I expected a different demographic distribution. For one thing, Agnes had assured me that the British are all, without exception, great walkers. Agnes watches

169

BBC America on the 'telly' just about all the time, and it was her contention that every British person except for the Queen and our guests wore sensible shoes, and was forever hiking up and down the hills of the Lake Country and along the cliffs of Cornwall. For some reason that she couldn't remember, Agnes was also 'almost positive' that the Grimsley-Snodgrasses would be dying to see the cemetery. She was certain, however, that they would stay out of the woods.

Agnes was partly right. Aubrey eventually wandered off towards the cemetery but I had too much to keep track of to allow me the luxury of accompanying her. The Beechy Grove Mennonite Church was rife with mini-miscreants – that is to say, other people's children. Oh, I'm sure that each and every one of them was a precious little saint, but not that day. They shrieked and ran about, turning deaf ears to their worried parents, or shrieked at their parents before running them over. It was absolutely horrifying. At any moment one of the little darlings could run right over the edge of the ridge, and *perhaps* all because their parents had asked them ever so nicely, a *thousand* times, to 'please, settle down.'

And then we heard it. It was a scream that was said to put the hens off laying in three surrounding counties, and for the next six months. It was a scream that caused Herman Hooley's mule to kick open its stall and run halfway to the Maryland State line (where none should venture without provisions, including animals). It was a scream that had some of our faithful citizens staring joyfully up at the sky in great anticipation, believing as they did that the trumpet of the Lord had at last sounded and they would momentarily be caught up into the heavens with their Lord and Saviour. It was a scream that brought a fair amount of consternation to the wicked woman, Wanda Hemphopple, who awaited trial in the county jail on one charge of murder and two charges of attempted manslaughter. Although she was a lapsed Mennonite, clearly of the progressive sort, she too thought that the scream might be the trumpet of the Lord, and she feared mightily that she would be left behind on account of the grievous sins that she had committed. This was a needless fear, I might add, for she had already repented of her sins, and God forgives all whose repentance is sincere.

At any rate, in the end it was indeed just a scream, not a trumpet. It was, in fact, a British scream. Although it may come as a surprise, allow me to assure all doubters that British women can scream just as loudly as their American counterparts. Also, since hysteria knows no accents, the 'aaah' part was pretty much a boiler-plate scream. But after a couple more really intense vocalizations, Lady Celia finally got around to sharing some information that seemed pertinent. Of course, it was incumbent on me to first supply her with many 'there, there's and 'it'll get better's, even though I already knew that this would not be the case.

Finally it was time to cut to the chase. 'What happened?'

I was astonished when she answered in a very calm and collected manner. 'I wanted to see

Lover's Leap. I'd read about it in the brochure that you sent to Mother. It sounded so romantic – two young Indians dying for love.'

'I think it sounds painful.'

'Yes, a dreadful way to die! That's why I screamed.'

'But dear,' I said, 'those young lovers – if they even existed – plunged to their deaths hundreds of years ago. It's the fires of Hell that they're feeling now because they were never saved, unless God in his infinite mercy has come up with an escape clause for all the nonbelievers who never had the opportunity to hear the gospel preached in his, or her, lifetime. But then, don't you think it would just be simpler if God didn't allow heathen people to live in other places until Jesus came and they had a chance to learn about the gift of salvation? I mean, I'm just saying – as you young people are so fond of saying.'

'Shut up!' Lady Celia said. When she said those awful words her eyes were tightly closed and her small porcelain white fists clenched at her sides. Clearly, such extreme rudeness did not come easily to her. As for me, I was so shocked that my thick cotton hosiery slipped free of my garter belt and puddled around my ankles. Had I not had my brogans securely tied, the little Lady from across the Pond might literally have knocked my socks off.

'I beg your pardon?' I said.

'Listen to me,' the teenager shrilled. 'My brother, Rupert, is dead; he has got to be. He just fell off this very same cliff.'

'*What?*'

172

'Are you suddenly deaf, you old cow?'

I was rattled by her claim and angry at being insulted, but I certainly was not deaf.

'Are you sure?'

'I saw it *myself*. I was right here.'

Perhaps I have a thing about the cliffs along Stucky Ridge, having been pushed off one by the most evil man in the world, the escaped murderer, Melvin Stoltzfus. I edged as close as possible to the cliff edge and peered over. Although the Good Lord saw fit to bestow my body with meagre blessings, He did equip me with vision worthy of a chicken hawk. Frankly, I've never quite felt it was a fair trade. I would rather have bottle-thick glasses and bazoombas large enough upon which I could rest a book instead of a chest that is a carpenter's dream (i.e. flat as a board). My point is that I could see the ground below Lover's Leap quite clearly. In fact, I could see into the nearest house which was a quarter of a mile away.

I gasped in indignation. 'I knew it! Jill Kaufman's pie crusts are *not* homemade!'

'What about my brother, you blithering idiot,' Cee-Cee said. 'Do you see him down there?'

'No; hence the blithering, I'm afraid. Are you *positive* that you saw him go over?'

'Aaah!' This second scream curdled bottled milk throughout Hernia, shattered even refrigerated eggs and convinced Wanda Hemphopple that the Angel of Death was headed directly for her cell. She even suffered cardiac arrest but unfortunately survived.

The second ear-splitting sound of frustration by Lady Celia finally brought a swarm of

173

concerned folk, including most of the Grimsley-Snodgrass family, my family, Agnes and a goodly number of our fellow picnickers from the Beechy Grove Mennonite Church. For the record, it takes two ear-splitting screams to get the attention of my church's merrily munching members and guests, so tasty are their comestibles.

'What is it, Hon?' the Babester asked. He was the first to reach us, given his long, strong legs. He also happened to be carrying Little Jacob astride broad shoulders.

'She said that her brother Rupert went over the edge here' – I pointed – 'but there isn't anyone down there.'

'How does she *know*?' Lady Celia shrieked. 'You can't *know* unless you go down there and actually look. No one has eyes that good.'

'Normally, I'd say that's true,' my sweet husband said, 'but my wife has perfect vision. She literally *could* find a needle in a haystack.'

Then the crowd surged around us along the edge of the cliff, and the situation worsened considerably.

'Mind the babies,' someone said. 'Take hold of your toddler's hand. I doubt if Magdalena has enough insurance to cover all of us. Ha, ha.'

'And be careful not to step on any specimens of the rare night-blooming *Libella wiscrapia*,' someone else said. 'It's a horrible little plant with ugly brown flowers and an obnoxious odour, but the government will sue you to Kingdom Come if you as much as crush one leaf.'

'Oh, don't worry about either of those things; falling babies or crushed wiscrapia. We'll just make Magdalena pay our expenses, ha, ha. Pastor says that she is richer than God and King Midas put together. Besides, isn't that what her insurance is for?'

My insurance? And *me* richer than *God*? Stucky Ridge was a village park, for crying out loud. It was in the public domain. Any flower-crushing dolts were irresponsible parents who were going to have to contend with their *own* insurance companies. I had quite enough on my own plate, thank you very much.

'Mother!' Lady Celia began jumping in place like a Masai warrior. 'Mother, where are you? These crazy foreigners aren't doing anything about Rupert.'

'Rupert? What *about* Rupert?' Suddenly Lord and Lady Grimsley-Snodgrass, and Rupert's younger brother, Sebastian, materialized along the edge of the cliff out of nowhere, much as if God had pressed the lever on His giant Viewmaster. It was a clear summer day, and with the soft greens of the valley behind them, backed by the purple ridges of our low Allegheny Mountains, it would have been a perfect photo opportunity had Little Lord Fauntleroy not been missing.

I hauled my poor, stressed, middle-aged body up to its nonetheless imposing height. 'Aubrey, your daughter has quite an active imagination. She thinks that she saw Rupert fall over the edge of Lover's Leap.'

'I did!' Lady Celia said. 'Mother, I know what I saw!'

'At any rate,' I said calmly, 'perhaps we should

175

all stand back a little ways. These rocks are some-what unstable.'

'Papa,' Lady Celia said, grabbing her father's well-manicured hand, 'there's more.'

'I'd shut up if I were you,' Sebastian snarled. 'No one will believe you.'

'Believe what?' Countess Aubrey asked.

Meanwhile, my fellow church members, who'd been too much in awe of British people in general, and nobility in particular, to get any closer to them than an arm's length, underwent a startling group metamorphous. Whereas before they'd been milling about like ants from a disturbed mound, now they pressed inward so as not to miss a word. In essence, they formed a virtual compression bandage of pious people.

Lady Celia was not afraid of her younger twin brother. 'The truth is that Sebastian *pushed* Rupert off the cliff.'

'Did not!'

'Did so!'

'Liar!'

'Cee-Cee,' Countess Aubrey cried. 'Say it isn't so! I shan't be able to stand it if that's the truth.'

'But it is, mummy. I swear on Granny's grave that it is.'

'Sebastian,' the earl roared, 'is your sister telling the truth?'

'No, Papa,' Sebastian said. 'Cee-Cee is always lying – you said so yourself.'

'Papa,' Lady Celia said, 'I swear on your best hunting dog's life that I saw Sebastian push Rupert over this very cliff not more than five minutes ago.'

176

The earl's eyes bulged to the point that his monocle slipped. Seeing both of his eyes free of obstacles sent chills up my spine. Here was a man who was not to be trifled with. 'What is my best hunting dog's name?' he said.

'J. Edgar Hoover,' she said without a second's hesitation. 'You named him after the head of the American spy organization that went after communists and homosexuals, even though J. Edgar Hoover used to dress in women's underclothes.'

'Allegedly,' the earl said. 'I won't be sued for libel on this side of the Pond!'

'Not to worry,' I said tiredly, 'it's common knowledge here. But let me remind you, you Brits don't get off scot-free. We all have skeletons in our closets.'

'Or in our elevators,' quipped the beautiful countess.

'Et tu, Aubrey?' I wailed.

'Magdalena,' she said, 'I don't know what is going on here but I positively don't like it. First, you bring us up to this wretched place, and then when my sweet, precious, darling daughter swore that she saw her beloved brother go over this cliff, you called her a liar.'

Well, *that* burned my barnacles, and I had yet to set a foot in saltwater. '*I* didn't call your *spoiled brat* a liar; it was your younger son who called his sister a liar.'

The Countess of Grimsley-Snodgrass, Mistress of Gloomsburythorpe Manor, looked as if I'd slapped her across the face with a bag of marshmallow fluff. 'Uh – well, you said that you

177

couldn't see Rupert at the base of this cliff, which is a totally ridiculous thing to say. No one has eyes that good, not even reporters who work for the *Guardian*.'

No one likes to be accused of uttering ridiculous verbiage, most especially a Mennonite motor-mouth such as myself. We have a reputation as peaceful folk, speakers of truth, whose 'yeas' mean yes and our 'nays' mean no. We are even exempt from having to swear upon the Bible in court. How dare this English-English woman, this Philistine, so-to-speak, dare to cast aspersions on my veracity? Forsooth, at times I have been known to embroider the truth, but not since high school have I out-and-out lied.

'You take that back, you over-pampered peeress,' I said in a most unchristian tone. Oh, rue the day that I set myself up as a shining beacon of light to the world. Here was one heathen Anglican who was bound to remain as such, thanks to my hair-trigger temper.

'That pretty little foreign girl is the one who's telling the truth,' someone said.

'*What?*' I said. I clapped both my ears to make sure that they were working correctly.

'In fact,' the speaker said, 'I've seen this skinny, funny-looking foreign man, and he's kinda struggling with this other man – he too was a foreigner. You can tell by their noses, I always say. They both had noses on them like the sails on one of them small boats, so I think they was British – yeah, like this man.' She pointed directly at Sebastian, who, admittedly, possessed a bit of a shnoz.

It is common knowledge that all English males have prominent proboscises, having only to lie on their backs in a stiff breeze and they can hitch a free ride to France across the Channel. In as much as that is true, it is common knowledge that all American women are loud and brassy and socially unacceptable, along the lines of Wallis Simpson. It is a fact, and so I state this out of a heart filled with charity, that Daphne Diffledorf is one of the loudest, brassiest, coarsest, crudest, homeliest – oh, but now I am beginning to judge.

The church members, who were dangerously close to crowding us all off the cliff, roared with excitement. They claimed to have witnessed fisticuffs, grappling and shoving, even Brit-on-Brit murder! Surely there could be no better way to spend an afternoon in Hernia, Pennsylvania. After Daphne started the ball rolling, it didn't stop until sixteen other people claimed to have seen poor, plain Mr Sebastian push his titled brother over the edge of Lover's Leap.

I wouldn't have blamed the younger son for making a run then, even if he wasn't guilty – and I was sure that he wasn't. After all, what was he supposed to do, just stand around and twiddle his thumbs? Was he supposed to wait for some overly excited male version of Daphne Ditherspoon to push him over the edge? Of course, no blue-blooded Brit could ever just melt into the American landscape, for we are a tacky and somewhat wacky people who do not put baked beans on our toast, nor do we eat with our forks held upside-down. Sooner, rather than later, Sebastian would be outed for his superior manners and I would still be no closer to finding Yoko-san's killer.

'I did no such thing,' Sebastian said. Then, quite unnecessarily, he added: 'You silly American cow.'

That did it; that sealed the young man's fate! Name-calling is one thing but bovine references in a dairy-farming community are beyond the pale. It's a wonder that some of the most bullish of our youth didn't tackle Sebastian right there and then. Fortunately, I was able to steer them away from such a foolish course of action but only by insisting that Toy apprehend Sebastian as a murder suspect in the death of his twin brother.

'Although it won't hold up,' I shouted in Toy's ear, 'unless we find a body at the base of this cliff.'

'Or parts of one,' Toy said. 'This reminds me of Crowder's Peak in Gastonia. It's not nearly as high as this but it still manages to keep the buzzards happy.'

'All God's creatures have to eat,' I said. I cupped my hands to my mouth and let out a yell that scared the feathers off any buzzards within a two-mile radius. Even a couple of trees dropped their leaves.

'People of Beechy Grove Mennonite Church and anyone else who can hear me, including atheists, pagans and members of the Church of England, let us all go quietly and respectfully, back to our vehicles. The picnic area will be officially closed shortly. Those of you who so desire, and who are over the age of eighteen, may join a search party that will form at the small parking lot at the base of Stucky Ridge. If the parking lot fills up, park single file along Stucky Ridge Road.'

'That's *single* file!' Toy interrupted. 'Folks who *double* park will be ticketed.'

'Amen to that,' I said. Beechy Grove members are pious folks, and so as long as Toy and I spoke in preacher voices a sacred hush prevailed which allowed me to continue. 'At the west end of the parking lot – west being where the sun sets – you'll find a little path that skirts the ridge. The path is sandwiched between the ridge and the south end of Rudy Swinefister's hayfield. Do not trample Rudy's hay! Ever since you voted him out of the church on account of him being a homosexual, he has become very bitter against we Old Order Mennonites.'

'It's not our doing; it's God's law,' someone whispered.

'Who said that?' I said, perhaps a tad too sharply. When no one answered, I continued, 'Odd then that Jesus, who was also God, had nothing to say on the subject.'

'Don't preach to us, Magdalena,' someone else said. 'You're going off topic.'

I was beginning to think that I was too liberal to remain an Old Order Mennonite. Perhaps it was time for me to shift gears and move into the Mennonite mainstream. By and large, even though mainstream Mennonites did not approve of gay marriage, neither were they opposed to inquisitive lay folk delving into ancient history – just as long as they didn't take it seriously.

The Babester pointed me to one text that suggested that the prohibitions against male homosexuality in the scriptures might have been based on male prostitution, as practiced in surrounding cultures. I can't begin to explain how confused I was after 'stretching' my mind that far. It is said that if you open your mind too wide, your brain will fall out. I am afraid that this might have been the occasion when the Devil jumped in and made himself at home.

'Given the fact that I pay half of Pastor Diffledorf's salary,' I said, 'and all of the church mortgage and maintenance fees, I believe that I have a right to preach.'

'Touché,' mumbled one of my few ardent supporters. No doubt it was a close cousin, one whom I supported financially.

I am happy to say that, for the most part, the congregants were well behaved and strayed from the path only when anatomical dictates, such as extreme obesity or *tri*pedalism made sticking to a narrow Indian foot path an impossible challenge. Fortunately the latter case involved only one individual: Cornelius Gerber, whose mother was a notorious chocolate addict. Although this most unusual case is still being hotly debated in scientific circles, the majority opinion is that the vast amounts of dark chocolate consumed by Prunella Gerber during her pregnancy must have been in some way responsible for the perfectly formed, *additional*, left foot that Cornelius possesses. It connects to his left leg at the ankle, and is rather like a second tyre on the rear of a lorry.

I feel that I must reiterate: I am not given to prejudice, nor do I set much stock in physical appearances. Indeed, as it says in the First Book of Samuel, chapter sixteen, verse seven: 'For man looks at the outward appearance, but the Lord looks at the heart.' That said, two identical feet working against one does tend to make even a well-intentioned young man walk in circles. At last, much to the relief of everyone, Cornelius made it safely to the base of Lover's Leap where the search had commenced.

As I said, the people of Hernia, and especially the members of Beechy Grove Mennonite Church, are good folks. Sure, if you've read some of the terrible books written about us, you'll discover that we've had a few rotten apples amongst us. But consider this: every barrel has at least a few rotten apples in it, and they're usually found at the bottom. Everyone at the base of Lover's Leap, early that Sunday afternoon, wanted to be helpful.

These good-hearted people had been willing to give up their picnic lunch in order to help search for the smashed remains of a *foreigner*. An English-English is about as foreign as one can get these parts; most of our foreigners are from countries like Hawaii and New Mexico. At any rate, every inch of the clearing was searched, and even some very careful forays were made into Rudy Swinefister's hayfield.

Finally, approximately two hours after we'd heard Lady Celia's ear-piercing scream, Hernia's Chief of Police, the devilishly handsome Toy Graham, blew on a small silver whistle that hung from his neck. Everyone seemed to freeze in place, reminding me of the game 'statues' that we used to play when we were children. As it happened, at that very moment I was standing not even an arm's length away from Lady Celia, who was weeping softly.

At the shrill blast of the whistle, she practically lunged into my arms and began to sob. 'Oh, it's horrible news; I just know that it is.'

'There, there,' I said helplessly as I patted her slender back.

'I'm afraid I've got bad news,' Toy said a moment later. 'No, make that terrible news.'

Lady Celia screamed one more time and then slumped in my arms, dead away. Seconds later, the dead weight of her dragged us both down onto the granite slab which formed the base of the cliff, with her lying on top of me. Unfortunately, Lady Celia's rosy English cheeks belied a youthful body that was no stranger to vigorous exercise, and I found myself trapped between a rock and a hard place.

Eighteen

It took two Mennonite men, one Mennonite woman and one lapsed Episcopalian to pull that pile of flailing noble limbs off me. It took one Jewish doctor, with our eighteen-month-old son strapped to his back, to pull my bruised and scraped carapace up, and enfold it, ever so gently, in his healing arms. Then finally it took the sometimes too timid, although always polite, Southerner, Toy, to blast away at his whistle yet again.

'Shut up, everyone,' he said. 'If you please. Especially you, young lady – Ladyship, whatever. You have no reason to be carrying on like a toddler with a popped balloon. It was Magdalena who took the brunt of the fall. You don't seem to have a scratch on you; clearly nothing's been hurt, but your pride.'

'It's her brother, you blithering idiot!' the earl roared. 'My son! He's been hurt; he's lying down here, no doubt broken into a million pieces. You're supposed to be searching for my son, not paying attention to the women. You find my son, and in one piece, or I'll have your head served up on a silver platter, I will.'

'Sir,' said Toy, his own cheeks drained of blood, 'your son must still be up there.'

'This is outrageous,' the earl shouted. He seemed to inflate with every word. 'Are you calling my daughter a liar?'

185

'No, sir,' Toy said as he appeared to shrink. But I've searched the parameter of this clearing and I've climbed those rocks, and nothing has disturbed that hayfield. Even if your son was pushed with great force off the top, he wouldn't have made it further than the edge of the field.'

'What a preposterous claim,' Lady Aubrey whispered. 'How could this young man possibly make such a claim?'

'*Because*,' Toy said, 'every spring, at graduation time, the high school boys throw a pair of fully-clothed store mannequins off Lover's Leap. Each year they try and set a distance record: which class can get their mannequin to land closest to old Swinefister's field. A mannequin weighs less than a human body, by the way – even less than a skinny English boy, like your la-dee-da lord of a son.'

'He was a viscount,' I interjected, to keep the record straight.

'Whatever,' Toy said. His left jaw muscle was twitching like the nose of a rabbit that has smelled a fox. This served to make Toy even more handsome than usual, but I knew him well enough to know that his jaw-twitching was an involuntary response that happened only to his left cheek. It could also be a precursor to tears of extreme *frustration* (but make no mistake, Toy was all man).

By now the earl was so overwrought that he was downright incoherent. Little puffs of steam escaped from between glimpses of yellowed teeth as he waved a fallen branch as a cudgel at us. Whereas once I had thought of him as dull and

186

pompous, now he was dull, pompous *and* dangerous. Had we been living in England during medieval times, Toy would have been strung up in the earl's dungeon and I would have been packed off to a convent: the sort of convent in which women wore clothes.

Poor Toy. It is times like this when I regret having hired such a young man for the job of Chief of Police, especially given the fact that he is the *only* police officer in the department. It takes a certain amount of life experience, or perhaps just the right combination of DNA, to give one the strength to stand up to the sort of bullying that the Earl of Grimsley-Snodgrass so excelled at. Given that I shared my birth mother with the evil murderer, Melvin Stoltzfus, *and* that I had also survived an uncanny number of attempts on my life by Melvin and other villains almost too numerous to count, I was indeed a strong woman. In other words, no one has the right to holler at my employees – *except* for me.

I set about selecting one of my long, slender digits to waggle in the earl's face, and being that I am a good Christian woman, and after a long struggle with the Devil, I settled on my *right* index finger. 'Shame on you for bullying this poor boy,' I said. 'Pick on someone your own size, you – you, Duke of Earl!'

Now I don't know why on earth those three words should have popped into my mind in that order, if it hadn't been for the Good Lord diffusing the situation on my behalf, even though those words, when strung together, form the title of a secular song. By the way, this isn't just a regular

187

secular song, like 'You Are My Sunshine'. No, siree Bob, to use an American phrase, the former is the type of song once found on dance records. Folks with longing in their loins pressed those longing loins together – sometimes with disastrous results – and did wicked things with said body parts, as well as with their tongues, hands and other appendages – most notably protuberances composed of adipose fat and baby-feeding milk ducts. Rock and roll was the Devil's music, and anyone who tries to tell you different is either my dear husband, the Babester, or else someone working for the Devil himself.

Now, where was I? Oh, yes! Speak of the Devil, one wouldn't think that many Old Order Mennonites would have even heard the song titled 'Duke of Earl', but apparently a number of them had once been young, and more than a few of them had been a mite rebellious. All at once, out there between the base of Lover's Leap and Rudy Swinefister's hayfield, a dozen harmonizing voices began to sing.

'*Duke, duke, duke . . .*'

To be honest, it was quite a pleasant experience. Borderline thrilling, actually. The harmony was superb; the deep baritone voices of George Plimpmeyer and Jonathan Throbswart, the sublime falsettos of Tim Hickey, Andy Cluckluck, and Geraldine Duwop, plus everyone else. Even Beverly O'Shea, who only sings in American Sign Language, was in fine fiddle that day as she belted out the lyrics in her incomparable bass. To have all these dear people, fellow church members, one and all, spontaneously sing this

188

secular song – why, it was almost like sinning and yet not sinning. I was living wild, for a change; I was living on the edge. Surely my meaning is a familiar one. It's walking on the line that gives it the thrill, isn't it? Taking my example one step further, it's akin to placing a crisp one-hundred-dollar bill in the offering plate at church but hesitating a second before letting go of it. Oh, what a sinful woman I can come close to being when I put my mind to it!

Needless to say, you can bet your bippy that the Grimsley-Snodgrass clan did not enjoy this wonderful entertainment. To the contrary, the earl began to inflate like a helium-filled birthday balloon. The two obviously surviving siblings *spittled and spattled*, which is a description totally original to me, but which, I feel, should substitute rather nicely for the phrase 'sputtered with rage' and thus should be incorporated into our mother tongue to help keep it fresh. That said, even the historically amiable Aubrey appeared nonplussed; a word, by the way, which is often used incorrectly.

'Magdalena,' she said tremulously, 'please forgive me for saying so, but you white Americans are a very strange lot. Before coming here I thought that you were merely transplanted Europeans with good teeth, who were addicted to gun possession—'

'Gums and good teeth are part and parcel of the same thing, dear,' I said.

'I said *guns*, Magdalena, not gums. Bang, bang, muck up the world kind of guns.'

'Well, *excuse* me, Your Ladyship,' I said. 'I

happen to be a pacifist, as has my family for the past five hundred years. That's one of the reasons that we came to America. Anyway, if it hadn't been for American guns, we might not be having this conversation, and if we did, you'd be speaking in a heavy German accent to say the least.'

Score one for Magdalena. Or not. The Book of Proverbs warns us that pride precedes destruction, and since I immediately saw that my sharp words and gloating tone had wounded my new friend just as surely as any gun, I felt deep remorse.

'I'm so sorry,' I said. 'Running off at the mouth is one of my main forms of exercise.'

Aubrey may not have heard my apology, however, due to the competing sounds of grunting and heavy breathing that were emanating from somewhere back down the trail we had just followed. Between Rudy Swinefister's wheat fields and Stucky Ridge grew a strip of woods – some of it rather dense and jungle-like – with the trail serving to separate the two. My first thought was that the strange noises were coming from a wild boar or possibly even a bear. Granted, both cases were highly unlikely, but not an impossibility. To my credit, it took me at least five full seconds before I *jumped* to the conclusion (another frequent form of exercise for me) that Janet Ticklebloomers and Norman Cornbrakes were breaking one of the ten big commandments, and maybe especially so, given that they were married to each *other's* spouses. Sadly, jumping to wrong conclusions has been known to add weight, rather than burn calories. Had I but waited five more seconds I could have positively

190

identified the panting party as my best friend Agnes, who, of course, had lagged far behind, along with her new best friend, the vociferous Daphne Diffledorf. They had to walk single file, of course (Agnes in the lead), with one hip brushing against bushes and brambles and the other hip laying low a swath of Rudy Swinefister's wheat. Someone was not going to be a happy camper.

The two women, however, seemed oblivious to any environmental destruction. 'Cheerio,' said Agnes with her flat American vowels, although no doubt she thought that she sounded 'tebbly' British. Given her laboured breathing, the word came out in three distinct syllables.

My doctor husband made both ladies sit on smallish boulders and took their pulses, while Pastor Diffledorf dabbed at his dearly beloved's brow with a white cotton handkerchief that was clearly in need of laundering. Meanwhile, my fellow church members milled about anxiously, and heedlessly, which is never a good idea when one is at the base of a granite cliff. Folks stumbled, ankles were turned, knees were scraped and little children cried out in pain – all this before either of the latecomers were capable of extended coherent speech.

It was the loquacious Mrs Duffleburger who truly found her tongue first. 'Why are there children here? They shouldn't be allowed as much as a peek at this poor boy's mangled corpse. Magdalena, I am putting the blame for this squarely on your broad but bony shoulders.'

There you have it in a nutshell; it was comments

like this from Daphne, as well as others made by her pastor husband, that had been getting under my paper-thin skin with increasing frequency. Could it have been all my fault because I was aging and my skin was literally getting thinner, or could it be that since I'd hired Pastor Diffledorf (with the elders' approval) the couple's behaviour had actually changed? We Mennonites are supposed to be soft-spoken, gentle, turn-the-other-cheek type of folk. True, I've sometimes been accused of being highly opinionated, and in possession of a sharp tongue, but I prefer to think of myself as being a woman who simply gets straight to the point.

Thank the Good Lord for my never-wandering Jew. 'You will apologize to Magdalena,' said my hero of a hubby.

Daphne *guffed* – that is to say, she gasped while she huffed. 'This is an outrage; I most certainly will not!'

'Wife,' said Pastor Diffledorf, 'that woman is not to blame – *this* time. I am afraid that a rather thorough search of the area has failed to turn up a mangled corpse.'

'Or even a slightly dented one,' I said. Heaven help me, I try so hard to be a good Christian but I am a hopeless case when it comes to my clergyman and his wife. And I am at least to blame for whatever comes out of my mouth, because I am the one who is responsible for bringing the Diffledorfs to my tiny piece of paradise on earth. *I* am the one who heard him preach a stirring sermon on 'the widow's mite' while visiting a cousin over in Holmes County, Ohio. The couple was originally from Xenia, believe it or not. It was *me* who convinced our sceptical board of elders that a Buckeye minister with his big city ways could mould himself enough to fit into our little inbred village of Hernia, Pennsylvania.

'B-b-but,' my dearest friend, Agnes, sputtered into speech like an old lawnmower when the ignition cord is pulled. 'M-Magdalena, I know that Daphne is not your favourite person, but you have to give your pastor's wife credit for possessing an eye as good as yours. Like you, she can literally find a needle in a haystack.'

The murmurs of renewed awe and support for my Mennonite nemesis were practically unbelievable. Had no one else in the congregation seen through this woman's thin veneer of peace and love? Was I yet again the most judgemental member of Beechy Grove Mennonite Church, the only black sheep in a flock of snow white, frolicking lambs?

'Why me, Lord?' I wailed, casting an eye to the heavens.

I've often heard it said that God answers prayer in one of three ways: yes, no or not yet. But apparently there is a fourth way, and this one stung my left eye and elicited peals of laughter from my supposedly pious peers.

'Stop laughing at my mom,' Alison said. 'She can't help it if pigeons hate her.'

As a matter of fact, it isn't true that pigeons hate me. And another thing: the dirty bird in question was a passing starling, one of a flock of thousands. The common starling, an alien species from Europe, made its debut in North

America in 1890 when one hundred of them were released in New York City's Central Park. It is alleged that the chairman of the American Acclimatization Society wanted to import every kind of bird mentioned by William Shakespeare. The starling was mentioned in Henry IV, Part 1. Today millions of starlings thrive across North America, and outcompete many native species for food and nesting sites. Of course, they are good for the owners of automatic carwashes but not much else.

'Shame on you people,' my doctor husband said sternly. 'This is no laughing matter. Would you be laughing if she got an eye infection? And here I thought that you were her friends.' Most fortunately for me, the Babester *also* carried a man's white cotton handkerchief, which he immediately put to good use.

As he dabbed gently at my eye, my handsome Jewish husband continued to lecture my Christian brethren. '*Schadenfreude* does not become you, by the way. I know that you have good hearts. I have been to your barn-raisings and served on your volunteer fire brigade. It is my firm belief that love is your guiding principle, and that is the way you live your lives – well, most of the time.' Gabe held up his hand, the one holding the soiled handkerchief, but it was not to show that he surrendered. 'I have just one more thing to say, and then I'll have said my piece: there is no one here who is more loving and more generous than my wife. Yes, it is true, she does have a sharp tongue at times – some folks claim it can slice through cheese – but there wouldn't even be a Beechy Grove Mennonite Church if it weren't for her.' No one laughed after the cheese remark. It seemed like no one was even breathing.

'That's two things,' Alison said after an agonizing second or two. Thankfully her quip cut through the tension just as smoothly as my tongue can slice through cheese.

Nothing would make me happier than to say that my fellow Hernians resumed behaving in the proper, Christian manner for which we Americans are best known and are wont even to export overseas. This was especially important to me because the benefactors of our good example would be the English-English, a morally bankrupt race, to be sure. I offer as proof their penchant for bestowing sexually suggestive names to everyday dishes. Spotted dick, indeed! Alas, however, the American immigrants among us were not quite as invested in being examples of proper Mennonite brotherhood.

'We're wasting time with this one family's drama,' said Daphne, who could now speak plainly. 'If it's really love and generosity that is important, then I suggest we start showing some of it to our guests by combing through Rudy's field for their loved one.' She turned to Aubrey. 'Royal Highness,' Daphne said, attempting a curtsy, 'I shall personally see to it that every inch of Rudy Swinefister's wheat field is flattened. You are not to worry; we will recover the badly mangled corpse of your beloved son in order that you may return to England with his bits and pieces in a suitably monogramed body bag. Why, I shall embroider it on myself.'

'Hear, hear,' someone said. I think it was Belinda Steelwater. In women's groups, she seconds *everything* that Daphne says, including her stated need to go to the ladies' room.

'Ach,' said Joshua Koenigsberger, shaking his head in frustration. 'If you'd only gotten here sooner, Daphne, you would have heard Toy explain everything. The wheat field is too far from the cliff, and even if the boy had sprouted wings and managed to fly that far – well, you can see for yourself that nothing has been disturbed.'

'Harrumph,' said Daphne. 'Maybe *you* can see that; but not me. I am not *unnaturally* tall like some people I know. Setting aside your giraffe-like proportions, I think that the issue at hand here is that we have a lazy Chief of Police.'

'Excuse *me*?' said Toy. He has never been a big fan of Daphne, ever since the day that she told him, quite unprovoked, that he would probably never make it into Heaven on account of he didn't believe in the physical resurrection of Jesus. Secretly, I have a hard time *not* agreeing with Daphne on that score, given that I was raised in the same tradition.

However, to be honest, believing in that dogma presents me with a huge dilemma: if that doctrine is correct, then my beloved husband and daughter are going to burn in a lake of fire for all eternity. An 'outsider,' one claiming to possess a logical mind, might suggest that a simple solution would be for me to abandon my belief in the physical resurrection. I suggest that said 'outsider' open his, or her, Bible to Proverbs chapter twenty-two, verse six.

I doubt if the pastor's wife opened her own Bible very often. 'There are two reasons that Chief Toy is content to leave Rudy Swinefister's wheat field alone,' she said. 'First is because he's chicken.'

'Buck-buck-buck-braaat!' That childish response was emitted by several people.

Encouraged by this shameful behaviour, even Daphne's physical demeanour changed. Ironically, she reminded me of my alpha hen, Pertelote, who occupies the tippy-top of the pecking order in my flock of Rhode Island Red chickens. Daphne's outsized chest was puffed to its maxi-Mother girth, and her throat wattles had assumed interesting shades of pink with crimson and magenta splotches. Whereas my fowl, Pertelote, has only one yellow beak with which to peck, the foul-tempered pastor's wife has a mouthful of yellow teeth which she bares when she grins in triumph.

'The *second* reason that Toy won't disturb this precious wheat field,' she cackled, 'is because he's on the take.'

'I'm on the *what*?' said Toy.

'Oh, don't play Mister Innocent with us,' Daphne said. 'We've all seen those TV shows where the cops are crooked.' She glanced around, seeking support from her husband's flock. Most unfortunately, for her at least, our sect of Old Order Mennonites watches very little television, with crime dramas being at the bottom of the list.

Toy was remarkably calm, given the demeanour

of his accuser. 'Mrs Diffledorf, until today, the matter of disturbing Rudy's wheat field to any great extent has frankly never arisen. True, from time to time, teenagers or hunters will do a little damage, but not so much that Rudy can't handle the problem by himself. And if he couldn't, I certainly wouldn't accept pay for my assistance.'

It pains me to say this yet again, but I have a younger sister in prison. Her crime was aiding and abetting a man who has been charged with kidnapping and multiple murders. This man is my biological half-brother. I repeat all this on account of it being a strange and terrifying world which we inhabit. The scary truth is that we are *all* capable of bizarre behaviour under the *right* circumstances, but it didn't take much more to drive Daphne Diffledorf completely over the edge.

Nineteen

'Brothers and sisters of Beechy Grove Mennonite Church,' Daphne said, her voice rising a full octave to where it wavered, rather like that of an inebriated cockatiel's, although to be honest, my experience with this avian species is rather limited. 'Might I have everyone's full attention?'

Given that her voice rose an incredible three notes even higher, there were dogs all the way down in the State of Maryland that had her full attention. In fact, the hairs on my arms were standing at attention (to be sure, they are very fine, blond and silky).

'Please, wife, be brief,' Pastor Diffledorf whispered. Frankly, it was the first time that I'd felt kindly towards him all day.

Daphne scowled at *me* instead of her husband. 'There are *those* in this community who wield a lot of power – financial power. *They* hold the purse strings. This purse opens and closes at *their* whim. The financial stability of Beechy Grove Mennonite Church depends on *them*. Indeed, the very welfare of Hernia depends on *them* and *their* disproportionate amount of wealth. Our scripture, however, tells us that it is the poor who shall inherit the earth, and that the rich will be kept out of Heaven, along with their camels.'

The gasps I heard in response to this nonsense were disgustingly loud; far more worthy of a

199

bedroom than God's green outdoors. Likewise, so many heads were nodding in agreement that I felt a wave of nausea.

'Stuff and nonsense!' I cried.

'What does that mean?' Lady Celia said.

'You ought to know,' I snapped, quite unfairly. 'It's an English phrase, after all.'

'Whatever it means,' Pastor Diffledorf said to his wife, his voice now just barely above a whisper, 'I don't think that God intends to keep rich people out of Heaven. Camels, on the other hand, won't be there.'

'Harrumph,' Daphne said. 'I wasn't through making my point, husband. I was only halfway there.'

'Then, by all means, finish,' Toy said.

'I intend to,' Daphne said. 'What sort of witness would we be to these godless Anglicans, these backward Europeans, if we didn't do our Christian duty and show them the kind of hospitality for which we Americans are so famous?' She wagged a stubby finger at me. 'Uh-uh-uh, don't interrupt!'

'I wasn't going to,' I interjected.

'Nice one, Mom,' Alison said. 'I just wanta know if God's gonna ban both kinds of camels. Them two-humped kinds are kinda cool-looking.'

'You see?' Daphne said. 'Magdalena, you are a bad Christian witness, even for your own heathen child.'

'She's not a heathen,' the Babester said. 'She's a teenager who is making up her mind about religion.'

'Same thing,' Daphne trumpeted. To my dismay, a number of church friends murmured their agreement.

'Et tu, you band of Brutuses!' I wailed.

'Behold, Magdalena is speaking in tongues again,' Pastor Diffledorf said. 'Wife, maybe it is time to lay off her.'

'I don't believe that she's speaking in tongues,' Lady Aubrey said, coming to my defence. 'She's merely trying to paraphrase a famous line that Shakespeare attributed to Julius Caesar in a play, but I'm afraid that she's forgotten her Latin declensions. Brutus was an individual, not a group of people, so one must use the plural—'

'Plural shmural,' Daphne growled. 'Why are *you* interrupting? Can't you see that I'm trying to help *you*? It's your son who is lying in this wheat field, his fragile, British body all smashed to smithereens. Don't you want to gather up the bits and pieces and tote the bloody fragments back to Westminster Abbey for a proper royal burial? Just think of how far that would go to strengthen the bond between our two countries. I mean, the funeral would be televised and we would get another chance to view those two princesses who wear fascinating table centrepieces on their heads.'

'Those are *not* table centrepieces,' Agnes said, not minding her business. 'They're called fascinators. And Magdalena's guests are not royalty!'

The Earl of Grimsley-Snodgrass snorted indignantly. 'You, my dear lady,' he said to Agnes, 'rally have no idea what blood runs through these veins of mine. Why, most of the crowned heads of Europe have rumpled the sheets of my ancestral manor, Gloomsburythorpe.'

'No doubt in an attempt to escape the bedbugs,' Janet Ticklebloomers said. She and her trysting partner, Norman Cornbrakes, appeared to be the only members of Beechy Grove Mennonite Church not under the influence of Daphne Diffledorf, and her shockingly subservient husband. I use the 's' word because our denomination, like many other conservative faiths, hold that it is the *man* who is the undisputed head of the household. For Christians such as myself, this teaching is thanks to an unmarried tent-maker named Paul (later made a saint by the Roman Catholic Church), who had many disparaging things to say about women, yet wrote such a beautiful treatise on love that it is often read at weddings. Go figure.

Now where was I? Oh, yes, the Earl of Grimsley-Snodgrass was not in the least tickled by Janet's remark. I will confess here that under less stressful circumstances I might have been tempted to stand back and watch the pair of them spar – so to speak. But the promiscuous Janet (for the record, she was a recent convert from Unitarianism) had never been my favourite person, and the earl was still my guest, so it behooved me to move the show along. Besides which, I didn't want Alison to be asking me about sheet-rumpling because I wasn't quite sure about the particulars myself. Let's face it, any nation that is capable of exporting a dessert named Spotted dick, (which I can purchase in the Foreign

Foods aisle of many large supermarkets Stateside), is bound to be a people without shame.

I waved my long, spindly arms with their preposterously knobby elbows as wildly as if I was deflecting a swarm of houseflies from my jam-covered face. 'Move it along, folks. We're heading back to the parking lot. That means *all* of us: nobility, clergy, innkeepers and commoners alike! March: two, three, four!'

But other than family, four was literally the number of people that I could coerce into marching back with me to the parking lot. They were Agnes, of course; the sensible, but adulterous Norman Cornbrakes; Janet Ticklebloomers and, quite surprisingly, Lady Aubrey of Grimsley-Snodgrass.

'Magdalena,' she confided when we were quite out of earshot of the crowd, 'I hope you're not offended by what I'm about to say, but—'

'You hate my pastor's wife?'

'Goodness no; I'm English, Magdalena, remember? Hate is far too strong an emotion for me.'

'Then perhaps you mildly disdain her actions in a genteel manner?' I said.

'By Jove, you've *almost* got it right,' she said encouragingly. 'Let's just say that I'm not amused by her behaviour. I find her a bit overbearing at times.'

'Ha, that's a good one,' I said. 'Most everyone around here would find it easier to stand up to a division of armoured tanks than to Daphne Diffledorf.' I was genuinely fond of the foreign woman, despite her overuse of adverbs.

'That certainly puzzles me,' Lady Aubrey said. 'I was given to understand that you Mennonites were a very softly spoken, kindly people; most especially your sort who wear the funny white caps perched precariously atop your massive coils of braided hair. Is it true that you never cut your hair, and how do you keep it looking so healthy?'

'We *are* so soft-spoken!' I wailed, not caring one whit about my locks at that point. About a mile away as the crow flies, the Kuneberger's ass, a wild species of donkey imported from the Arabian Peninsula, responded to my cry by braying piteously. The Kunebergers have this asinine idea that they are going to improve the bloodlines of their donkey herd with an injection of wild blood. Well, it may be good science, but the male donkey that they imported has taken a liking to my voice, and every time I raise it the stupid critter tries its level best to court me.

'As for Magdalena and her sect's massive coils,' Agnes said, 'they believe that a woman's hair is her crowning glory.'

'One Corinthians, verse fifteen,' I said.

'Well, it certainly saves time at the beauty salon,' Lady Aubrey said and chuckled.

'Really, Lady Aubrey,' Agnes said, 'I don't mean to be disagreeable, but how can you be so blasé when your own flesh and blood lies somewhere in Rudy's wheat field, flattened as thin as a Swedish pancake. Why, if those pious women from Magdalena's ultra-conservative church, with their funny caps perched atop their massive coils of braids, don't stumble upon the remains

204

of your son before dark, he is bound to become a buzzard buffet at first morning light.'

I gasped in horror. Given that it was high summer, and we were twixt woods and crops, I inhaled a mouthful of bugs of some sort or another. Since supplemental protein is nothing to be sneezed at, I swallowed my unexpected snack gratefully. We must always remember to thank the Good Lord for small blessings, don't you think?

The control exhibited in Lady Aubrey's voice proved that she was worthy of her title. 'My dear woman,' she said, 'the scenario that you described couldn't possibly happen – not in a million years. Whereas I agree with you that the bellicose pastor's wife, along with her spontaneous search party, comprised of civilians as it is, are likely to destroy that poor farmer's wheat field, they shan't in any way damage one cell on my beloved son's body. I say this because my son is *not* lying in that field flattened like a Swedish pancake, as you so gruesomely put it.'

'Hear, hear,' the Babester said, although how *he* could hear was beyond me, given that he and Alison had taken the lead on the walk back to the parking lot and were at least ten yards ahead of us. Even the adulterous Ticklebloomers and Cornbrakes pair, who were walking between Gabe and us three, didn't seem to hear Lady Aubrey's response to Agnes.

'You seem to have a mother's innate sense of certainty,' I said. 'I am, after all, a mother twice over. Even though my older child is adopted, my heart would know if she were dead. Of that I am sure.'

205

Lady Aubrey grabbed my elbow, an intimacy which proved that surely she must have had at least one American ancestor somewhere in the upper branches of her family tree. From what I'd learned from Agnes, no pure-blooded Englishwoman would as much as set eyes on another person, much less a hand.

'Magdalena, that is it exactly! Only another mother could possibly understand.'

'I resent the heck out of that statement,' said Gabe. Actually, he said a stronger word, one that references Satan's permanent abode, and can be heard by reading the name of Helen of Troy aloud.

'Gabriel,' I said sharply, '*must* you?'

'Must I what?' my clueless husband retorted.

'You swore in front of our child,' I said.

'Oh, stuff it,' Aubrey said. 'What a trifling thing to worry about at a time like this.' Then, still firmly grasping my elbow, she practically pushed me down the narrow path ahead of her as if I were a perambulator and she a nanny racing to escape a swarm of bees.

'S-s-stuff it?' I stuttered. 'Why I never, in all my born days! You, dear, are a shady lady, if indeed you even are one. According to Agnes, we're having more bodily contact now than most Brits have their entire married lives. Surely you're an imposter. I have half a mind to call the Department of Homeland Security.'

'And you, Magdalena, are a silly woman,' Aubrey hissed, sounding rather like a tea kettle, which should not have been surprising if she really was a Brit. Hissing American women sound more like snakes in my opinion, and I do have a right to an opinion, you know.

Nonetheless, I'd just been insulted by someone whose husband's ancestors had quite possibly been ennobled for *slaughtering peasants*. My ancestors, on the other hand, were most assuredly *persecuted peasants*. Frankly, she may as well have slapped my face. I yanked my Yankee arm free from the countess's claws and ran to the highway as fast as a knock-kneed woman in a midi-skirt and clodhopper shoes could go.

Alas, I wasn't fast enough to escape the countess's clutches. 'H-have a heart,' she panted. 'I am in dire need of your assistance.'

'For what?' I wailed. Having run away from trouble on numerous occasions, I wasn't even breathing hard.

'The loo!' she wailed. 'The looooo.'

Who knew that English nobs could wail, much less sound like a coyote when the moon is full? Clearly the woman wasn't bluffing, and when a gal's gotta go – well, a gal's gotta go.

'Full steam ahead,' I hollered, and made like it was the Devil Himself who was right behind.

Needless to say, we left poor Gabe, Little Jacob and Alison in our dry summer dust. When we got to the car we tumbled in and off we drove, lickety-split, far exceeding the speed limit. I was so focused on helping Aubrey that I didn't stop to consider that breaking traffic rules is also a sin, and stranding my family without a ride home is downright inconsiderate.

Twenty

ORANGE MARMALADE

4 oranges
1 lemon
Cold water
Sugar

Wash fruit; cut in half; remove seeds and stem end. Slice rind very thin or grind fine. For every cup of fruit add 1½ cups water. Let stand overnight. Pour in preserving kettle; let cook slowly from one to two hours or until tender. Again let stand overnight. For each cup of fruit add one cup of sugar and cook for twenty minutes or until it jells. Pour into hot, sterilized glasses; cover with paraffin.

Twenty-One

Unfortunately, there was no way to drive all the way back to the inn in time to attend to poor Aubrey's needs. She later revealed that she'd ventured to nibble on some sort of refreshment offered to her at the Convent of Perpetual Agony (her words, not mine). She wasn't able to identify the treat, except to say that it was disgusting, vile, nauseating, etc. I wasn't able to help on that account, as her description applied to everything that I'd ever sampled there as well.

My pioneer ancestors could not have gotten as far inland as Hernia had not every single one of them been willing upon more than one occasion to sneak off behind a bush to attend to their bodily functions. Lady Aubrey made it abundantly clear, via more wailing, that the grand mistress of Gloomsburythorpe was above taking a squat in the woods, even if her high-born hinnie was hidden. At that point, we either made it back to the PennDutch in time or I surrendered my cream-coloured Cadillac to the hang-ups of the English upper class.

Actually, there was a third option, albeit an unpleasant one; that option was to stop in at Rudy Swinefister's farmhouse and beg to use his facilities. However, since at that very moment my co-religionists were trampling his wheat crop, my request might possibly be met with a modicum of hostility. I dare say, it would be rather like a lioness asking a herd of zebras if they might babysit her cubs while she strolled down to the river for a drink of water. Well, I have never been any good at drawing analogies, so perhaps that one is too extreme. Or not. After all, I certainly didn't expect Rudy to open his door while holding a double-barrel shotgun. What's more, one of the barrels was pointed directly at me, which meant the other one most probably was as well.

'Go away,' Rudy said softly. Curiously, he didn't sound angry.

'Rudy, we have an emergency,' I said.

'Funny,' he said, 'but I didn't figure *you* for a Judas as well.'

'This woman needs to use your bathroom,' I said.

'I don't need the bath part,' Aubrey said, 'just the toilet.'

Rudy stepped aside and pointed to a hallway. 'Second door on the left,' he said. 'You'll have a good view of Lover's Leap from the john.'

'Thank you,' Aubrey said gratefully, her words trailing behind her like a stream of toilet paper as she ran.

'That was very nice of you,' I said. 'Rudy Swinefister, you are a good man.'

He grunted. 'Magdalena, follow me.'

Rudy led me through a traditional farmhouse living room, still decorated with antique Victorian furniture that had belonged to his mother, now deceased: Zelda Swinefister. The wide entry hall was flanked by a parlour on one side and a formal dining room on the other. In the dining room, the heavy oaken table had been shoved to one side and most of the matching chairs piled on top. This was to make room for a large elaborate telescope at the south window, the one facing Lover's Leap. Beside the telescope was a wooden TV tray bearing the remains of a half-eaten Sunday dinner.

Sometimes my brain can be as dense as my homemade bread; on those occasions I foolishly jump to conclusions. Then again, since jumping to conclusions is yet another of my regular exercises, I shouldn't beat myself up whenever I do. Come to think of it, beating oneself up might even be considered to be a form of exercise – just not one that is suitable for a pacifist.

'Please tell me,' I said, 'that you're not one of those UFO nut jobs.'

Rudy frowned. 'If a witty woman is half right, does that make her a half-wit?' he asked.

'I beg your pardon!'

'I accept your apology, Magdalena, if only because your theology keeps the essential *you* boxed in. You're like a hamster who thinks that his cage is the entire universe – *if* hamsters were capable of thinking about the universe and their place in it.'

Of course my feathers were ruffled, given that I hadn't actually apologized, but his analogy was so ludicrous that showing him up would be more satisfying than getting angry.

'Don't be silly, dear,' I said smugly, 'because if a hamster *could* think about the universe and that it was limited to their cage, how would they

211

explain the giant hand that reaches in to care for them from time to time?'

'Perhaps in this analogy they think of those hands as God.'

I was stunned. 'What a shocking thing for you to say, Rudy. What is your point, besides trying to insult my faith?'

His frown long gone, Rudy sighed. 'I was not trying to be sacrilegious; I was trying to make a point. If you'll recall, Magdalena, I started out believing, as you do now. I know that you believe that aliens from another planet cannot possibly exist because they are not mentioned in the Bible, in God's plan of salvation. And I'd be willing to wager a bushel of my finest wheat that you are fully aware that I am open to encounters with extra-terrestrial visitors. Am I right?'

'Yes, but you are also wrong,' I said. 'I mean that your beliefs are wrong.'

'Spoken like a true conservative,' Rudy said.

That hiked my hackles. 'Don't put the blame on me, dear. It was God Almighty who chose not to create your little green men.'

'There you go again with another absurd conclusion,' Rudy said. He sounded a little peeved himself.

Simultaneously, we were made aware of Lady Aubrey's presence at the dining-room door. Rudy and I froze like naughty children with our hands caught in the cookie jar.

'We didn't do anything,' I said, 'except verbally spar with each other. Isn't that the case, Rudy?'

'Come on, Magdalena, be totally honest; is that *all* that happened?'

212

'Of course! What else could have happened? Even if you're implying what I think you are, that takes at least three minutes now that I'm older, and she wasn't gone but two.'

'Oh, do tell everything,' said Lady Aubrey. 'You Americans are just as wicked as your films portray you.'

I gasped. 'W-w-w-wicked? Little Mennonite *moi*?'

Despite his rather obvious faults, Rudy had an agreeable laugh. 'I was about to show Magdalena my telescope. I have it focused on Lover's Leap. Contrary to what our self-described *little* Mennonite believes, I have no time for star-gazing.'

'I believe that Mars is not a star,' I snapped.

'Quite right,' Lady Aubrey murmured as she hurried toward us. 'Might I have a look?'

Rudy helped the countess adjust some knobs until she had the cliff edge 'practically in my lap.' In fact, he had to dial back the view a bit because even the sight of a chipmunk scurrying along in the background made her recoil and left her pale and shaking with fright.

'It was a bear,' she said when she could speak. 'I've never seen one – we don't have them back home – but yes, I'm sure that this was a bear.'

Rudy did a quick check on the scope. Black bears have been known to find their way atop Stucky Ridge to raid the trash bins, but normally they wait until we noisy humans have left. This, I'll have you know (in all modesty, of course) is largely due to me educating my fellow Hernians not to feed our neighbouring members of the family Ursidae.

213

'Chipmunks,' he explained to our panting visitor, 'are no larger than a hamster. Think of them as tiny squirrels with stripes – only cuter.'

'Yes, of course,' Lady Aubrey said. 'Silly me.'

Oh, what stoicism those Brits possess! Keep calm and carry on, indeed. What a plucky, lucky people to live in those Sceptred Isles where a stiff upper lip is the result of a brave attitude and not an injection of Botox.

I sighed wistfully. 'If I could have been born in any other country except America, it would have been somewhere in the United Kingdom. You know, Agnes feels the same way.'

'That's no surprise,' Rudy said, rudely interrupting my moment of sweet reverence. 'Many Americans are Anglophiles and think of England as the motherland, even though their ancestors came from other countries. It is because we were once a British colony and English is our mother tongue. Also, the language one thinks in contributes to one's world view.'

'To be fair,' Lady Aubrey said, 'I'm not sure that the love that you Americans have for us is reciprocated – at least not to the same degree.'

'*What?*' I refused to believe my ears. Her remark was simply unacceptable, and as for Rudy's reaction, he looked like a scarecrow minus the straw and supporting framework.

'But more's the pity,' Lady Aubrey said as if absolutely clueless. 'Let them eat cake, tally ho, and God Save the Queen!'

'*Excuse* me?' said Rudy. 'Are you having a nervous breakdown? Insults are one thing but incoherence is quite another.'

214

'Well said for a farmer, dear,' I said most sincerely. Perhaps I shouldn't have been surprised at Rudy's eloquence; I'd long known that he subscribes to *O Magazine*.

Lady Aubrey plopped unceremoniously atop the lone chair next to the telescope. 'Unfortunately I am still in possession of all of my faculties, which is precisely my problem. At least if I were bonkers I might enjoy seeing your reactions to my next bit of news.'

'Holy guacamole,' Rudy said, clasping his hands in a prayer-like stance. 'I knew it; you really *are* Kim Jong-un in drag. I'm sure that you had Magdalena fooled, but I knew it from the moment that I met you. It's that awful wig. It reads more like a dirty floor mop crossed with a steel wool pad than it does human hair. Really, girlfriend, the least that you could do is wash that retirement home for rats on top of your head. Maybe use more roach spray and less hairspray next time.'

I glanced around for a hole large enough to crawl into and, not finding one available, resorted to telling a harmless white lie. 'Why, I'll be a monkey's uncle,' I said. 'I never met this man before in my life!'

My guest rose from the chair in a stately manner, squared her noble shoulders, narrowed her eyes and set her chin just so. Even a colonial rube like myself could read that body language. Lady Aubrey, the Countess of Grimsley-Snodgrass, was clearly not amused by our jesting.

She cleared her throat but in a genteel way, of course. 'What I have been trying to tell you two is that I have only one son.'

215

'My dear,' I cried, 'you mustn't say that!' A true blue-blood, Lady Aubrey could speak without moving her lips. But she'd spoken so calmly about her son's death that he might as well have been an overwatered houseplant.

'No, no, you don't understand,' she protested.

'But I do,' I said, placed one spindly Yoder arm around her left shoulder and gave her the gentlest of squeezes.

'Ouch,' she said.

'Oh, it's the princess and the pea syndrome,' I said with a wink. 'It's *you* who has royal blood; that's why you're so sensitive to touch.'

Before Aubrey had a chance to react to my latest accusation, the usually misanthropic Rudy threw both of his well-tanned and heavily-muscled arms around the countess and pulled her in tight against his bulging pectoral muscles.

'Thanks for the hug, dear,' Lady Aubrey said as she patted his biceps, 'but I'm quite all right. Rally, I am.' She patted his bulges again.

'How can you say that, Aubrey,' I said, 'when your daughter just murdered your son?'

'Murdered? Are you daft? Or didn't you listen to a word I just said? I have just the one son. Not twins, not two sons, just *one*. That would be the Viscount Rupert.'

Now it was *my* turn to throw back my broad peasant shoulders, furrow my easily puckered brow and narrow my faded blue eyes into slits. 'Are you saying that you've been lying to me?' She began to nod her head so I picked up steam. 'This has all been a deception? A con game of some sort?'

216

'Oh, no, Magdalena,' Aubrey said in a sudden burst of emotion. 'It is nothing nefarious, if that's what you mean. If the two of you swear to keep my secret I will tell you everything. And I mean *everything*. You have to swear to secrecy on a Bible – on a King James version. That should suit you, I would think.' Then, using up several years' worth of British emotion, she stepped forth and caught up my hands in hers, flesh actually touching flesh. And let me tell you, those aristocratic little hands, as bare as a new-born babe's, were as smooth as mother-of-pearl and as light as Charleston biscuits.

Her aristocratic little hands were so light, I'm telling you, that when I let go of them they floated back to her sides. It wasn't fair. Why, Lord, did you create some folks with perfect features, peaches-and-cream complexions, curvaceous figures, shapely limbs, give them wealth, titles of nobility and good health? OK, so there was the matter of her rather unattractive husband, but all in all it just wasn't fair.

'Aubrey,' I said, 'forsooth, I would swear on just that version of the Holy Book, *if* swearing is something that I did. However, we Mennonites are forbidden to swear. Come to think of it, one would think that James chapter five, verse twelve would apply to all Christians. It commands us to let our yes be "yes," and our no be "no."'

'How very quaint,' the countess said. 'Although surely that doesn't apply to *everyone*. What I mean to say is that I have watched American telly. *The Good Wife*, for instance, is one of my favourite programs. Am I mistaken, or is your

Mennonite sect rather like the Quackers? Because that would explain this strange custom of yours.'

'No, dear,' I said softly, to minimize her embarrassment, 'it's pronounced Quakers. They named themselves that because they quake in awe and fear before God – as any reasonable person ought to.'

'Bullocks. I've met the Queen on numerous occasions and we've always gotten along quite splendidly. She's never once caused me to quake, and seeing as how she is the Head of the Anglican Church, she is pretty close to being God, if you ask me. Therefore I am quite sure that the name of the sect that I have in mind is Quackers. Now, how dreadfully boring this conversation has gotten, so do let's move on.'

Quackers is exactly how she continued to pronounce Quakers, as if my fellow pacifists were a flock of emoting ducks. This was getting to be a bit much; the rose-coloured film was all but washed from my glasses, and in the light of high noon, the mistress of one of England's finest families was forever tarnished in my estimation. I don't know what I would have done had Rudy not at last stepped up to the plate.

'Ahem. Your Highness, I hate to break it to you, but Magdalena is right. As for the swearing, how about I do that twice – once on her behalf, before Magdalena calls the county sheriff down from Bedford. I already know, by looking through the scope, that she has our local police involved. And by the way, I should mention that appearances can be deceiving; Magdalena might look like a simple Mennonite farmwoman but she's as sharp as a steel pitchfork and as well-connected as a barn built from Legos. She might not cast much of a shadow; nonetheless, you don't want to get on her bad side.'

Lady Aubrey's smile showed a measure of relief. 'My, what picturesque speech. Mister – uh—'

'Call me Rudy, Your Highness.'

'Well, that's just it,' Lady Aubrey said. 'I'm not Your Highness; I'm not a Royal.'

'Hmm. You certainly could have fooled me. I can see those teensy veins in your wrist and they look mighty blue to me.'

'Pardon?' Lady Aubrey said, her eyes twinkling.

'Blue blood, get it?'

'Oh, give me a break,' I moaned. 'Who is kidding who? Aubrey, he is not going to switch teams just because you're making goo-goo eyes at him. And Rudy, you know what they say about—'

'That's quite enough,' Lady Aubrey said. 'I will not have you besmirching an entire race with those vicious rumours, which I believe were started by the French – or maybe even by the Italians. We English women most certainly do *not* lie comatose during the act of reproduction! *Au contraire!* Once during the throes of heated passion, I unclenched a fist. Why, it is possible that I might even have moved my foot a few centimetres. At any rate, I am quite confident that the earl was fully aware that I was awake throughout the entire ordeal.'

'TMI!' I cried. 'Too much information.' I

219

swallowed. 'Were both fists clenched in the beginning? Just asking.'

'I think that I'm going to be sick,' Rudy said. 'If you're not going to spill the beans then I will have to ask you to leave.'

'Beans?' Lady Aubrey said.

'Secret,' I said.

'Yes, well, it's like this. We really *did* have twin sons, and their names really were Rupert and Sebastian. Then a year ago today – to be exact – Rupert was killed in a polo accident. His horse stumbled just as a player on the opposing team was in full swing. That mallet connected with my dear Rupert's jaw and virtually' – she paused to let a trio of tears trickle down her right cheek – 'tore his head off. It was a double tragedy for our family, you see, for the other player was his brother, Sebastian.'

I was gobsmacked. I should have been gag-smacked, however, because I just couldn't keep my big trap shut.

'Something's rotten in the country of Denmark,' I said.

'State of Denmark,' Aubrey said.

'*Excuse* me?' I said.

'You said *country*, but the word is *state*. That comes from Hamlet, Act One, Scene Four. The line is spoken by Marcellus just after they've seen the ghost.'

'You're in shock,' I said. Perhaps in a more perfect world Aubrey and I would be Italian. I could throw my arms around her with ease and she would graciously accept my comfort and succour. But given that my people are even more reserved than hers, I would be like a tree falling in a forest – but against another tree. In this case there would be Rudy to witness the sound we would make, if any. The odds were that we would both crash to the floor without making a peep.

'I-am-per-fect-ly-fine-Mag-da-len-a.' Aubrey carefully enunciated each syllable and spit them out like ice cubes from a dispenser.

'But—'

'Shut up, Magdalena,' Rudy said, 'and let the poor woman finish her terrible, agonizing tale.'

'Yes, that's right, it's a tale,' I muttered. 'Why else would the earl and his other two children still be out there searching for a body?'

'I heard that,' Aubrey said as she wiped away a crocodile tear. 'You make a good point. But you see, they do it to humour me. Until now – until this very hour – I have refused to face up to the fact that my beloved Rupert is dead. Dead! Dead! Dead!'

At that the Countess of Grimsley-Snodgrass, Mistress of Gloomsburythorpe, Former Friend of Magdalena, aka just plain Aubrey, cast herself into the bulging biceps of one Rudy Swinefister, who just happened to be Hernia's most liberated gay man. As I didn't have an exclusive claim on either of these two individuals, it should not have affected me one way or another that Aubrey should seek solace in Rudy's arms as opposed to mine. The truth is that it did matter to me. I don't mean to belittle these two human beings but it was rather like having a friend's new pet prefer one's husband over oneself.

'There, there,' said Rudy. Frankly, it is just

about the lamest phrase one can say when words of comfort are needed, yet we Americans use it all the time. I fully expected the countess, since she was a foreigner, to ask: '*Where?*' Instead, Aubrey did calm down, and considerably so.

'The earl, Sebastian – even young Celia – have all been ever so supportive of my fragile mental state. This trip to America, for instance; it was my son Sebastian who thought of this as a distraction for *me*, yet it was he who lost his identical twin brother. Can either of you even begin to imagine that?'

'No, I most certainly can't,' said Rudy graciously.

'Uh,' I said, just for the sake of answering.

Fortunately, Aubrey was too focused on Rudy to hear. 'Identical twins are two halves of the same person,' she said. 'We sent the boys to different boarding schools so that they would develop a modicum of independence, but one would always ring the other if they had a head cold, scored at rugby, went into town – that sort of thing. They were psychically connected, you see. Always were, ever since they wore nappies. To be honest, I never could tell them apart, so I had nanny dress Rupert only in blue and Sebastian only in green. Later, when they outgrew nanny, they switched clothes and all bets were off.' She paused to squeeze out a second tear. 'Yes, we had ever so many laughs when the twinsies played "dress-up," as they called it.'

'How positively droll,' Rudy said.

'Oh, please,' I muttered. Tell me, what Old Order Mennonite man (even a gay fugitive from that faith), not only has the word 'droll' in his lexicon but is ready to trot it out at the drop of a tear?

'What was that?' Rudy said. 'Magdalena, I fear that you're being frightfully unkind.'

'*Frightfully*, dear?' I said. 'Rudy, you're *not* Oscar Wilde, you know. You might be gay and an Anglophile, but you are *not* English and you never will be. You *can't* ever be. British, yes, but *English*, never.'

'Hmm,' Rudy said. 'Well, hmm. More's the pity, rally.'

'Stop it, Rudy, and open your eyes. Aubrey's supportive, grieving family has every member of Beechy Grove Mennonite Church trampling through your wheat field looking for a bogus body, and she finds their behaviour admirable.'

Upon hearing my accusation, Aubrey extricated herself from Rudy's carnal embrace. This is not to say that the couple had been engaging in anything at all adulterous; after all, who am I, of all people, to judge? I am merely stating that constant flexing and reflexing of so many bulges of various sizes and the sight of so many throbbing veins and so much pulsating skin certainly made it hard for me not to think of anything other than those urges that should only be expressed within the confines of a marital bed. Even then, what I beheld between Rudy and Aubrey should only happen at night, with the lights off and with one, or more, of the participants blindfolded, and with at least one of them tied up, or otherwise restrained, so as to limit the amount of groping, which, as we all know, can be dangerous to one's health.

That said, if one is *intent* upon sinning, rather

223

than committing adultery or engaging in wanton fornication, one would do well to consider an unbalanced washing machine, or a lovely deep bathtub named Big Bertha with thirty-nine jet sprays. When all is said and done, one is left with either clean clothes or a clean body.

'Magdalena,' Aubrey said, 'I can't take any more of your accusations; I'm going home.'

'Say *what*? Do you mean, by *yourself*? And just wait a minute, by the way; it is one thing for your family to play along with you but why on earth did Celia take it to the extreme that she did? Why did she pretend that Rupert was pushed over Lover's Leap? Didn't that tear the fresh scar off your grief? That sounds like cruelty to me! That, for sure, was not support!'

'Magdalena, Magdalena,' Rudy said as he shook his balding head in exasperation. 'Celia was undoubtedly close to her brother, Rupert, and she was trying to get back at Sebastian for killing him with his polo hammer.'

'*Mallet*, dear,' I said. 'And when did *you* become such an expert on psychology and so familiar with the Grimsley-Snodgrass family? Have I just now awoken from a ding-dang coma?' By the way, that was the foulest language I have ever used.

Rudy was still shaking his head, and believe me, the Devil made me want to shake it even harder. 'I'm not an expert on anything,' he said, 'although I do know something about farming. However, about Lady Aubrey and her family – all I did was listen to her, Magdalena. I didn't judge like you did.'

'Oh? You mean, like you're doing now?'

'Magdalena,' Rudy said, 'your slipups are showing.'

I glanced at the hem of my skirt; my petticoat was certainly *not* visible. 'What?'

'That was a misfired joke,' Rudy said. 'I meant your mistaken assumptions – the net product of all those jumps that you make to your hasty conclusions. Your so-called exercise routine.'

I was silent for several very, very unnaturally long minutes. If the Good Lord had wanted us to be mute he wouldn't have given us the instruments of speech. This is a proven fact. I mean, just look at apes and monkeys. Chimpanzees – which aren't related to us because we're made from dirt and they're not – screech and hoot all day, and the Good Lord didn't even give them the entire speech package. Ditto with the so-called talking birds like parrots, ravens and magpies. How much more so then, must our Creator expect from us; we who have the power to say what is on our minds?

'Oh dear,' Aubrey said, breaking the silence. 'Rudy, perhaps you've gone too far.'

'Yes, Rudy, perhaps you have,' I said. I was trying very hard not to cry. I'd brought Aubrey to Rudy's farmhouse to be helpful, not to be reminded that I am, indeed, a capricious, judgemental woman.

'Sometimes the truth hurts,' Rudy said.

'*And?*' I said.

'Nothing further,' he said.

'You weren't going to add an apology?' I said.

'No,' he said. 'Why should I? I was just stating a fact.'

225

'But Rudy, do you know all the times that I have stood up for you? I am constantly defending you – even still at church – at Yoder's Market, Miller's Feed Store, in the community. Aren't you in the least bit grateful?'

'I *am* grateful, but I don't ask you to defend me. And I'm certainly not going to apologize to you just because your conscience is telling you to do the right thing. You speak your truth and I'll speak my truth, and that's how it should be.'

I later learned that my sigh of exasperation was so intense that it could be felt a thousand miles away in St Louis, Missouri, where it stirred up a dust devil, which is something akin to a miniature tornado. This one was totally harmless. In fact, it had quite a positive effect on that community in that it caused the cancellation of an outdoor concert of sinful rock and roll. Perhaps that is just a slight exaggeration, but needless to say, I was peeved. I didn't have a drop of English blood in me, and when my tear ducts opened there was no telling what might happen. In the worst-case scenario, the countess might have to swim her way out of the farmhouse, and at the very least, my upper lip would become soggy and fall off, like papier-mâché that has been left soaking too long.

'I'm done,' I said. 'I quit. Out of the kindness of my shrivelled heart, I brought a foreigner here because she had an emergency and now the two of you have ganged up on me.'

The Countess of Grimsley-Snodgrass, Lady Aubrey, smart as ever in a robin's egg blue silk frock and a triple strand of nine-millimetre pearls, stretched her long, elegant neck to an impossible length and patted her immaculately coiffed hair. So gentle was her touch that not a strand was put out of place. And when she smiled, so evenly did her lips part that I was reminded of stage curtains being drawn open on my senior class play. Oh, to be a lady of her ilk, even for just one day, instead of being a clumsy, country bumpkin like myself.

'Now then,' Aubrey said as the smile shrank from her lips, 'now that you're quite done throwing your little tantrum, perhaps you'll do me the kindness of driving me to the nearest airport.'

'*Excuse* me?' I said.

'I'm afraid there is no excuse for you, my dear; your behaviour just now was abdominal, to say the least. Nonetheless, I need a lift, since I presume that there is no taxi service this far out in the middle of nowhere.' Her voice lilted upwards, in that peculiar fashion so favoured by the Brits and Canadians.

I jiggled my ears with my pinkies to make sure that I had heard correctly. The need for this rather impolite but sublimely sensual activity was becoming so frequent that I was in danger of having to add ear-jiggling to my list of exercises.

'Let me get this straight, toots; after speaking to me so rudely, you actually expect *me* to drive *you* to the nearest airport? Why, that would be Pittsburgh International, and it's fifty miles away!'

Aubrey tilted her head a wee bit, just enough so that I could get the full effect of her smirk and her partially closed eyes. 'Of course I expect that from you. After all, you are the innkeeper, are you not?'

I shut my eyes completely, as a proper Christian should when they pray. 'Oh, Lord,' I said, 'guard my tongue from speaking evil, for indeed I find these foreigners most taxing.' I opened my peepers. 'Ha, I just made a pun. Taxing! Get it? You need a taxi, and—'

'Tell you what,' said Rudy, 'how about if I drive the gentlewoman?'

'The *what*?' I said.

Rudy placed his hands on his hips, which is something he *never* would have done as a practicing Mennonite, seeing as how we view it as a prideful stance. He even dared to look at me, iris to iris.

'It means a woman of noble birth,' he said.

'How do you know she's of noble birth?' I said. 'You've only just met her. For all you know, her mother was a lap dancer who has never been to Lapland.'

'Rudy's quite right,' Aubrey said smugly. 'My father was the Duke of Bigoldtoadingham.'

'So what? I used to keep tadpoles in a jar.' That's when I hung my oversized, horsey head in shame. I had truly been acting abominably. I had been giving tit for tat, which is truly ironic, given that the Good Lord had not seen fit to bless me with the former, and I have never had the patience to learn the delicate art of tatting.

'I see by your posture that you're ashamed of your behaviour,' Rudy said.

'Yes,' I agreed.

'And you haven't been humble like your faith requires of you,' Rudy said.

'Quite so,' I said softly.

'Nor have you been placing your oversize feet in the footprints of our Lord,' Rudy said. He turned to Aubrey. 'In other words, she hasn't been doing what Jesus would do.'

'He's right,' I whispered.

'You certainly haven't been turning the other cheek,' Rudy said as he absentmindedly scratched his left buttock.

'I'm no saint!' I roared.

'Clearly,' Her Ladyship said, exhibiting unconscionable temerity.

'Give me your car keys,' Rudy said, 'and we're off.'

'Excuse me?' I said. Believe it or not, I'd actually taken it down a notch.

'If we don't leave now,' Rudy said, 'given your infamous temper, you might start throwing things. I may not be rich like you, Magdalena, but that framed needlepoint on the wall was done by my Grandmother, Rubella Swinefister, and it is very precious to me.'

'Ah, yes, I remember her; she was your German grandmother, the one who died from measles. Rudy, you are *not* taking my car.'

'Don't start in again, Magdalena. I have to use your car; mine is in the shop being repaired.'

'Well, then, how am I supposed to go anywhere?'

'I'll drop you off at the inn; it's right on our way to the Pennsylvania Turnpike.'

'I thought we were going to Pittsburgh and the airport,' Aubrey said.

'You have to take the Pennsylvania Turnpike,' I said, 'or haven't you even bothered to open a map of Pennsylvania? I certainly would have opened a map of the UK by now if I'd visited your country.'

'Tut, tut,' said Rudy, 'mind your Mennonite manners.'

'Manners bannaners,' I growled, having never been much good at rhyming. 'Rudy, I don't wish to return to the inn. I want to get back to that crazy bunch over yonder.' I flapped my arms at the window. On the side of it Lover's Leap loomed as a backdrop to his cornfields.

'Then take Constance, my tractor,' he said. 'You do know how to drive a tractor, don't you?'

'What do you think? I'm a farm girl, born and raised. It wouldn't surprise me to learn that I'd been conceived on a tractor, were it not for the fact that every woman in my family, since the time of Eve, has died a virgin.'

Rudy laughed, which pleased me immensely.

'Well played,' he said.

'Well, I think that Magdalena's common,' Aubrey said. 'I would never permit such vulgar talk around my table at Gloom-and-doom-let's-not-bury-the-hatchet-glop-shire.' By now I'd become a bit of an expert on deciphering the English habit of shortening their place names so that they don't bear any resemblance to their spelling, and I was quite pleased that I was able to reconstruct the aforementioned estate name from just Gmbshr. Although, frankly, since it wasn't quite the same word that the earl had scrawled in my guest register, perhaps at least

230

one of my antennae should have been tingling with suspicion. But to quote Christopher Robin, I am 'a bear of very little brain.'

'Magdalena's a queer duck,' Rudy said, 'but she's really all right. You just need to get to know her as well as I do.' He dug into the pocket of his sinfully tight jeans and yanked out a pair of keys.

Twenty-Two

It has been said that I possess an active imagination. Mama used to say that I never knew where the truth left off and the imaginary began. My high school creative writing teacher, Mr James D. Sodt, even suggested that I might consider trying my hand at fiction writing. More's the pity that I don't agree with them. I don't think that I have what it takes to write a recipe for boiling water.

Thus it was that while mounted high in the custom-made saddle of Rudy's John Deere tractor, the only scenario that I could place myself in was the Jewish nation of Palestine in the third century BCE. I was Alexander the Great, astride my war elephant, leading my army up to conquer Jerusalem and destroy the city. However, I would soon change my mind and spare this holy city. In the account given by Josephus, in his history titled *The Jewish Wars*, I would be met by the Jewish High Priest, Eliezer, dressed in crimson robes. The reception given me, and the glory of the temple, would so overwhelm me that I would spare Jerusalem and, in fact, offer a sacrifice of my own. From that day, until this, the name Alexander would be popular with Jews around the world.

Of course, lacking an imagination, I had only to pretend that I was Alexander the Great. The rest was recorded history, and recently corroborated by the excavation of an ancient synagogue in Galilee which has a mosaic floor that depicts a war elephant, presumably that of the great Greek general. All that, by the way, I managed to glean from an issue of *Hadassah* magazine in the gynaecologist's office, followed up by a visit to my local library.

Whereas Alexander the Great was met by anxious Jewish officials, I was met by a most curious Jewish husband. 'What the heck are you doing riding a tractor, Mags? And where have you been? While these morons have been looking for a non-existent battered corpse, I've been looking for you!'

'Did you try calling?'

'Only a million times.'

I fished for my phone in the pocket of my modest, calf-length skirt. If you ask me, the world was a much simpler and therefore better place before these ding-dang things were invented. Family was never meant to be separated further apart than shouting distance. If you don't believe me, then look to nature. Wolves live in packs, birds live in flocks, fish live in schools and starlings swirl in magnificent murmurations. If that is not enough to convince you, just try to imagine the twelve disciples, each with their own smartphone. I don't mean to be sacrilegious, but instead of following Jesus they might well have wandered off to wherever reception was the best and totally ignored their Lord and Master. Yes, siree, and Bob's your uncle – wireless devices are one of the Devil's favourite playthings, just like women's lingerie catalogues are His favourite reading material.

I glanced at the cursed object in my hand, which had clearly been turned off. 'Oops,' I said. 'It must have accidentally got turned off.'

'Great Danes and butterscotch cookies!' My Beloved was becoming quite fluent in the art of Mennonite swearing.

I smiled as winsomely as is possible for a woman who is getting long in the tooth and who would do well to begin standing on her head for eight hours a day to counteract the forces of nature. I also relied on a trick I picked up from watching a TV program; this one while waiting to see my dentist.

'You really look good in that colour,' I said.

'*What?*'

'Your royal blue shirt,' I said. 'It sets off your tan and frames your face beautifully. That's one that you picked out, right?'

'Mags, you know that I choose all my own clothes. I always have – not that I don't trust you; it's just that you're kind of – uh—'

'Conservative?'

'Yes,' the Babester said, 'but that's what I like about *you*. What the heck, why are we talking about the clothes? Let's get back to the tractor.'

'Oh, this little old thing?' I climbed down, taking care to gather my skirts, for by now the so-called morons had crowded around us, and among them were at least half-a-dozen sexually repressed teenage Mennonite boys.

'I see London, I see France, and I see Yoder's underpants!'

234

I felt myself turn a shade of Scottish white after a long, soggy winter. After all, only two men had ever seen my underpants – my current husband and Aaron Miller, my pseudo-husband, he of my inadvertent adulterous affair.

'My Land o' Goshen!' I yelled. 'Shame on you, you naughty earl. You're supposed to be a gentleman, not a peeping Tom.'

'I've a mind to punch his lights out,' growled the Babester. He might have done it too, except that he was holding Little Jacob in his muscular arms.

'Hit him, Daddy,' hollered Alison, and she made smallish girl fists as she danced up and down in the small space allotted her by the crush of people. 'Punch him in the nose.'

'No one is getting punched,' I said. 'Although, shame on me, because I am supposed to be a pacifist and, truth be told, I would dearly love to have my husband avenge my honour.'

'Oh, poppycock,' the earl said. 'Teasing a grown woman about her knickers is hardly a crime that merits vengeance.'

'You tell her!' The bleating voice belonged to none other than Daphne Diffledorf, my pastor's wife.

'Shut up,' Agnes said, her voice seemingly coming from nowhere.

My best buddy is, to put it frank, squat. She is short and round. She is most easily spotted from an aerial shot – taken perhaps from a drone or a helicopter. However, she can be hard to find in a crowd when one is searching for her on the ground, unless one is adept at reading signs. One such sign is the birds hovering above her in hopes of crumbs falling from her omnipresent snacks. That Sunday, I had been too focused on the oily earl to pay attention to swooping sparrows and swirling starlings.

'Did you hear that?' Daphne demanded of her husband's flock. 'And me, a *pastor's* wife?'

'Perhaps you should act like one, then.' The speaker was a woman, but she spoke so softly that I couldn't identify her. Never mind, I would ferret her out later and have Freni bake her a cake.

'Amen,' Ned Baumgartner said.

Trust me, old Ned was getting a cake as well.

'Magdalena,' handsome Toy said, making an appearance for the first time, 'where's the princess?'

'She's a countess, Toy, and she is on her way back to England as I speak.'

'Come again?' Toy said.

'She is returning home to Doomsburythorpe,' I said.

'For your information, Miss Yoder,' Sebastian said, pushing his way to the forefront of the crowd, 'the name of our estate is *Glooms*burythorpe – but only if you must pronounce everything in that dreadful American accent. With your mouths so full of vowels it is a wonder you have any room for all those blinding teeth. Rather like Chicklets, I should say. Ha!'

'Jolly good, that,' said his father, the Earl of Grimsley-Snodgrass. 'Now what's all this nonsense about my dear Aubrey returning to the proper side of the pond?'

'Nonsense, is it?' It had been a struggle not to sound harsh. Here was a man who loved his wife enough to play along in a very complicated charade in order to ease her pain. But the earl was so unlikeable!

'Miss Yoder,' the earl huffed, 'Her Ladyship would never abandon her son. Surely not while his broken and bleeding body lies somewhere at the base of this cliff waiting to be discovered.'

I thought fast. Thinking fast is something that I am quite used to doing, as a matter of fact. I'm not boasting, mind you; it is a genetic trait that I inherited from both of my biological parents who were double second cousins, third cousins four different ways, and fifth cousins so many times over that I *am,* in fact, my own cousin. Give me a sandwich and I constitute a family picnic.

'Where is the lovely Lady Celia?' I asked.

'I'm standing right behind you,' a young British girl answered. 'I am surprised that you didn't sense me. I've been boring holes through your head with my eyes. Usually people turn around, you see, given that I have these psychic powers with which to command them.'

'If you're so psychic, why can't you find Rupert?' Those words just slipped out of my mouth, like those lima beans did one Sunday dinner with Granny Hostetler.

'How dare you!' said the Earl of Grimsley-Snodgrass in the most convincing bit of play-acting I'd ever witnessed. His stiff upper lip must have been reinforced with steel bars if he truly believed that his son's broken body lay unclaimed somewhere at the base of Stucky Ridge.

'Whoa, Mags,' the Babester said, and he actually tried to physically restrain me with one of his strong, tanned arms. Believe me, one can count on less of a reaction by throwing petrol on a fire.

'I'm sorry for your loss, Mr Grimsley-Snodgrass, but Lady Aubrey told me what's really going on.'

The earl stiffened, seemingly frozen in place as if he were playing the children's game that we called Statues. Meanwhile, his two children searched his face for guidance.

'Oh, it's quite all right, dears,' I said. 'The charade is over; I know *everything*.'

'This is going to be good,' Alison said, stepping up beside me to get a ringside seat of the action. I can't say that I blame the gal; she is a very bright young teen and life in Hernia can be rather boring, if farm chores and cleaning guest rooms are not your cup of tea.

Hearing that the charade was over, the starch went out of the earl's face, along with the colour. Forsooth, his cheeks sagged so much that his monocle slipped but was quickly jammed back in place. In that microsecond, however, I saw something that raised the fine hairs along the nape of my neck and set to ringing an alarm bell in some seldom-used corridor of my mind, as it were. I can't define my feelings further other than to say that they were quite unsettling. Then again, I'd nibbled on one of Janet Ticklebloomers' egg salad sandwiches an hour earlier, and given my

238

luck that day, salmonella was a possible explanation for them.

'What do you mean by *everything*? Rally, I should tread very carefully if I were you, Yoder. You Americans have this silly notion that one is innocent until proven guilty. Ha, ha, what a preposterous idea. We Brits, on the other hand, make one *prove* that one is innocent of a crime. That is a far harder task, you know.'

'Hold it right there, Your Highness,' Toy said. 'No one is accusing you of crime, and if someone was, it would be me. I am the law around here, not Miss Yoder – I mean, Mrs Magdalena Yoder Rosen.'

'Whatever,' the earl said. 'I don't care about her name. And it is not me who is in danger of being accused of a crime, but she!'

'*Moi?*' I said.

'My *mom*?' Alison said.

'Yes, you,' the earl said. 'If you say anything libellous, I will sue you in Her Majesty's court, and upon winning, which I shall, you will be left with nothing but your string of worthless names.'

'Why, I never,' I wailed.

'And it is no wonder that you haven't,' said Daphne Diffledorf, my pastor's wife. 'With all that wailing, you sound like a fire engine station!'

'Hey lady, leave my mom alone,' Alison said.

The assembly murmured, many approvingly. 'Hear that?' said Daphne. 'This woman with the unsaved Jewish husband is causing our flock to wander astray, each man to his own way. Scripture warns us against that.'

'You're misquoting that scripture verse,' I said.

239

'And for your information, Earl, I have no intention of slandering you. In any event, I have decided to address my remarks to the good folks of Hernia' – I paused to give Daphne Diffledorf a meaningful look – 'and I repeat, the *good* folks of Hernia. According to the woman known as Countess Aubrey of Grimsley-Snodgrass, who has since departed for a gentler, moister clime, her eldest twin son, known as Viscount Rupert, perished approximately a year ago in a polo accident.'

Alison isn't the only one in our village who is starving for entertainment. Virtually every one, including the pastor and his wife, pressed in to hear what I would say next, and since I am but slightly claustrophobic, I managed to keep my wits about me by scrambling back aboard the tractor.

'I see London, I see France—' the earl began childishly.

'Oh, shut up,' said Daphne Diffledorf in a most un-Mennonite way. Two seconds of silence followed her outburst, and then the mostly Mennonite crowd gasped with such strength that their combined suction caused the wheat that had not been trampled to ripple in waves across the field.

'Now she's done it,' cried Alison gleefully, and she hopped from foot to foot, slapping them in turn in an impromptu heathenish jig.

'Spit it out, Mags, I'm begging you,' said the Babester, 'before our daughter causes you-know-who to bust a gut.'

'Aye, aye, Captain. You see, folks, the

240

countess's grief at losing her son has been so intense that she has been in denial all along.'

'Moses was in the Nile,' said Nora Shnootheimer, 'but that was a long time ago, I reckon. Didn't know the Nile was still around.'

'Well, it ain't,' said Harvey Gruber. 'They closed that thing down years ago on account of the virus; West Nile Virus, they even called it. Margaret, it ain't a sin to read the papers, you know?'

'*People*,' I hollered. When I put my mind to it, my pipes can be heard three counties over. Once, just the sound of me bellowing caused a tree to drop its leaves simultaneously, all the way down in the State of Maryland. I know this to be true, because my fourth cousin, once-removed, Prudence Mast, wrote and told me this on her hand-pressed, lavender-scented stationery, something that she would never do had it not been so.

Having got everyone's attention, I kept nothing back. 'And so you see,' I concluded, 'I have here, as my honoured guests, three of the kindest, most self-sacrificing human beings on the planet. This bereaved father, albeit an earl, and his two grieving offspring were acting like a normal family on an American holiday – that's what the Brits call a vacation, Nora, Harvey – just to ease Her Ladyship's breaking heart.

'But' – I paused dramatically – 'just as a rubber band can be stretched too tight, so it is with the human psyche. Up there at Lover's Leap, poor young Lady Celia experienced a break from reality and thought that she imagined her deceased brother, Rupert, being pushed over the cliff by his twin. This doesn't—'

'I protest!' Cee-Cee cried as she raised a dainty white fist high above her golden head.

'Hear, hear,' roared her father as he punched the air with an impromptu walking stick made from a length of dead sycamore branch.

'Fine,' I said. 'Ascribe your own motive to lying to these good people and depriving them of their much-needed Sabbath rest. And since this was not an emergency, and therefore cannot be construed as an act of charity, Rudy Swinefister will be more than happy to assess you for the damages. Hmm, let's see: ten rows of trampled wheat comes out to be . . .' I turned to my husband. 'Are you good at converting dollars into pounds?'

Well, that certainly did the trick; that took the wind right out of the earl's sails. 'Yes, yes,' he said without moving his lips the breadth of a human hair, 'weh tebbly close, you see. But you must undahstand that the dual role that my son Sebastian played was only to ease his mothah's aching hawt.'

So it was that when the wind left the earl's sails it took with it his ability to pronounce the letter 'r.' All of a sudden the most incomprehensible switch was flipped in my brain: whereas hitherto I have insisted that the only way to say a word is to pronounce all the letters, like the Good Lord intended, I now found the earl's dropped consonants functioned as an aphrodisiac.

Now, a thoroughly modern woman like Millie

242

Freedenbauer would tell you that it was the stress that made me think like that. The truth is, however, that it was the Devil – or one of his minions – plain and simple. Fortunately, I knew a sure-fire if only temporary remedy for routing them.

'Get behind me, Satan,' I bellowed.

Perhaps I should have given the earl a heads-up, or at least a primer on sexual repression, guilt and redemption. The poor man reared like a horse chancing upon a snake – which indeed he might well have been, given that the Devil was so near.

'What the blazes?' he demanded. 'Has this woman lost her mind?'

'Are you implying that she ever had one?' Daphne Diffledorf said.

'Ha, jolly good that,' the earl said, and whether or not he intended to do so he poured petrol on difficult Daphne's metaphoric fire.

'I suppose now you'll be changing your mind about spending tonight at her den of iniquity,' Daphne said.

'Say what?' the earl said.

'Well,' said Daphne, 'any number of murders have been committed there, and since murder is the worst of sins, it only stands to reason that other sins, such as fornication, usury, lying, envy, dishonouring one's parents – and of course, *adultery*, have all taken place under her roof.'

'It was *inadvertent* adultery,' I wailed. 'And I have never knowingly engaged in usury; I'm not even sure I know what it is.'

At that, the new Viscount of Grimsley-Snodgrass, the surviving twin, Sebastian, jumped

243

to my defence. 'If you were to seek my opinion,' he said, 'Mrs Rosen Yoder is inadvertent in just about everything that she says and does. It surely isn't her lifestyle that bothers me; it's the desiccated corpse that she keeps on her lift.'

You could have heard a frog fart all the way over from Miller's pond. Unfortunately, that golden silence lasted all of two seconds, and then a torrent of noise broke loose. Thanks heavens that Toy was the first to react, and he did so by blowing a small, silver-tone whistle that had become tangled in his chest hairs.

'*You*,' Toy said, pointing at Sebastian, 'do not have diplomatic immunity, so get that notion out of your head, if that's what you were thinking. One more word about what you saw at Miss Yoder's this morning and I will have you put back on the first plane to London. Do I make myself clear?'

'But sir,' Sebastian said, his lower lip quivering, although his upper lip did remain rather smooth and stationary. 'I meant no harm; truly I didn't.'

'We shall see,' Toy said. 'In the meantime, the rest of you – with the *exception* of the Grimsley-Snodgrasses, Magdalena and family – ah, yes, and Agnes; the rest of you go home and don't repeat a word of what you heard here. Otherwise you might be charged with hindering an ongoing investigation. Now, *get going*. All of you. Out of here.'

'Harrumph,' said Daphne Diffledorf, and with such force that even her third chin wobbled like an undercooked soufflé. 'I don't think that "hindering an ongoing investigation" is even a charge.' Nonetheless, as directed, she obediently shuffled back to the parking lot along with the rest of her husband's hapless flock. Since Daphne is so contrary that she would give me the shirt off her back – but only if I told her that I didn't want it – I knew in my bones that she was certainly up to something no good.

Twenty-Three

With the madding, and very maddening, crowd gone, Toy surveyed the surrounding destruction thoroughly before climbing up on the tractor. In my eyes, at least, the extra height added to the young man's authority.

'Rudy is going to be really pissed off when he sees this,' he said.

'I'll thank you not to swear in my presence, Toy,' I said. 'Just because one has authority it does not give him the right to be crude.'

'I dare say,' the earl dared to say, 'I would hardly count that as swearing.'

'My mom says that folks should mind their own business,' Alison said.

Toy winked at my daughter, which made her blush. 'Getting back to business,' he said, 'since these foreigners were your guests, and their lies, however well-intentioned, were the root of all this' – Toy clutched the tractor seat with his muscular thighs as he stood to wave his arms – 'you will, of course, compensate Rudy for his loss.'

'Hold your horses, young man!' I said, perhaps a mite too belligerently for a good Christian, especially on a Sunday.

'I think that it is quite fair,' said the Babester with a chuckle.

'Oh, you do, do you?' I said. 'That means that there'll be less for you to inherit.'

'Who says you're going to die first?' he said.

'I'm definitely going first if my blood pressure gets any higher,' I said.

'Waa!' Alison sobbed and flung herself into the ample arms of my best buddy, her 'Aunt' Agnes. 'I'm going to be an orphan,' she cried. 'A *real* one this time.'

Agnes glared at me. 'Stop being a cheapskate, Mags, and pony-up for the damages. You are traumatizing your poor daughter for, what to you, amounts to a widow's mite.'

From beneath the fleshy folds of Agnes's arms I saw Alison winking at Toy. Even now, on the brink of womanhood, that girl is already a master manipulator. Someday she is going places; I'm just afraid that none of them are going to be Pennsylvanian addresses.

I sighed so hard that I practically exhaled my ability to hyperbolize. 'OK, OK,' I said in a breathy voice. 'Far be it from me to cause my beloved child any more emotional trauma. Now permit me the luxury of thinking aloud. Poor Rudy is much disliked in this community, so what if I turn my entire estate over to him? We could go live in some cold, barren room at the convent, eat only vegan meals – that wouldn't be so bad. No TV, no radio, no books, no allowances to pay – that would be very freeing.'

Suddenly Alison was back in the long, bony arms of the *master* manipulator. 'Ya wouldn't really do that, would ya, Mom?'

'Grandma Ida,' I whispered.

'Yeah,' she said, 'no way you could live there.'

'I heard that,' Gabe said. Believe me, if someone

247

in Kuala Lumpur were to whisper his mama's name, his ears would swivel in that direction.

'Actually, Magdalena is on the right track,' Toy said. 'You are all going to be quartered at the Convent of the Sisters of Perpetual Apathy for the foreseeable future; the PennDutch Inn is now an official crime site.'

The earl sputtered like a diesel engine with sugar poured into its tank, while Gabe the Babester looked like a man torn between two lovers and feeling like a tool.

'What about me?' Agnes said. 'Do I get to stay at the Convent of the Sisters of Perpetual Apathy? I mean, I really don't care if I do, but then again it would be nice.' I've known Agnes since we shared a bathtub when we were babies; it was gin clear that my newly widowed friend was dying for company, even if that meant being quartered with the miserable apostates.

'Yes, yes,' I said with hyper-enthusiasm. 'Hie thee to a nunnery. Ha, ha.'

'I believe she is speaking the Pennsylvania Dutch language,' the earl said to his children. 'It really isn't Dutch, but an old form of Swiss-German.'

'My,' I said, 'you are surprisingly well-informed, for a *foreigner.*'

'Was that kind?' Agnes said. 'This man is our guest.'

I hung my horsey head in shame. 'Please accept my apology, Your Lordship. It's just that most folks don't read through the brochures that I send them through the mail.'

His Lordship jumped back as if I were about

to touch him with my coarse, peasant hands. His noble noggin wobbled on his spindly inbred neck – not that I'm judging, mind you – and he was hard-pressed to keep the monocle in place.

'We're not "most folks," I'll have you know. I'm the Twelfth Earl of Grimsley-Snodgrass. My ancestor was given his titles by King Henry the VIII. In fact, I have more royal *English* blood than—'

'Stuff and nonsense,' Alison said in what I thought was a ding-dang good imitation of Lady Celia's accent.

Of course everyone was stunned, and truly none were more horrified than Alison's father. 'She didn't mean that,' the Babester blurted out before bedlam could erupt.

'I did *so* mean it,' Alison said stoutly. 'We don't get to choose our ancestors so we shouldn't get credit for who they were. And anyway, we read about this Henry guy in school, and he was a really mean man. He kept getting rid of his wives, and all because they couldn't give him a son. He'd have their heads lopped off, like they was chickens or turkeys. Then he'd go and marry him another one.'

The Earl of Grimsley-Snodgrass grasped hold of his monocle tightly and leaned in to inspect Alison as if she might have been a polo pony that had suddenly begun to speak. Of course, it brought to mind the story of Balaam's ass in the Bible.

'Jolly good,' he said at last. 'This child makes a good point. Perhaps if I ever were to divorce Countess Aubrey I could send for this one, and

249

then *she* could become the next Countess Grimsley-Snodgrass.'

'*Eew!*' Alison said. 'Yuck!'

Thank heavens that Toy can think fast on his well-shaped feet. 'Gabe, stop! If you punch the earl in the nose you'll be charged with assault and it won't be worth it. If vengeance is what you're after, then tell your mama, Mother Superior of the Sisters Who Feel Inferior.'

Even the Babester had to laugh at that. Before long it was all sorted out, and the mob of nobs and their minders – that would be Gabe, Alison and Agnes – were headed over to bed down at my mother-in-law's supposed convent, where folks were free to frolic about in the altogether like the heathens that they were.

I insisted on tarrying behind with Toy. This time it was me who carried Little Jacob on my hip.

'What is it?' Toy asked when he was quite sure that the others were far enough away so that we could not be overheard.

'I'm not sleeping over at the Den of Iniquity,' I said.

'Then *where*?' he said. 'You can't go back to the inn.'

'You can't stop me. I *have* to go back; I have two cows and a horse to feed, not to mention twenty-three hens and a very large cock – I mean rooster.'

'I know what a cock is, Magdalena; I'm not stupid.'

'I'm sorry. Anyway, I intend to sleep in my own bed tonight, and I will be taking Little Jacob

250

with me so that I can give him a bath and he can sleep in his own bed. But you needn't worry; we won't touch your precious crime scene. My bedroom is on the ground floor and the corpse is upstairs, lying supine – albeit a wee bit flattened – across the roof of my lift. Uh, that means elevator.'

'Yes,' said Toy, 'I know what that means, as well. Big cock and a lift. Gotcha.'

'Don't be coy, Toy,' I said. 'I'm not going to have my toddler living over there in the pigsty of apostasy.'

'So an open tomb is better?' Toy said. 'Somehow I fail to see the logic. Besides, doesn't it spook you out the least little bit?'

'Logic shmogic,' I said. 'Yoko-san has been in that shaft all along; why should this night be any different? Little Jacob will not be getting upstairs, I can promise you that, and if Yoko-san was going to haunt me, she would have done so by now. Anyway, good Christians don't believe in ghosts.'

'Funny, but I could swear that you did. I've seen you talk to your granny.'

'I was giving you the benefit of the doubt, officer.'

Toy shook his sinfully handsome head. 'I'm really sorry, Magdalena, but I can't allow it. Not until I can get a forensic team in here from Pittsburgh, and that could take days.'

'Harrumph,' I said as I furrowed my brow so deep that one could plant corn between the hillocks. 'In this one-horse town it is the mayor who hires and fires the police force. Since I art the mayor, and thou art the police force, I say that

251

either thou wilt allow me to sleep in mine own bed or I shall be forced to fire thee.'

Toy looked like a wounded boy. I wanted to throw in the towel that second. Almost . . . sort of. I would be willing to eat off the so-called convent floors, even the chairs where all those naked bottoms had been – no, not that, but almost – not to see the way that he looked at me.

'I quit,' he said.

'What?' I cried.

'Magdalena, you're making it impossible for me to do my job. Just because you're by far the wealthiest individual in this village and single-handedly pay for all the services, that doesn't give you the right to be a dictator.'

'But I'm a benevolent dictator,' I cried. 'I don't lop off heads or compel anyone to pray before school – even though, Lord only knows, those Episcopalian twins, in junior high, could stand a demonstration of how a proper prayer is done.'

Toy raised a groomed yet heterosexual eyebrow. 'Are we being a bit judgemental?'

'I was observing, not judging. Just to show you how impartial I am, it is my observation that the children who attend the church with thirty names, out near the Turnpike, would do well to lay off the sweets and fried foods.'

'Now, that is just mean,' Toy said.

'How is that mean?' I asked. 'The Bible says that we are to maintain our bodies as temples for the Lord, but some of those kids have added enough extra space to their temples that they are competing with the Vatican City for size.'

'Never mind; I give up,' Toy said.

'But you don't quit, right?'

'I guess. But I am counting on your word, as a God-fearing woman, that you won't be sneaking upstairs for one more peek at poor Miss Yoko-san.'

'Yes, sir.' I gave him a clumsy salute.

'Cut it out. But hey,' he added, just as he started to turn away. 'One more thing. When you went off to speak to Rudy, I got another call. This one was about the owner of a convenience store on the east side of Pittsburgh.'

I felt like a tray of ice cubes had been dumped down the back of my dress. 'Oh?'

'The owner of the convenience store claims to have seen your brother in his store this morning.'

'*Pittsburgh?* That's just an hour away! What was Melvin doing in Pittsburgh? How did this convenience store owner know that Melvin was my brother? How did Melvin behave in the store?'

Toy turned entirely so that he faced me square on. 'So many questions. For starters, I don't know why Melvin was in Pittsburgh – but at least he's *there*, and not *here*, even if it is just an hour away. As for how he behaved himself; he robbed the poor fellow, who had only recently arrived from India with all his savings to purchase the franchise. Fortunately, Mr Rashid was a portrait painter in India and he did a bang-up job on his own police sketch, which in turn, matched the FBI's most-wanted poster perfectly.'

'Jiminy Cricket! So then it was the FBI who called you?'

'No,' Toy said, 'it was local. No doubt the FBI has their hands full at the moment.'

253

'Quite so,' I said. 'No doubt that their hands are full of soap and warm water as they blithely wash them.'

'Say what?' Toy said. 'Was that sarcasm? If so, whatever for?'

'Let's just say that my problems with Melvin, with him wanting to kill me and members of my family, must be really small potatoes to the FBI. That serial killer, half-wit, half-brother of mine has been running across state lines for nigh on two years, and these phone calls you've gotten lately are the first real evidence that the Preying Menace still lives.'

'I thought that you called him the Praying Mantis,' Toy said.

'He's both,' I said.

'Magdalena, do you want me to crash at the inn tonight?'

'No!'

'Good,' Toy said with a smile. 'Because I hate ghosts – no offense, Granny Yoder.'

'But,' I said, 'you can still do a huge favour for me.'

'Anything – but *that*. I have boundaries, you know, and I respect your husband's fists.'

'You also have *chutzpah*,' I said. I allowed a broad smile to lift the corners of my pale, thin lips. 'Believe me, dear, I was not asking you to dance the mattress-mamba with me.'

'Of course not,' he said quickly. 'Besides, I'm a virgin.'

'You are not!'

'Yes, ma'am, I am.'

'Get out of town and back!' I said. It was a

phrase of incredulity that I had picked up from Toy himself.

But how could such a thing possibly be true? Toy had 'movie-star' good looks. That was back in the day before I opened the PennDutch Inn and stars such as – well, never you mind. Let's just say that some of today's crop don't bear a strong resemblance to Rock Hudson and Paul Newman but look more like Rocky the Flying Squirrel.

'I was painfully shy,' Toy said. 'I still am.'

'Well, well, well, how very interesting,' I said. I said it quite kindly, of course. 'Perhaps I can help you overcome your shyness – just not today. What I need from you now is help to get a message to the Babester.'

'The *who*?'

'My studmuffin – Gabriel.'

'Oh,' Toy said. 'So you really don't have designs on *me*?'

'Well, you *are* very handsome; there is no denying that. But even if I were considering such a heinous sin, the fact that you are yet a virgin puts me way out of your league.'

'Come on, Magdalena, you know I'm just *toying* with you.'

'Toy! Just pay attention – *please*. I need you to go across the road to the Convent of Dismal Anarchy and tell Gabe that I'll be staying the night over here. Tell him not to worry; that I'll be all right. You got that? Tell him that if he gets scared his mother keeps *Winnie the Pooh* videos in a big wicker basket, located up in the coat closet of the main sitting room. And tell him that

255

I said that it was OK if she cuts his meat for him just this once.'

'Hmm,' Toy said. 'I thought that they were vegetarians.'

'Not all of them. Just some of the leadership.'

Toy sniffed the air, even though we were too far away to pick up even a trace of a scent. 'I wonder what the meat choice is for tonight,' he said.

Twenty-Four

An empty inn can seem as large as Buckingham Palace. Granted, I've never been to Her Majesty's house (I'm still waiting for an invitation) but I've read that she has a pack of corgis barking at her heels and servants melting in and out of the woodwork just as regularly as the ants climb up my walls. I rather enjoy my own company, being the cheerful soul that I am, but my periods of solitude are usually short-lived and definitely bracketed by my family's comings and goings, not to mention the many volunteer tasks I undertake on behalf of Beechy Grove Mennonite Church. Now, with most of my family under the stubby wings of Ida Rosen, aka Mother Superior, and most of my church members being difficult, thanks to the daffy Daphne Diffledorf, I was largely by myself.

Of course, I wasn't *all* by myself, because I had Little Jacob with me. That little Cutie Pie is always doing *something* kinetic. He slobbers and kicks when he is asleep, but when he's awake he toddles, babbles, plops, cries, sings, grabs, scrabbles, laughs, reaches, climbs, screams, eats, poops and, well, I guess that his Grandmother Ida Rosen was right; the two of them *do* have a lot in common.

Perchance I longed to hear the voice of another adult, then there was Granny Yoder's ghost to keep me company. If one is in the mood for a lecture, she's good for several hours of entertainment at one sitting – but mind you, one must be sitting straight, lest bad posture become part of said lecture. Granny, however, never leaves the parlour, so that she can be easily avoided, if that is what one so desires, and that is exactly what I intended to do that night.

As for the ghost of poor Yoko-san, how could I really be sure that she existed without experiencing her myself? Just because Lady Celia had claimed to converse with her, even divulging information that she could not have been privy to, that was no reason to be convinced that the Japanese girl's spirit had remained stuck to my lift. No siree, I take pride in being a sceptical woman, and if I want to believe that dinosaurs coexisted with man, despite the fossil evidence, or that somehow Noah managed to take woolly mammoths, as well as Asian and African elephants, and their subspecies, aboard the ark, not to mention all the giraffe and zebra species – since there is no such thing as evolution and therefore they could not have evolved *after* the flood – nevertheless, I am a very logically-minded and sceptical woman. I will admit that sometimes, when I ponder that there are perhaps a million species of animals overall – well, never mind. *Faith!* We must have the faith of a small child! And blinders! In my humble opinion every new Christian should be issued a pair of metaphorical blinders, so as not to be unduly frightened by logic and reason. After all, we Amish and Mennonites put blinders on our horses before

258

taking them out on the highway so that they aren't frightened by cars.

Suffice it to say, I fully intended to keep my promise to Toy. The master bedroom was an afterthought when the farmhouse was converted into an inn, so it is on the ground floor and can be reached only by going through the large country kitchen. We like it this way, as it makes it inaccessible to guests, whom Freni shoos out of 'her' kitchen with the business end of her broom. After fixing comestibles for the little one and myself, I retired to the bedroom to eat and – there is no way to say this without sounding worldly – watch a little television.

But let me hasten to add that I do not countenance programs that contain violence or sexual acts of any kind. Why, once I even turned off the television after watching a nature show that dared to air a clip of two rhinoceroses doing the horizontal hootchie-cootchie. When the Babester demanded to know my reason for this, I said that if the Good Lord had wanted us to view this act, He would have seen to it that we were born in the African bush. While it is true that I was born and raised on a dairy farm, there is no comparing the bulls of the two species when it comes to their endowment. It is said that rhinos have poor vision, and this is surely a blessing bestowed upon Mrs Rhino by The Creator. For if Mrs Rhino could see that Mr Rhino had five legs, she would run until she encountered an ocean and then swim until she drowned. Forsooth, it is no wonder that they are such crotchety beasts.

259

Now, where was I? Ah, yes, I was set to have a quiet evening with a suckling babe at one breast and a copy of the Good Book propped against the other while I played a rousing game of Bible Roulette. The rules are very simple: one simply flips the pages at random, stops, places a finger on a verse, without looking at it, and then tries to determine what message the Lord has for you embedded in that verse. I decided that in order to be fair to the Lord, I'd give Him three chances to get His message across to myself.

The text that my bony index finger happened to pick first was Proverbs chapter twenty-five, verse twenty-four. *'It is better to dwell in a corner of a housetop, than in a house shared with a contentious woman.'*

'No fair,' I wailed aloud. 'That doesn't count; that was just a practice prophecy, Lord. I want three more verses – *please!*'

I laid Little Jacob on the bed next to me – he had somehow managed to fall asleep – turned my Bible upside down and gave it a good, if somewhat useless, shake. Then I righted the book and, sight-unseen, flipped through it forwards and backwards before picking my next verse. But again, it was from Proverbs; this time it was Proverbs chapter twenty-six, verse eleven. *'As a dog returns to his own vomit, so a fool repeats his folly.'*

'OK, I get your point, Lord,' I said. Frankly, I wasn't just disappointed; I was a bit miffed. Like any good Christian, I am constantly in conversation with my God and always striving to grow in my faith. But God is my father, and just as any child might feel, it stung a little bit to be reproached by my Father in Heaven.

No sooner had I uttered those words, however, than I heard a noise emanating from somewhere in the house – somewhere other than the bedroom! I yanked the sheet so that it covered Little Jacob up to his button nose and then slid out of bed. While it is true that my feet are the size of tennis rackets, I can tread as soundlessly as one of our American mountain lions. It is a skill honed from years of creeping up my impossibly steep and creaky staircase to check on my guests' welfare. I feel that I should explain, perhaps even illustrate, although I'm quite sure that one example should suffice.

For instance, on one occasion I heard loud, angry voices coming from room four in the wee hours of a morning. I also heard what sounded like the breaking of glass and the splintering of antique wooden furniture. The room had been rented over the telephone to Donald Mallard and Mozella Whiplash, both of whom were winners of the Universal Sausage and Bacon Eaters Championship. I had been loath to rent them a room, for fear that my stairs would collapse or, Heaven forfend, the toilet would be smashed into smithereens. I was quite shocked when the couple presented themselves at my front desk.

Donald did indeed resemble a soccer ball, albeit an angry soccer ball, with sausages for arms and legs, but Mozella was a tiny thing. What a strange pair they made; a fat barnyard goose with a fledging sparrow chirping along behind it! That night I must have sneaked up my impossibly steep and squeaky stairs a dozen times in order to check on poor Mozella's undoubtedly pitiful plight, given the girth of her husband, and the gruffness of his demeanour and earlier behaviour. I have had a few too many murders committed under my roof to sleep easily when I sense an emotional storm brewing overhead.

At any rate, on my final check, after hearing my property being destroyed, it was not the mere slip of a lady whom I found to be in need of protection but her half-tonne hubby. That little gal had him pinned to the floor like a roped steer, and had tied him up, hands and feet, with one of my best buttercup yellow guest sheets.

'This varmint ain't running off nowheres till he gives me my half of the winnin's,' she said.

'Run off?' I said. 'I don't mean to be too rude but I rather doubt that a man his size is capable of running at all.'

'Ma'am,' Donald said, 'I'll have you know that I am a good Christian man who don't gamble, take up with loose women, drink or smoke on account of my body is a temple for the Lord. If I want to eat me some grub, then I say 'Praise the Lord and pass the mashed potatoes.'

It took me a second or two to scan Donald's entire body. 'Mr Mallard,' I said, 'if your body is a temple for the Lord then you've been building him a mighty large annex.'

Mozella yelped with delight. 'You hear that, Donald? I always told you that you was an—'

'That's not what I said, dear,' I cried, absolutely mortified. I won't even allow Alison to shorten the word 'buttocks' in my presence.

'We ain't married,' she said. 'We lied so as we could save money on getting only one of your famous rooms.'

'And now you have none of my famous rooms,' I said as I dialled the police.

It may appear that I have digressed, but once again there is a method to my madness. The point was to illustrate that it is quite possible to navigate my impossibly steep stairs undetected *and* that looks can be quite deceiving. Therefore, when I heard the noise again, and it seemed to come from above, I had to seriously give credence to the possibility that an intruder had already managed to gain access to the second story of my pseudo-historical, Pennsylvania Dutch inn.

A much more comforting thought was that the End Times were at last upon us and that the Rapture had begun. Perhaps a brief word of explanation is in order for non-Christians, and those eighty percent of folks in the UK who are too lazy to go to church. I am referring to the day when Jesus Christ will return triumphantly to the earth and true believers everywhere, even the dead ones and perhaps a few Roman Catholics, will rise up to meet him in the air. The Bible does not go into details, but I should think that roofs will have to come off buildings and vehicles and soil off the tops of graves in order for this to happen. Faithful Christians across the globe have been eagerly waiting for this event their entire lives, as have their forbears for millennia.

The question remains, however, at least in my mind: *where* in the sky will Jesus reappear? If he makes his landing over the Holy Land, as he promised his disciples, the curvature of the earth will prevent *me* from witnessing that great event over here in Hernia, Pennsylvania. And if *I* rise straight up through a hole in my inn's roof, no matter how conveniently it is prepared for me, I might miss the great reunion, since I would have no idea how to steer, once I was airborne, and thus I might shoot straight out into Outer Space and spend all of eternity on some distant planet. Oh, the thoughts that trouble this woman's soul; it is a wonder that I can function at all!

Since the Rapture happens as quick as a blink, and I heard no further preparations on an exit hole, that left the first theory as the most likely: I had an intruder. I lunged for my bedside telephone. The line was dead. No signal. I looked around for my cell phone. Ding, dang, where was my cell phone? Oh, yeah, I'd tossed it on the kitchen counter while I'd heated up some supper for Little Jacob and myself. We don't get very good cell reception in the inn anyway, and the phone was constantly banging against the cupboard doors, which I found most annoying. Truth be told, by then I was easily annoyed, and the little phone was not behaving, as inanimate objects are sometimes wont to do. Even when I slammed it on the counter it skittered to the edge and slid to the floor, where I just left it. If that's where it wanted to stay the night, so be it. I wasn't about to continue a battle with five inches of steel and circuits.

Then, horror of horrors, I heard a sound directly outside my bedroom door. *Rap, rap, rappity-rap.*

It was faint, to be sure, but it certainly wasn't the blood throbbing in my temples or the more familiar sound of wood-eating termites.

It was high summer, and since I eschew paying a premium for electricity, I had to keep the windows open rather than turn on our central air conditioner. In Hernia, where even our heathens are generally law-abiding (aside from the odd murderer) the only people with locked doors are those folks engaging in various forms of sexual expression. So it was that it did occur to me that perhaps a raven had chosen to share my home for the night. And yes, I do possess a healthy imagination, but I owe this train of thought to my eleventh-grade teacher, Miss Lehman, and a rather unusual bout of irrationality brought on by fear.

'Say something, you stupid bird,' I shouted through the door. 'Don't just stand there rapping. Identify yourself! I have a cudgel here in my hand and I'm not afraid to use it.' To be honest, I didn't even know what a cudgel was, and I was actually gripping the wire handle of an old flyswatter that we keep on the window ledge by the bed.

The raven mumbled something which I couldn't understand, then it continued to destroy my antique door with its sharp, corvid beak.

'Can't you at least say "nevermore"?' I hollered.

'Nevermore,' came the faint response.

That did it; a massive dose of adrenaline kicked in and I yanked open the door with such force that the raven barrelled into me, almost knocking me over – except that ravens don't barrel, they fly, and they certainly don't look like Lady Celia Grimsley-Snodgrass.

'I'm so sorry,' she said in a flat American accent. 'Are you OK?'

'Not really,' I said. 'I think I'm having a nervous breakdown – in which case, you're a figment of my imagination.'

'Miss Yoder, I'm quite real, I assure you. May I come in?'

'You're already in,' I said. 'Can I pinch you?' Under the circumstances it seemed like a very reasonable request to me.

'Uh, I'd rather that you didn't,' the young woman said.

'May I flagellate you then?' I said.

Lady Celia blanched. 'Miss Yoder, please don't take this personally, but I am *not* attracted to women. *Any* women – not just you.'

'Then welcome, dear,' I said and stepped further aside. 'I also have no interest in mammals with corresponding body parts. I was, as they say, just yanking your chain with my last comment. To flagellate means "*to whip*". I figured that if you didn't know what I was talking about then I wasn't imagining you.'

'You have a strange way of making sense, Miss Yoder. I've always sort of liked you. In fact, that's why I'm here.'

I led the young woman – I still was not quite sure of her identity – through my bedroom and into an alcove that is furnished with two recliners that swivel to face a seventy-inch television that rises from the floor. This is as close to a 'man cave' as the Babester gets. Trust me, no other

266

house in our Amish and Mennonite community boasts such an expensive and worldly setup – nor ought they. I have conceded this one great pleasure in order to keep the love of my life happy. And now I must confess that I may not have been entirely truthful earlier, for there have been times when Gabriel has persuaded me to sit alongside him as a dutiful wife and watch television shows with deceptive names, such as *The Good Wife*, who does not act like a good wife, but more like a wanton harlot in my opinion. But what am I to do? The New Testament states quite clearly that it is the husband who is the head of the house, and that the wife should obey him. *Oy vey*, I realize now that I brought this on myself when I became unevenly yoked with a nonbeliever. And since the New Testament also says that I am not allowed to get divorced unless he commits adultery – *which he never will* – we shall forever remain yoked together like an ass and ox. Besides, I adore Gabe. I love every hair on his manly chest and even the ones that are beginning to creep across his shoulders and back.

'Wow!' said Lady Celia's doppelgänger. 'You have a humongous bedroom and this place back here is really cool.'

'Hang on, toots,' I said, 'because you ain't seen nothing yet.' I pressed the button on a remote that made the television rise silently from the floor. Then I pressed another button, one that caused a pair of heavy floor-to-ceiling drapes to part, revealing a set of French doors, and through them a well-lit patio.

'Wow again,' said the girl, her jaw scraping the floor. 'How romantic!'

'A gal has to work hard to keep the romance going,' I said, 'especially when she's an ugly duckling married to a prince charming.'

She scowled. 'Perhaps. But what does that have to do with this?'

'*Moi* – ugly duckling,' I said, rolling my eyes in exasperation. 'Mr Rosen, the most handsome man you've ever seen.'

'Wrong,' the girl said. 'He might be an eight – in the eyes of an older woman – but certainly no more than that. And you, by the way, are not an ugly duckling. If you stopped dressing so severely and wore a little makeup, you could easily be a nine. A femme fatale.'

Believe it or not, I had heard this same spiel coming directly from the lips of a psychologist. He tried to convince me that I suffered from a mental disease known as Body Dysmorphic Syndrome. Supposedly, I was incapable of seeing myself as I really was, and the ugly reflection that I viewed in the mirror was the result of low self-esteem. Of course, he was wrong; for me to agree with him would have been proud and quintessentially un-Mennonite.

'Flattery might get you everywhere,' I said to the girl, 'but not with me, dear. I don't swing that way, if you get my drift, and I wouldn't even drift that way, if I was a swinger, which I'm not, since I'm happily married to a man who is a solid *ten* in my eyes, so there!'

'You are a hoot, Miss Yoder, I'll grant you that.'

'And a holler.'

'Undoubtedly so.'

'Then come outside and sit on my private patio,' I cried. 'Because you agreed with me, you are now back in my good graces. There is one caveat, however – no, make that two.'

'What are they?' she said. Talk about looking a gift horse in the mouth!

'First you must agree to sit here and sip a cup of tea like a civilized person, maybe even have a slice of Freni's homemade bread, slathered in Amish butter, and then covered with heaps of strawberry jam.'

'Agreed,' she said. 'What is the second condition?'

'The second condition is that you put the kettle on and make the tea. We Americans are Philistines, I'm afraid. We use tea bags which, I am sure, horrify you civilized Brits. But, as the saying goes, "beggars can't be choosers." You'll find real cream, from my very own Holstein cows, in a pitcher in the refrigerator, as well as the butter and jam. The bread is in a wooden box on the counter, and it is clearly labelled bread in shiny gold letters. Just scrounge in the cabinets and drawers until you find the necessary cups, plates and tableware.'

'But, Miss Yoder—'

'No "buts," dear, this is America, where everyone is equal and must pull their own weight. Now hop to it before I decide to charge you for the privilege of making tea in an authentic Pennsylvania Dutch kitchen.'

'Yes, ma'am.'

Quite frankly, the speed and efficiency with

which the noble lass performed her duties impressed me. One would have thought that she'd been born to an American. I barely had time to use my private facilities and check on the status of my precious bundle of joy. For the record, Little Jacob was snoring ever so softly, thanks to the remnants of a summer cold.

Not only was Lady Celia quick, she was remarkably resourceful. Tea was served on a wood tray that I'd forgotten I owned. This she placed on a small wicker table that separated a pair of Adirondack rocking chairs. The traditional English tea pot, the bone china cups and saucers, had all belonged to Gabe before we were married and were part of our 'melded' things. Somehow, in those few minutes the girl had not only found time to make jam sandwiches, she'd even removed the crusts. Believe me, if she ever immigrated to the United States and wound up impoverished, I would offer her a job as my housemaid in a heartbeat.

'Now, dear,' I said, 'pour us each a cuppa and then settle into your rocker, whereupon you must get straight to the point.'

'Miss Yoder, what's a cuppa?'

'Aha! I had my suspicions! Pretending not to know what pancakes are – that was Aubrey's first mistake. Every Englishman knows what pancakes are; on Shrove Tuesday you even have pancake races.'

'Busted,' the erstwhile Lady Celia said. 'But I still don't know what a cuppa is.'

'It's a *cup of tea*, you twit – oops, you sweet little thing. Dear Lord,' I prayed aloud, 'guard my tongue from speaking evil.'

270

'Miss Yoder,' said my youngest guest, 'you shouldn't be so hard on yourself. We all agree that you have a razor-sharp tongue, but you also have a razor-sharp conscience. That's obvious from the constantly changing expressions on your face.'

'Come again?' I said.

'You're like a one-woman character study of good and evil. No offense, Miss Yoder, but you do possess a rather large face, and one can observe your emotions battling across the screen, just as real as if they were actors.'

That offended me. 'What would you, young lady, who is *not* a lady, know about actors?'

'Miss Yoder, I am an actor.'

'Aren't we all? But shouldn't you have said "actress?" Unless, of course, you changed genders – not that I have a problem with that, mind you.'

'No, I did not switch genders. Nowadays we try to avoid sexist terms like "actress" since it really serves no important function. Anyway, when I said that I was an actor, I mean that I am a professional actor. More specifically, I was paid to act the part of Lady Celia Grimsley-Snodgrass; my real name is Joyce Toestubber.'

Even in the patio light I could see that my long-drawn-out sigh appeared to blow the steam from my tea in a straight line. Lady Celia's doppelgänger was sorely trying my patience.

'Pay attention, Celia, dear,' I said as I leaned over the table in her direction. 'Read my lips, if you can. I am quite capable of playing mind games all by myself. Coming across as weird to

271

others is one of my skill sets. Faking an American accent, and a very bad one at that, is one thing. But choosing an alias like Joyce Toebuster – why, that's just laughable!'

The young woman leaped nimbly to her feet while holding her tea and without spilling nary a drop. 'I take umbrage with that, you old bag. My name *is* Joyce Toestubber – not Toebuster! Whoever heard of a stupid name like Toe*buster*? And I am most certainly *not* faking my accent; I come from Chillicothe, Ohio, which is the heartland of America, and our English is the purest of the pure. So you better apologize to me right now if you want to learn anything – *anything* at all – about the others, and how they came to be fooling you.' She paused. 'You old bag,' she added quite needlessly again.

There is at least one thing good about living a life filled with bad things; you start to recognize the truth when you hear it repeated for the umpteenth time.

'Oh my heavens,' I said. 'Oh my stars! Fiddlesticks and pickup sticks! I have been fooled yet again. I *am* a fool, yet again. My poor brain is swirling around in my oversized noggin, like bathwater going down the drain. Speak to me, Joyce Toejam; lay the truth upon these misshapen ears so that I might eventually – perhaps after the fifth telling thereof – absorb an inkling of what is really going on. Lay the truth upon me, I beseech thee, Ms Toejam. Henceforth I shall shut up; the stage is all yours.'

'Somehow I doubt that, Magdalena Yapper.'

'It's *Yoder*, dear, not Yapper!'

'I'll say your name right when you say mine correctly. Although, frankly, your second attempt to butcher my name is at least understandable. I really should wash my feet more often.'

I hung my horsey head in shame. 'Apparently I owe an entire nation my apologies.'

'At any rate,' Joyce said, 'the truth is that I am a trained actor who has been scratching out a living in a professional company of actors who perform Shakespearean plays. We call ourselves the Boarshead Players and there used to be thirteen of us. We were quite famous, you know. We performed all over the country: Los Angeles, St Louis, Chicago, New Orleans, Miami, Washington, Philadelphia and even New York. Not quite on Broadway, but very close. You must have heard of us.'

'Nope.'

'Hmm. Well, it's your loss, then. We were good, as you can tell, because we fooled you, Ms Eagle Eyes Yoder.'

'*Really?* You think I'm sharp? Because flattery really will get you everywhere, except not *there*, as we've already established – unless your name is Angelina Jolie. I saw her picture on the cover of one of those gossip magazines in the grocery checkout line and I just had to buy it. I thumbed through the pictures out of curiosity, of course, but I soon found that I had to tell Satan to get behind me numerous times. This proved to be a rather tricky task for Satan, I'm afraid, seeing as how I was seated in my private bathtub – the one with thirty-two jets, and which I have named Big

273

Bertha. Goodness me, I don't know why I'm telling you such a personal story.'

'Maybe because you're worried about being a lesbian?'

'I most certainly am not! I have made a lot of rash decisions in my life, but that is one choice I have yet to make.'

'It is *not* a choice, Ms Yoder. Just like the fact that you were attracted to Doctor Rosen wasn't a choice. Or *was* it?'

'Stop right where you are, young lady; I will not be confused with facts. Back to the subject at hand. What happened to the rest of the Boarshead Players, and why on earth did you answer poor Agnes's ad when she went trawling for nobility?'

'What happened to the others, and us, was the economy. Unlike your beloved Angelina Jolie, most stage actors – unless they have achieved a certain level of fame – do not rake in huge salaries. Besides, these days people would much rather see *The Lion King* for the millionth time than a stage production of *Hamlet*.'

'That's not true,' I snapped – albeit gently, as is my style. 'Gabriel dragged me all the way into Pittsburgh to see *The Lion King*, and what a bitter disappointment that turned out to be. There wasn't a lion in the show! It was just people prancing around in costumes. Even the supposed cub was a real-life boy. I would have much rather watched some men in tights waggle their swords at each other.'

Joyce snorted. 'That's because you take

everything literally. The Bible – everything. I bet that you even believe the newscasters on TV.'

'Ha,' I said, 'I got you there, because that all depends on which channel I'm watching.'

The second time that Joyce snorted, she sounded exactly like Saul Lieberman's stud bull. 'Actually, you probably hear very little of what's on the screen because you're constantly talking back to it, like a drunk who's washed down a handful of LSD pills with a bottle of gin. Am I right?'

'Maybe, but you don't have to be so rude about it. Now tell me the story about the not-so-noble Grimsley-Snodgrasses, and I promise not to interrupt. I'll even stop breathing, if you signal me to stop. Now start yammering. I'm all misshapen ears.'

Twenty-Five

GRAPEFRUIT MARMALADE

2 grapefruits
2 lemons
2 oranges
Sugar

Wash fruit. Remove core and seeds of grapefruit. Remove thin yellow outside rind and cut ½ of it in fine strips. Remove the thick white peel, but do not use. Mix shaved rind with the cut-up pulp. Put into preserving kettle with three times as much water and let stand overnight. Put on stove, let come to boiling point and boil for ten minutes. Repeat this for two days. On the third day, measure and add an equal amount of sugar and boil for one hour or until thick. Turn into jelly glasses.

Twenty-Six

'It was a dark and stormy night,' Joyce said. 'Literally. We had just performed our last paid production – a much condensed version of *Hamlet* – in Morgantown, West Virginia. Incidentally, there were eight of us then.'

'What happened to the other five?' I couldn't help myself. Besides, it was a reasonable question that needing asking.

'*Tch, tch, tch*,' Joyce said, and wagged a finger in my face. 'Naughty, naughty, Miss Yoder, you promised that you wouldn't interrupt.'

'Give me a break,' I moaned. 'You look seventeen and you're an actor, but don't tell me that your day job is that of a grade school teacher.'

'No ma'am, I am not a teacher and I'm twenty-five. If I act like a teacher it's because I have twenty-six brothers and sisters, half of whom are younger than I am.'

'Get out of town and back!'

'Pardon me?'

'It's just an expression of incredulity I picked up from one of my guests. Anyway, it seems to me that having so many children is an irresponsible thing to do in this day and age, the first commandment notwithstanding.'

'Agreed. That is why my family got their own reality television show that liberals loved to hate. It was titled: *Be Fruitful, Multiply and Deplete*

277

the Planet. It was a very wholesome show, all about how God gave us animals to slaughter as we please – I mean, everything was created for us, and not the other way around. God says so right there in Genesis, chapter one, verse twenty-seven. We are supposed to have *dominion*, Miss Yoder. Liberals forget that.'

'The word "dominion" just means "authority," dear, it—'

'Do you want to hear my tale or not?'

'Yes,' I said as I mimed locking my lips with a key and tossing it over my shoulder. In real life, however, I eschew mimes. In fact, I so dislike mimes that I might even overcome five hundred years of pacifist inbreeding to gently slap a mime's face – miming it, of course.

'So,' Joyce said, 'it was after the last show and we were sitting in a Morgantown bar, having a farewell drink to our careers when this well-dressed Englishman walked over to our table and introduced himself as the Earl of Grimsley-Snodgrass. He asked us if we had ever watched the masterpiece theatre show, *Downton Abbey*, which, of course, we all had, being the Anglophiles that we were. He then showed us photos of his own place, Gloomsburythorpe, which he compared to Downton Abbey.'

'Yes, but—'

'The only "but" is "butt out," ma'am.'

I nodded vigorously; up and down, then from side to side.

'Ahem, Miss Yoder, for a senior citizen, you're acting extremely childish. If I *were* a teacher, I'd keep you after school for detention.'

278

I jumped to my Jeep-size feet. 'I beg your pardon, young lady! You take that back. A senior citizen is someone who is sixty-five years of age and older, and I am only fifty!'

Joyce Toestubber smiled cruelly. 'Oh, sit down, already; I was only yanking your chain. I know how old you are and I've already told you how marvellous you look. Now zip it – *please* – because this is your last chance.'

So I plopped my patooty back down on the balcony chair and prayed that God would hold my jaws tightly shut, just as shut as the angels had held the lions' jaws shut for Daniel when he was in their den. 'Continue,' I said. By the way, with one's lips pulled back, it is possible to speak any number of words without opening one's jaws.

'The earl came across to us as a broken man. He said that he had recently lost all of his family in an automobile accident while on a family holiday in the Scottish Highlands. I mean, that's how he spoke: trotting out words like 'while' and 'holiday' and making it sound all English and upper-class stuffy. Although frankly, the way he pronounced some words, like 'rally', didn't seem right to me. Then again, what did I know? He was the first, real live earl whom I'd ever met.

'So anyway, after four or five drinks – that he bought – when we were all feeling pretty soused, he offered us a job impersonating his deceased family. I know, it's kind of gruesome, but you see, he was – is – a lonely man. He'd come to the States in an effort to heal his grief. He and his wife had always been planning to come, and at first he thought he could do it alone. But it didn't work out that way. So then, when he came to our performance and saw that we could do accents and that we were approximately the same ages as his dead loved ones, well, that's when the idea of a substitute family hit him. The only trouble was that back in England, in real life, he had had twin sons. So poor Michael – known to you as Viscount Rupert *and* the Honourable Mr Sebastian – had to do double duty.'

Well, a gal has to do what a gal has to do, which means I couldn't help butting in. 'But you said that there were eight of you.'

For some reason, Joyce didn't seem to mind this interruption. 'Indeed, there were eight of us in the beginning, but five of our number were apparently not quite as stupid, nor as greedy, as we three. Those five immediately bowed out. George "Georgie-Porridgie," we called him, on account of he was always kissing us girls and making us cry – he even called the earl a charlatan and a scammer. Right to his face. The earl just smiled and peered at him through his monocle like he was an insect or something. You know how he can be.'

'I do. What made *you* take the job?'

'His offer of five thousand dollars a week.'

'Holy baloney! Get out of town and back!' Those colourful phrases may not be Pennsylvania Dutch, but my former guests assured me that these words are not blasphemous.

'You see? Believe me, Miss Yoder, that is a lot of money for a struggling actor like me.'

'Were your parts scripted?' I said.

'You better believe it,' Joyce said. 'We had

280

pages and pages of background material on you Mennonites, the Amish, the village of Hernia and especially you and your PennDutch Inn. We were given two weeks to memorize everything, and then we were put through these gruelling rehearsals until I had *schnitz* pies crawling out of my ears.'

'Mm, *schnitz* pies,' I said and licked my thin, colourless lips. 'I can certainly think of worse things than fried apple pastries. But wait a minute! What about your conversations with the ghosts? With Great-granny Yoder and Yoko-san? Were those bogus?'

Joyce – aka Lady Celia – bit her plump, glossy lips. 'Yup, I'm afraid so. Those were scripted as well. Come on, Miss Yoder, don't tell me that you really believe you can converse with ghosts?'

'With Granny Yoder's ghost, yes,' I said. 'However, I have never talked with another ghost, nor do I ever wish to do so.'

'Well, I don't believe in ghosts, nor do I believe in life after death. And I don't believe in magic, but I do believe that people skilled in the art of illusion can trick others and fool them into believing that a certain event took place that in all actuality never happened. Take the miracle of the Feeding of the Five Thousand in the New Testament, for instance.'

'*What about it?*' I said, sounding perhaps a wee bit testier than I had a right to sound. I hate it when people try to disprove my faith with rationality.

'Well, once that little boy in the story trotted out his two fish and five loaves of bread, the

281

other 4,999 people felt guilty and brought out the food that they'd been hiding in their loose-fitting robes. You see, they hadn't wanted to share it with their neighbours. It's as simple as that.'

'Pshaw,' I said. 'I've heard that explanation before and I totally discount it. If your explanation were true then the Bible would have used that story instead in order to teach the lesson of being unselfish. The same thing can be said for the story about the feeding of the four thousand people, which occurs a few pages later. That story is not as famous, and doubters like you often say that it is simply another version of the feeding of the five thousand. False, I say! False, false, false! Every word of the Bible is true, and therefore, there can't be one story with two different versions. God does not make mistakes, and don't you try to tell me otherwise.'

Joyce shook her pretty, youngish head. 'Oh, Miss Yoder, you have a mind like a steel trap – one that's been sprung.'

'I'll take that as a compliment, dear. At least my brain won't fall out, seeing as how my brain *is* the trap.'

'Touché.' She gave me an admiring, and therefore endearing smile. 'But how would you explain the *earl* knowing about you and your Granny's private conversations?'

My heart thumped extra loudly in my bony chest. 'It had to be that ding-dong-dang Agnes Miller. She was obviously so enamoured of the British upper crust and that silly television program of hers, Downtown Aggie, that she sold me out. She pulled out all the stops to convince

282

the Earl of Grimsley-Snodgrass to make the PennDutch his holiday destination. You know how the Brits love their ghosts.'

'Miss Yoder, I hope that you are only teasing about the name of that program. In any case, it seemed to me that the discovery of the Japanese woman came as an unpleasant surprise, even to you. If that's so, then what would explain the script that the Earl of Grimsley-Snodgrass had me memorize? The one where her ghost talks to me?'

That's when I felt my heart do a somersault, followed by a backward flip and possibly even a few steps of sinful Latin dancing. 'This might sound like an absurd question,' I said, 'but have you ever seen the Earl of Grimsley-Snodgrass without his tweed jacket and starched, high-necked shirts?'

'Uh – yes, and yes. During those weeks in which we were learning our lines and rehearsing them endlessly, he put us up at a seedy motel. It was connected to the seedy bar where we first met him. We would rehearse in the earl's room, which was called a garden suite. That's because it was large enough to have an alcove containing a stained brown corduroy couch *and* a plastic *ficus* tree that was never dusted.

'At any rate, I got to rehearsal just a few minutes early one morning and I opened the door without knocking. The earl always left it unlocked for us, you see, it being Morgantown and all, and it was broad daylight. That day, however, the Earl of Grimsley-Snodgrass was clearly running late. He had his back to the door but he was dressed

only in trousers and a "wife-beater" undershirt
– you know, the sleeveless kind. At first I didn't
recognize him because he had this enormous head
bobbling around on the thinnest neck you have
ever seen. If I drew it on paper it would look
like a tennis racket. I'm not kidding. It even
occurred to me that his head might just topple
over, and that if I didn't run and catch it I could
be liable. You know, if it crashed to the floor and
split open like a watermelon.'

She paused, so I urged her on. 'Then what?
Tell me everything!'

'Well, he sensed me staring so he whirled
around, and that melon-like head came whipping
around as well, straining at the end of the finger-
thick stem, and just as I was about to scream my
last words, he found his voice.'

'"You tell anyone what you saw," he said in a
kind of squeaky voice, "and you're not getting
paid." Miss Yoder, I am not a gossiper, and I
might not have said anything to anyone anyway,
but there was something maniacal in the earl's
eyes. You see, he wasn't wearing his monocle
then, and his eyes were not only bulging but
aiming in different directions. One of them was
even rotating, if you can believe that. I'm sure
that you don't believe in aliens, Miss Yoder – not
the outer space kind – but that's what he reminded
me of. Either that or a giant—'

'Praying mantis?' I croaked, for my throat was
as dry as an Amish home's wood-burning stove.

'That's right; how did you know what I was
going to say?'

'Get inside!' I shrieked. 'Now!'

Joyce needed no more encouragement than that. She seemed to move intuitively on my heels. I dived through the French doors, threw myself on the bed and scooped up Little Jacob, after which I clasped him to my heaving excuse for a bosom. Meanwhile, Joyce locked the French doors behind her and shoved a large oak armoire in front of them.

I had just finished locking the main door to my bedroom when we heard the thump overhead. Having grown up in this house, or an exact reproduction thereof, I am familiar with its many means of expression: moans, groans, creaks, screeches and scrabbling sounds. These noises have been traced back to tree branches, sagging timbers and various animal species such as: raccoons, squirrels, doves, pigeons, cats, bats and even a family of opossums.

'Miss Yoder,' Joyce whispered, 'tell me what is going on. If I am going to be scared out of my wits I at least deserve to know why.'

'You're right,' I said. 'Here's the real deal. The so-called Earl of Grimsley-Snodgrass is really a serial killer named Melvin Stoltzfus.'

'No way!'

'And not only that,' I said, for I always enjoy exposition, no matter how dangerous the moment, 'but Melvin also happens to be my half-brother, through our birth mother, Elvina Stoltzfus, who almost let her precious son kill me.'

'You're kidding!'

'You poor, misplaced child,' I said.

'Then you're *not* kidding! Spit it all out, Miss Yoder, because I can't take it in dribs and drabs.'

'OK, but hold on, toots, because it's not a pretty picture. That murderous, maniacal, monocle-wearing mantis, Melvin, is my brother-in-law through his marriage to my baby sister, Susannah. There are those who say that she is even more eccentric than I am, based partly on her penchant for carrying around a miniature Yorkshire terrier in her brassiere. To be fair, she has currently abandoned the practice of packing a pup in her bra because she's serving time in the big house for aiding and abetting a fugitive from justice. That is to say, she's in prison. Oh, did I mention that, although Susannah was born to my adoptive parents, she and Melvin are my second and third cousins respectively? In other words, we're a scary bunch.'

'No offense, Miss Yoder,' Joyce said, and I could hear her teeth chatter from where she stood in the middle of the room, 'but I just want to go home.'

'So do I, dear, and I *am* home.'

'What do we do now? Call nine-one-one?'

'And tell the dispatcher that we heard a thump overhead while we were cowering in an old farmhouse? Besides, I *am* the go-to-person for emergencies in Hernia. It's me and Toy.'

'Then call Toy. Please, Miss Yoder?'

I rolled my eyes. I didn't do it to be mean; I did it partly in resignation and partly as a way to relieve stress. But just as I did so, the knob to the interior door of my bedroom began to turn. My eyes must have widened, as well as rolled, because Joyce whirled round.

The scream that Joyce produced was worthy

286

of a six-year-old girl. Any keen observer of the human condition can testify that such a scream is far superior to the usually touted nine-year-old example. I couldn't help but scream in response. As for Little Jacob, the tyke had had no option but to follow suit.

Each person's vocalizations only served to rev up the other two, so that the bedlam in my bedroom reached decibels of truly frightening magnitude. One might imagine how much more frightened we were when we noticed that a man in a clown suit suddenly materialized on the deck just outside the French doors. The clown's greasepaint mouth was an upside-down smile, and in each hand he grasped a headless, life-size baby doll which he pumped rhythmically up and down. When he saw that he had our attention, the clown tossed the dolls aside and began to do what is called 'break-dancing.' It is an activity in which the performers appear to be demonically possessed. If you ask me, it is quite possible that they are.

I knew that the person in the clown suit was not my half-brother, the deranged Melvin Stoltzfus. For one thing, the man on the deck had rhythm. My nitwit, serial-killing sibling couldn't take three steps without tripping over his own shadow four times. For another thing, it is darn hard to fake a sturdy neck. When this fellow got down and spun on his white clown pate, as if he were a round-bottomed top, I was a thousand percent sure that he wasn't Melvin. The clown and I shared absolutely no DNA – not that such a thing as DNA exists, mind you.

'Close the drapes,' I managed to yell even as I dove for them myself, all the while keeping Little Jacob as safe as a dozen eggs in the crook of my arm.

Twenty-Seven

Both bedroom doors were locked and the heavy deck drapes had been pulled. For an illusory moment my world felt safe and familiar again. Then I began to imagine that I heard my half-brother, Melvin Stoltzfus, breathing just outside the interior bedroom door, the one that was connected by a short hallway to the kitchen. The psychopath Melvin has a deviated septum, the result of his sheer stupidity. How else can one explain a farmer's son who tried to milk a bull and then got kicked in the head for his efforts?

Melvin was stupid enough to try anything; that's what made him truly dangerous. But Melvin was also a coward and a loner; he was unlikely to work with outsiders who dressed as clowns. On the other hand, I had to hand it to him for hiring a down-on-its-luck Shakespearean theatre troupe. The Melvin whom I thought that I knew was now much more sophisticated in his thinking, and therefore unpredictable.

Lord, I prayed silently, please help us. That really *was* Melvin just outside the bedroom door. But *what* was he waiting for? Was he trying to toy with me like a cat with its prey? Undoubtedly that was it: Melvin knew how to force his way in somehow, and the waiting was part of my torture.

Then the breathing stopped. That's when dread crept up my spine like a line of whiskery cockroaches feeling their way out of a greasy drain. Dread didn't have cold fingers; dread was hundreds of hot, pricking feet that climbed up my back and my neck, then across my scalp, making every hair stand at attention, leaving my cheeks smouldering in its wake. Dread settled in my eye sockets where it burned, forcing out hot liquid from eyes that seldom, if ever, saw tears. Magdalena Portulacca Yoder Rosen never cried out of pity, or sadness, but she might cry if she was afraid for her child. Little Jacob was everything.

But then the grip of dread was broken by laughter. High-pitched giggles really. It was the type of sound one might expect to hear emanating from a demon's mouth in Hell. Yet it was coming from the plump red lips of Joyce Toestubber and not one of Satan's minions – *or was it*? The Bible warns us that Satan and his angels are capable of assuming any shape or size, and I am firmly convinced that at least one of the American Presidential primary election candidates hails from the Devil's fiery kingdom.

'What issss it?' I hissed, with enough s's to make up for at least a few bestselling writers' shortcomings.

'You had me going for a while there, Miss Yoder, you really did. I almost believed you about the earl being a serial killer, and all because he has a head like a bobble doll and eyes like a dragonfly. Oh, well, then there's your acting ability. Props to you, Miss Yoder. You have what it takes, and I mean that. Of course, you're too old to be a leading lady, but you definitely could carve out a niche for yourself as a character actress, what with your – uh – unique look.'

Like I said before, flattery will get me almost anywhere, apparently even close to being dead. I momentarily forgot about everything except for my less-than-perfect appearance.

'What's wrong with my look, missy?' I demanded.

'Are you familiar with the painting *Whistler's Mother*?' Joyce said.

'Yes,' I growled. 'I may be a Philistine but I'm neither a hayseed nor a rube.'

'Well, to be honest, the way you dress – that's what people call you behind your back.'

'They call me *Whistler's Mother*?' I could feel the blood rushing to my cheeks, despite everything else that was going on.

Joyce's giggles turned into guffaws. 'Really, Miss Yoder, you're too sensitive! I paid you a compliment when I said that you were a good actress. As far as your clothes go, with your kind of money you can change out of those fuddy-duddy duds for some really cool things without leaving the privacy of this room. But you have to tell me why it is that you're so freaked out by a clown showing up at your patio door.'

I jiggled both pinkies simultaneously in my ears in order to make sure that I was hearing correctly. Alas, both cartilage protuberances were in perfect working order. The woman was bananas – certifiably crazy.

'He's no ordinary clown, don't you see? That

291

man out there is one of murderous Melvin's accomplices!'

'Ah, come on, Miss Yoder,' Joyce said. 'No offense, but I think that you're being paranoid. I bet that clown is really just Michael Tugonitvich, whom you happen to know as Viscount Rupert or Mr Sebastian – depending on which role he is playing.'

'*What?* So you're in on this too?'

That slip of a girl, who was barely out of her teens, had the effrontery to toss her head like a thoroughbred mare. I will say this, however: she needed to work on her snort if she were to compete with *moi*.

'I'll say it again, Miss Yoder; you are paranoid.'

'*Paranoid?* You think that *I'm* being paranoid?'

'Yes,' she said, 'and now I think that you're being hysterical as well.'

'*Me?*' I shrieked as tears of frustration washed down my cheeks. 'How dare you say that?'

I'll say one good thing about the males in my family: neither of them can stand it when one of their two females cries. The elder male is quick to comfort with his strong, encircling arms, whereas his progeny is prone to throw back his oversized toddler head and wail like a banshee from a Sherlock Holmes novel.

Joyce Toestubber clapped her hands over her ears. She strode back to the drapes that hid the French doors and freed one hand long enough to pull on the drapery cord. The other hand dropped to her side when she saw that the clown, whom she'd thought was her friend Michael Tugonitvich, was now inches from the left panel of glass. Both his fists were tightly clenched, and at shoulder level. In one he gripped a butcher's cleaver, and in the other a small hand axe. Although his forehead was pressed against the pane, the sad clown's mouth hung open and his shockingly long tongue hung loose. It could have been a dog's tongue or even a donkey's tongue, except that the clown's tongue had been pierced with a gold stud. Then, as Joyce and I stood watching like a pair of transfixed fools, the crazed clown began wagging that awful appendage from side to side, as if it were the pendulum of a grandfather clock.

'Miss Yoder,' Joyce whispered, for now even Little Jacob seemed eerily mesmerized by the evil sight, 'if that *is* Michael, then he isn't the *same* Michael that I knew. Your brother has obviously gotten to him.'

'Look here, toots,' I said, my Christianity momentarily deserting me, 'don't you be laying *that* one on me. You claimed that Michael was your friend. Now *do* something!'

Unfortunately, Joyce didn't even have time to swallow before we heard what sounded like fingernails raking the length of the other bedroom door. We leaped backward as if we'd been splashed with droplets of acid.

I couldn't stand it anymore. I grabbed the bull by the horns.

'Melvin,' I called, 'is this you?'

'Huh?'

'I *know* it is you, Mely-kins,' I said, using

293

Susannah's disgusting term of endearment for her husband. 'What is it that you want this time?'

'Baby,' Melvin said.

'*Excuse* me?' I said.

'You forgot to add baby to my name, Magdalena. My Sweetykins never forgets that.'

'It's really him,' I mouthed to Joyce. 'It's the maniac monster.'

The look on Joyce's face was one of confusion. No doubt she wondered how even a skilled actor could pull off such a convincing British accent – despite the occasional gaff like *rally* – and still sound like such a pathetic nincompoop of a Pennsylvanian. Clearly she needed more convincing.

'Pretend you're saying sweet nothings to Susannah in a posh English accent,' I said. 'Then I'll know that it's really you; I'll fling open the door and extend my long gangly arms in a wide embrace.'

As I put no time frame on the door opening, or the arm flinging, strictly speaking, what I'd said to Melvin was not a lie. Also, I have become more or less convinced that Melvin began life as an identical twin and that he absorbed his brother in utero, as sometimes happens. However, while becoming Melvin's breakfast, lunch and supper for nine months, his identical twin absorbed Melvin's brain. This theory of mine explains so much, and I do not wish to be dissuaded of it by such a shaky thing as science.

'Oh, my dahlin' Susannah,' said Melvin, 'sweet nothings, sweet nothings, sweet nothings.'

'The man has a brilliant imagination,' I said.

'Yoder,' Melvin whined, 'are you being sarcastic?'

'Indeed, I am.'

'Yoder,' he said again, 'you could at least thank me for my gift.'

'What gift would that be, Lord Smuttbottom?' I said.

'Hey,' Melvin whined, 'you don't have to be mean just because I want to kill you. After all, I did supply the answer to the riddle of what happened to that Japanese girl. I even gave you the answer twice. What more could you want?'

'Hmm, let me see, dear. How about a padded wagon and four strong men to carry you away? You, pretending to be the earl, dropped your passport – wait! What did you mean when you said that you gave me the answer to the riddle twice?'

'I meant that I wrote those lines for that scrawny little actress, Joyce. You know, when she *supposedly* has a conversation with Yoko-san herself. Right there, as plain as daylight, I let you know how that Japanese tourist died and where she's been all this time. But did you even bother to listen? Ha, and you say that you believe in ghosts, Yoder.'

'You're right,' Joyce Toebuster whispered. 'It really is him.' Having been persuaded that Melvin and the earl were one and the same, she proved to be a woman of action. She grabbed one of my elbows and tried to yank me away from the door. Now, we Yoders may be tall and spindly or low and roly-poly, but the odds are that we have ankles like tree stumps. It takes a mahout and

295

his mount to move me when I'm sufficiently motivated to stand my ground.

'OK, Melvin, let's say that you recognize the evilness of your deeds. You killed the very personable young lady from Japan who said that she loved everything Mennonite and Amish. *Why* did you do this? What was your *motivation*?'

I could hear the murderous mantis mashing his mandibles in frustration. 'I did it for you, Yoder. She caught me relieving you of some of your excessive wealth, on account of the Bible that says it's hard for the rich to get into Heaven. So I was just helping you out a little bit, that's all.'

That got me so steamed up that I almost slapped *Joyce*. Then again, I am a peaceful, Mennonite woman who wouldn't hurt a male mosquito. By the by, they're the large mosquitoes; they don't bite.

'*When* and *where* did this happen?' I demanded.

'Oh, don't get so bent out of shape, Yoder. It happened years ago when I was Police Chief. I knew that you kept piles of cash down in the old root cellar beneath the parlour, the same place that you keep the village records. I *am* married to your sister, who grew up in the same house – well, close enough. The things that she and I would do down there—'

'Shut up, Melvin!' Joyce bellowed. This time the strength and timbre of her voice caught me off guard and she succeeded in yanking me into the master bath. 'What are we going to do?' she demanded when we were safely out of earshot. 'You collected our cell phones when we checked in, remember? You claimed that having them

296

would invalidate our authentic Amish experience. And when I went out to make tea for you, like I was a slave or something, I saw your phone lying on the island. You'd better have a landline.'

I wrenched free from her grip. 'Calm down, dear. I did have a landline – but you know how the phone company is with their layered fees, and the constant sales calls—'

'Really, dear,' I said in my most soothing manner, 'you could have an aneurism or something if you keep this level of tension up. I once had to force castor oil down the throat of a constipated sheep, one whose eyes were bulging as wide as yours are.'

'You're serious?'

'As serious as a Supreme Court judge. Mama used to say that castor oil is good for what ails you, but tell that to the sheep, because it died.'

'*Oh, Magdalena! I'm coming to get you and your little friend Joyce.*' It was Melvin calling out in a warbling falsetto.

Don't think for a second that I didn't pray for a solution to our dilemma. The Bible says that we should pray without ceasing, and that women should pray with their heads covered. It is for this reason that we Old Order Mennonites, such as myself, and the Amish, wear little white caps that we refer to, fittingly, as prayer caps.

I can't speak for anyone else, but I pray for strength, peace and inspiration, and not things that would bespeak of favouritism. I have no way of measuring it, but I am pretty sure that I am capable of praying as 'hard' as the next person.

Or am I? Every time that there is a plane crash or a devastating tornado that is responsible for many fatalities, a survivor will appear on television and credit their good fortune to having prayed 'real hard.' God forbid that I will one day be the corpse found in Seat 32A, who didn't pray *quite* as hard as the occupant of Seat 32B.

Hence it was that, while I was praying, I happened to remember our tornado shelter. Tornados are not a common occurrence here in south-western Pennsylvania, but this house was taken down by one once a few years ago, and when it did I ended up face down in a cow patty. So when I rebuilt my genuine replica of my authentic homestead, I built a large 'safe room' under the walk-in closet of the master bedroom. Given that God has blessed me and I am a very wealthy woman, the idea that this room could protect my family from bandits also brings me a measure of peace.

My doctor husband has seen to it that the space is stocked with enough food and water to last for a month, that it is well ventilated, that there are battery-powered lights for reading, some medical supplies and four cots. He even has a name for this shelter: the Rabbit Hole – although Alison, with her incomprehensible teenage mind, refers to it as the Hernia House of Horrors.

When the need arises, my long, knobby fingers can morph into fearsome talons, and thus I was able to grasp Joyce by *both* elbows. Then, holding her in front of me, like I might a dining room chair, I rushed her out of the bath and into the master closet before she had time to say 'Bob's your uncle' which, for the record, he is not. In the meantime, the Son of Satan continued to rake his fingernails up, down and across my poor, innocent bedroom door.

'I'm waiting, Magdalena. First I'm going to huff, then I'll puff, and then I'll blow your door down with this hand grenade which I have in my pocket.'

'I don't want to die!' Joyce sobbed.

'Shh, dear,' I said. 'Sob softer, if you can. With any luck the Mantis will blow himself up. But even if he doesn't, I have a plan. It may sound far-fetched, but we are grasping at straws here.'

She nodded.

'Now, step outside, dear. You're standing on the better mousetrap – er, rattrap.' I shoved the gal gently, and when she was clear of the hardwood closet floor, I whisked up a beige area rug that had been positioned in the middle of the space. Then I pressed a spot on the wooden slats and a trapdoor popped open to reveal a gap that was four feet square. Because I had yet to turn on the closet light, what Joyce could see was only a void as black as Melvin's heart. I'm sure that she couldn't see the ladder that was firmly screwed to a floor joist.

'Holy guacamole,' she said softly. 'You want me to go down there?'

There was no time to be annoyed. 'You're not the rat, dear; he is. Drastic times call for measures, so listen closely. This hole drops straight down: ten feet into a tornado shelter. Melvin doesn't know that it exists. What you're going to do is go right back into the bathroom and lock the door. I'm going to turn off the light in the bedroom, then I'm going to let him in and I'll race back here. At the last second, I'll duck in, step aside, and he'll—'

'You can't,' Joyce whispered.

Actually, Joyce might even have been shouting for all I know. Melvin was pounding so loudly on the door with his hard little fists that I couldn't hear a thing. At any moment that freakishly over-sized insect was going to break through my cheap plywood door and do what the *female* praying mantis usually does to her mate.

'Just go,' I said to Joyce, and gave her a mighty shove toward the bathroom, even as I threw myself at the bedroom door. Fortunately, the light switch was located adjacent to it and I managed to flip it off unhindered. My once colourful boudoir turned fifty shades of grey, but being the owner, I would have known my way around the room while wearing a blindfold. However, I had to engage in some knuckle abuse of my own in order to get Melvin's attention. Then it was in for the penny, in for the pound.

'Oh, Mely-kins,' I purred, 'this is Magdalena, the woman whom you hate most in the entire world; I'm the person responsible for your sweet Susannah serving time in a state penitentiary. Who knows, she could be assigned to hard labour. She might even break a fingernail or put a ladder in her stockings, and all because of me. Think about that, you measly little weasel. OK? Right, so I'm going to open the door now and let you do whatever you want to me. Of course, you have to catch me first.'

My half-brother snorted like a horse trying to rid its nostrils free of flies. 'I'm not a complete idiot, Yoder. I could see the light go off under the door when you turned it off. I know that you won't touch guns but you're going to hit me with something, aren't you?'

'Nope. We're just going to play hide and seek, like we did when we were kids. That's all. Correction: when you and your sweet Susannah were kids and I got stuck with babysitting yinz.'

'*Yinz?*' The incomplete idiot chuckled.

'Yes, yinz – the two of yinz.' The word in question is a colloquialism used in Pittsburgh, and much of Southwestern Pennsylvania, for 'y'all,' or 'youse,' or 'you,' second-person plural. In this case, it was a ploy to make Melvin feel like we could bond over culture and bad grammar.

If the resulting pause had indeed been pregnant, it might have produced two sets of twins, but at length I heard a long sigh. 'OK,' he agreed. 'We'll play hide and seek in the dark, just like old times, but if I catch either one of yinz I get to do whatever I want with her – even if it is *you*, Magdalena. But you can't tell my sweet little Susannah-kins if we do any grown-up stuff. Agreed?'

Wow! On the plus side, if I wasn't to tell my sister, that meant he planned to keep me alive. On the negative side, if I wasn't supposed to tell his sweet, innocent wife, then that meant that her husband intended to do sexual acts with whomever he caught, including me. Never mind that my baby sister was anything but innocent (she is, after all, a *divorced* Presbyterian!).

True to my word, I yanked open the door and,

301

thanks to the grace of God, who gave me the arms of a gibbon, I was able to jump safely back from the serial killer's reach. So far, so good. Then it wasn't. What I'd forgotten to take into account was that Melvin's eyes bobbed in his head like ice cubes in a pitcher of gently shaken lemonade. They never worked together. Whereas his dominant left eye was supposed to follow me into the closet, his right eye caught a glimpse of light as Joyce closed the bathroom door behind her.

Ding-dang that right eye of Melvin's! It may as well have been a pruning hook embedded in his brain and pulling him forward, for he lurched along behind it, even though he couldn't have seen where he was going now that the room was dark.

'Yoo-hoo, Sweetykins,' I said in a perfect imitation of my sister Susannah. 'My Mighty Muscled Love Machine, my Mel Cakes, my Basket of Love!' I am ashamed to admit that many is the time I've stooped to cover for her and call in sick at her places of employment while she's been off cavorting with the halfwit who now wanted to murder Joyce and me. And believe me, I wanted to retch when I repeated my sister's names of endearment for Melvin Stoltzfus.

I could hear Melvin clomp to a stop. 'Is that really you, Baby Doll, sweet little Susannah of my heart's desire?'

Twenty-Eight

'Coochie-coochie-coo, Loveykins.' Strictly speaking, it isn't lying if one says sweet nothings instead of answering a question directly.

Unfortunately, Melvin is merely dull-witted and only occasionally delusional. I say that charitably, but frankly a serial-killer can hardly be classified as sane. Still, Melvin had moments when one and one could add up to two, and that's when he really becomes dangerous.

'Wait a *bleeping* minute!' he screeched. Take it from me – a pigeon-chested mantis is incapable of roaring despite any amount of rage he might be feeling. 'How can Susannah be here when she's locked up in the state penitentiary because of her blabbermouth, turncoat and disloyal sister? That's you, Magdalena! And that's why I'm here! I've come to kill you, and that's what I'm going to do, and I'm going to do it now.'

Then Melvin did something I had *not* anticipated. He started spraying the room with bullets! That son of a gun had an automatic weapon. Who ever heard of such a thing? An ex-Mennonite acting like a gangster? There are those who won't believe me, but I say that it was a miracle that Little Jacob and I weren't hit until I had a chance to drop to the floor. Given my exceedingly great height, that took longer than it would have the average person.

Once on the floor, I cradled Little Jacob under my body while I crawled toward the closet on my hands and knees, all the while praying really hard that God would forgive me for being so judgmental about the airplane survivors and spare me.

When I reached the door, I crouched to one side and called out to my nemesis. 'May God have mercy on your soul,' I shouted above the hail of bullets.

The shooting stopped.

'That's what the chaplain will say before your execution,' I said.

'They're not going to catch me,' he said as he stumbled forward in my direction.

'What if I told you that you've already been caught, because this house is surrounded by State Troopers, and that any minute now they'll come crashing through the door?'

'Ha! I'd say that you're lying again, Yoder. I'm paying that idiot clown you knew as Rupert big bucks to guard the patio door, and he's keeping a lookout. He would have warned—'

To say that Melvin screamed like a little girl when he fell through the trapdoor opening would be an insult to my sex. He emitted a shriek that could only be duplicated electronically using the high-pitched buzz of cicadas as a starting point. It would have been very Christian of me to have felt sympathy for him when I heard him moaning in pain at the bottom of the hole. Instead, I felt nothing but immense relief.

I immediately slammed the trapdoor shut and screamed for Joyce's help. Then I stood on it, cradling my child close, until Joyce appeared and helped me push a heavy dresser over the trapdoor. Then we both fled into the kitchen.

It was my responsibility to call Toy and Sheriff Stodgewiggle, which I did. In the meantime, Joyce called Agnes over at the Convent of Perpetual Apathy where, of course, nobody cared about our situation except for Agnes and assorted members of my family. Within minutes my son and I were safely in my husband's arms, and we both had our arms around Alison, making it a family huddle. Alas, the stubby arms of my mother-in-law, the supposedly apathetic Mother Malaise, tried to envelop me in an embrace empty of empathy, but her enormous bosoms extended beyond her stubby arms and left her frustrated but, sadly, not beyond words.

'*Nu?*' she said. 'Und dis eez de tanks dat I get for making dee classy velcome for Heez und Her Royal Highnesses?'

Quite frankly, her self-centred comment rather peeved me. I had not invited her into our intimate circle, her 'velcome' had not been classy, and she was kvetching while poor, traumatized Joyce was sobbing her heart out to Agnes in the adjoining dining room. If pity was what Ida Rosen wanted, then she could take the 'a's' out of 'apathy' and insert an 'i.' I disentangled myself from the heap of love, leaving Little Jacob safe in his father's strong arms. Despite the fact that Toy, or the County Sheriff, could burst into the room at any second, I pulled off my long, cotton flannel nightgown.

'Oy!' Mother Malaise leaned forward on the

305

bed, her eyes as large as latkes. 'Vas eez dis? A strip show?'

'No. But look at my nightgown and my sturdy brasserie. You can see where one of the maniac's bullets grazed me – right here along the left side of the bra cup. If it hadn't been for the fact that I wear sturdy Christian underwear to bed, well—'

'Oh, hon,' the Babester said as he squeezed me tighter in his loving arms, which were still holding our youngest, mind you. 'If you'd been standing just two inches over he'd have hit you in the heart.'

'Oh, mom,' Alison cried, 'I don't want to ever lose you!'

'Oh, daughter-in-law,' Mother Malaise said in perfectly unaccented English. 'I couldn't have asked for a better daughter of my own.'

'At last we agree on something,' I said.

Her pudgy hands shoved my balled up nightgown in my face. 'But geet dressed again, yah? You look like a hoosey.'

'A *what*?'

'She means hussy,' Alison said with a giggle.

'Ida Rosen,' I hissed through clenched teeth, proving that Papa was wrong and that I could have been a ventriloquist, with just the slightest bit of encouragement. 'Unhand me now, you *hypocrite*, and go back to the nudist colony that you run under the guise of a pseudo-religious establishment for tax purposes.'

'But hon, pretty *please*,' the Babester said, using his sad voice and flashing his long, dark lashes at me in sad little boy fashion. 'She's an old helpless woman.'

306

'So was the Wicked Witch of the West. Go, Ida, go. You can come back during visiting hours.'

'Yah? Vhen eez dat?'

'We'll let you know.'

'But who'll cut my meat for me?' my husband said when his mother was gone.

'You're a surgeon, dear,' I said, not unkindly. 'Maybe you can figure it out for yourself.'

'Daddy, I can help you,' Alison said.

'My, what a generous offer,' I said, 'but Daddy needs to do it for himself or he won't get his allowance.'

'Daddy still gets an allowance?' the dear child asked.

'Indeed,' I said. 'That's what made your little brother possible.'

I couldn't believe my ear pans when Sheriff Stodgewiggle returned to the kitchen and reported that the Rabbit Hole was empty. Police Chief Toy was quick to back him up. That information did not compute; the floor might as well have been up and the ceiling down.

By that time Agnes and Joyce had joined our number, which, as it turned out, was quite fortunate for me. I'd been waiting closer to the bedroom door, slightly in front of the anxious Agnes, and when I heard the perplexing news I fainted dead away. Shame on me for ever having judged my friend's prodigious appetite, for it was her pillowing plenitude that saved my noggin from a possible concussion.

Sheathed in that noggin is a fair-to-middling brain, but that brain houses a will that makes it impossible to keep me 'out' for as long as it takes to count to three. In fact, Alison is convinced that I missed my calling and that I should have been a boxer. With my exceptionally long and spindly arms, rather like an octopus's tentacles (without the suction cups, mind you) I could weave in and out of my opponent's reach. If I was ever knocked down I could pop up again, much like a weighted punching bag.

Thus it was on that occasion. 'What happened?' I gasped. 'What did I miss?'

'Almost nothing,' Agnes said as she propped me back up. 'And *nothing* is what they found. Are you sure that murderous Melvin fell down your so-called Rabbit Hole?'

'It's *the* Rabbit Hole,' I said. 'And I'm positive. I heard him scream as he fell. Then I immediately slammed the trapdoor shut. After that, Joyce and I pushed the dresser over it to keep him from escaping. There's no way he could have gotten out.'

Sheriff Stodgewiggle cleared his throat. It was not a straightforward process. He thrust out his three chins, and opened wide a cavernous maw lined with teeth no larger than grains of millet. Then we were treated to the sounds one might expect from a tiger throwing up a hairball. The ritual turned his face the colour of rancid, pickled beets. I, for one, dared not breathe again until he shook his massive wattles to signify that, at last, actual words were forthcoming.

'*While* one is under great stress,' he drawled, in a West Virginia accent, 'it is possible for even the sharpest *among* us to hallucinate.'

308

Agnes patted my arm as if I were her child rather than her best friend. 'Mags, at least you have to give the sheriff props for using words like "while," and "among," even if he did prove that you've been acting a little bizarre lately.'

Boy, that did it! That hiked my hackles until they practically caught in the hooks of my sturdy Christian brassiere. 'I was not hallucinating, I was not acting bizarrely. Melvin Sticklegoober Stoltzfus really *has* been pretending to be an English earl.'

Alison giggled. 'Sticklegoober. Come on, Mom. Can'tcha come up with a better name than that?'

'Hush,' her father said. 'I happen to know that you had a grandmother by that name.'

'Oops,' Alison said. 'Strike that.'

I was gobsmacked, then, when Joyce walked around the kitchen island and put a slender arm around me. 'This kind of talk angers me,' she said. 'What all of you are really doing is calling Magdalena and me liars. Magdalena did not hallucinate; neither did I. And yes, Melvin did impersonate an English Lord.'

'But how could he?' Agnes protested. 'That man has always been so – well, so *very* incompetent.'

'He's managed to impersonate a human being,' I said.

'Way to score, Mom,' Alison said.

The Babester frowned. The dear man isn't necessarily 'holier than thou,' but he is definitely holier than *me*, and he hates it when I am judgemental, even when the man I am mocking is a serial killer.

Joyce clapped her hands as if calling a class to order. 'Look, you *knew* me as a somewhat ditzy, telepathic Lady Celia, a teenager. But I'm really twenty-five and I'm a graduate of Julliard. I'm originally from Chillicothe, Ohio and I'm as American as grass lawns, oversized food portions and Christmas music in September. But I had nothing against this Melvin Sticklebooger until today. Not one thing – until he started shooting at us.'

Even Sheriff Stodgewiggle laughed when Joyce Toestubber said Sticklebooger, which, if you ask me, is skating on pretty thin ice. Fortunately, Joyce didn't take the laughter personally, and she was able to pick up her tale in a minute. She told our little group everything that she'd told me, but also added a few details that she thought might be pertinent.

'The man whom you call Melvin worked very hard on his accent. By the time he caught up with us in West Virginia and asked us to work with him, he'd already watched all of the *Downton Abbey* TV shows. He had taped every episode, and was always referring to this one or that whenever we rehearsed. If he'd had his way, we would have shown up here as an aristocratic English family from the twenties.'

Sheriff Stodgewiggle sighed deeply, sending ripples through his jowls and down through the many layers of flesh contained in his ever-expanding neck. It was a fascinating and truly wondrous sight; the sort of thing one ought to thank the Good Lord for having had the chance of witnessing. Our neighbour, Marnie, went to

310

Nova Scotia once and saw a whale breach in the Bay of Fundy. She said it was a moment which she'd never forget. I'd like to think that my moment with the sheriff's jowls was akin to that.

At any rate, miracle of miracles, Joyce was able to describe her theatre troop's training period with Melvin in such agonizing albeit hilarious detail that anyone who knew him really well could not doubt that her story was indeed true. Of course I had already fainted, so my quota of acting out various points had already been met. That meant that I could only bite my lip and roll my eyes as she took centre stage and regaled them with story after story about the time that she spent training to be one of the family of Grimsley-Snodgrasses.

'What I still don't understand,' Sheriff Stodgewiggle said at last, bringing us all back to earth, 'is what was to be gained by having the viscount disappear over the edge of Lover's Leap? That was just a major distraction for everyone, and it had to be an enormous headache for you, Magdalena.'

'That was it, exactly!' Joyce said. 'In fact, I overheard Melvin offering Michael a thousand-dollar bonus if he could pull off a decent job of disappearing. I got a measly two hundred extra for claiming to have seen Rupert being pushed. But anyway, the whole point was to cause Magdalena grief. The fact that the townspeople trampled the field – that's what Melvin was hoping for.'

'And you were *OK* with this?'

311

'No one is perfect, Magdalena,' Joyce had the temerity to say.

It was time for me to clap my hands – either that, or I was going to wring Joyce's neck; a decidedly unchristian activity.

'Listen up, folks,' I said. 'We can stand here all day, admiring the way that Melvin, that wicked weasel, nearly pulled the wool over our eyes and turned me into hamburger meat, tenderized by a gazillion bullets, or one of us can actually go down into the Rabbit Hole and take a close look-see. Just sticking one's head in there and calling out his name – what does that prove? There is a sofa in there, for pity's sake. The man weighs about three stone, naked. He could be lying flat under the cushions and you wouldn't see a bump. There is a mini-fridge down there as well, for crying out loud. He could probably fit in that if he curled up. There are oodles of possibilities – that's all I'm saying. Why hasn't anyone gone down there?'

Then, to my embarrassment, it dawned on me why not. It was, in fact, as plain as the ring around Sheriff Stodgewiggle's collar. The good man was not going to be able to fit through the opening, not unless we stuffed him down the hole like sausage in a casing. As for Toy, he'd already made it painfully clear that he could barely tolerate sleeping under a sheet, so severe was his case of claustrophobia.

'You know what?' I said next. '*I'll* go. After all, he's my hallucination.'

'No, *I'll* go!' said my fourteen-year-old without a second's hesitation, and not only did she step

right in front of me, she stomped on my toes –
by accident, of course.

'The heck *either* of you will,' growled the
Babester as he grabbed a torch off the kitchen
windowsill. He pushed his way past both lawmen,
and if either of them intended to stop him they
sure didn't exhibit much of that intention. We all
just followed in my brave husband's wake and
then gathered in a semi-circle around the entrance
to the secret room. By then, I was so overcome
with emotion that I fell to my knees.

'If I thought that I could get up again,' Sheriff
Stodgewiggle rasped, for he was breathing hard
from the exertion of walking, 'I would likewise
fall to my knees in prayer. As a devout Roman
Catholic, I believe that Lord Jesus can work
miracles on our behalf if we but ask, and most
especially if we beseech Him through the mercy
of His mother, the Blessed Virgin Mary.'

'My mother doesn't think that Catholics are
real Christians,' Alison said.

I gasped, which was very hard on my respiratory system at that moment. 'Alison, that's not
true!'

'Yes, Mom, it *is* so; you're always praying for
their salvation.'

'Maybe, I do, but that's only because if they
were real Christians, they'd give up this Pope
and Mary business and become – well, you know,
Protestants.'

'Like us Episcopalians?' Toy said. 'Are we
Christians, Magdalena?'

'Don't be silly, dear, of course you are. You
gave up Mary and the Pope when you put a

serial killer, one by the name of King Henry VIII, in charge of the Church. But to be honest, Toy, there are some in your church who like the smells and bells part of it, the so-called High Church end of your spectrum, perhaps a wee bit too much. Knees hitting the floor in near constant genuflection – I don't see why God would be interested in any of that.'

'Ooh, ooh,' Alison said, as she is wont to say when she is excited. 'I went to one of them High End churches with my girlfriend, Cyndi. I loved that genuine inflection stuff, and the incense burner thingy was awesome. The rabbi kept swinging it around and around until it made enough smoke that all the old people choked. Yeah, that was so cool.'

'I'm pretty sure that the man in question was a priest, Alison,' Agnes said, 'and not a rabbi.'

'Yeah, whatever,' Alison said.

Sheriff Stodgewiggle was still chewing on my judgement bone – or was it his? 'Tell me,' he said, 'does your husband possess the same narrow view of Christianity that you do?'

'Her husband is a secular Jew,' Alison said. 'He don't care what kind of Christian that she is, just as long as she stays off the Hell Train.'

'I beg your pardon?' Sheriff Stodgewiggle said.

Just about then, the Babester came back into view and looked up through the Rabbit Hole. 'Although I am a secular Jew, and not religious, I would like to point out that Satan is not mentioned in our Torah; neither is Hell mentioned. Eternal damnation has never been a Jewish concept. Just as long as the most beautiful woman

314

to walk the face of this planet – that would be Magdalena – stays out of my spiritual life – I will keep my opinions out of hers.'

'Hip, hip, hooray for you, Gabe,' Toy said through cupped hands. 'I would so marry you if we were both unattached gay men – which neither of us are.'

My Dearly Beloved laughed as he scrambled up the ladder. 'Mags,' he said, even before he had cleared the opening, 'Melvin was definitely down there but he escaped.'

'That's impossible,' Sheriff Stodgewiggle said. 'I actually got down on my belly and shone my torch into every corner of your safe room. That's a pretty nifty setup you have down there: sleeping cots, chemical toilet, tinned food, bottled water and even a little primus stove. However, and maybe it's because you used to be a heart surgeon, everything is so neatly folded or stacked in such a way that there is no place for anyone to hide. Chief Toy, will you concur with my finding?'

'Absolutely,' Toy said. 'I mean, I concur.'

'How did you get off your belly?' Alison said.

'Alison!' I said in dismay. Meanwhile, her father, the heart surgeon, smiled wryly.

'Chief Toy lent me a hand,' Sheriff Stodgewiggle said.

'Be sure to return it when you're through,' Alison said.

The sheriff laughed and winked at me. 'Out of the mouths of babes,' he said.

'She's fourteen; she's not a baby. What she said was very rude.'

'Still, I like kids,' Sheriff Stodgewiggle said.

315

'Got to cut them some slack, I say. Growing up is hard these days.'

I shrugged off the child-rearing advice and threw myself unabashedly upon my now-fully-emerged husband. 'Darling! What do you *mean* by saying that the monster was down there but isn't anymore? How can you be *certain* of these things?'

'Evidence,' my hero said. 'The weasel managed to crawl out through the ventilation shaft.'

'Impossible!' I cried. 'Even a small child couldn't squeeze through that, and the mantis has an enormous, bobbing head.'

'Ah,' the Babester said, 'could it be that he has only a somewhat largish head and an extremely thin neck? Because the screen is removed from the vent opening and there is an empty bottle of cooking oil beneath it, and the shaft is smeared with oil as far as I could see. The edge around the opening is a little jagged, so no doubt he left a little DNA behind that will confirm that he was there. Oh, and then there was this.'

Gabe reached down the back of his shirt and pulled out a second shirt. There was no mistaking the shirt that Gabe held out as the same, mono-grammed dress shirt that I'd seen at the start of the day on the Earl of Grimsley-Snodgrass, and then later on the serial killer of Southwestern Pennsylvania.

'I think I'm going to faint,' I said. Pride at being vindicated and fear of Melvin still being on the loose were two emotions that do not mix well.

'I think I'm going to puke,' Alison said. She has always been more pragmatic than I.

'Before either of you ladies do your thing,' the Babester said, 'in the spirit of full disclosure, I feel that I should inform you that I also found a pair of shoes, socks, underwear and trousers stuffed into the shaft, which means that Melvin Sticklegoober Stoltzfus is running around outside as naked as a jaybird.'

Then Alison followed through on her threat.

Twenty-Nine

Epilogue

It was almost six weeks later and the daytime temperatures had cooled considerably. In fact, light frost was predicted in the valleys any night now, and the change of seasons had brought with it, much to my surprise, some closure. Melvin Sticklegoober Stoltzfus was still on the lam, but at least Yoko-san's remains had been definitively identified and respectfully removed from my lift car roof. I had yet to reopen the PennDutch Inn, but if – or when – I did, it would no longer house a lift. Instead, I envisioned a wider, less steep staircase built in honour of Yoko-san.

Gabriel had heeded my advice, which was to stock the car with provisions before driving the children to a county fair all the way down in the State of Maryland. There they planned to gaze upon a big orange gourd – and happily so – without me whispering loving words of criticism into their jug ears. '*The world's largest pumpkin. Large enough for Peter to keep his wife in,*' the ad claimed. Ha! I mean, who can believe advertisements these days?

'But it really is true,' Agnes said as she put the first pin prick into my hot air balloon. 'I was down there yesterday and I saw it for myself.'

'*What? Where* were you yesterday? And most importantly, with *whom*?'

For the record, this conversation took place at Agnes's house as we were having tea and shortbread biscuits on her veranda while the afternoon sun still held some warmth. Agnes had been about to hold the plate of biscuits out to me, but snatched it back when she heard my tone of voice.

'Why Magdalena, you sound almost jealous.'

'I do *not* sound almost jealous,' I said. 'I *am* jealous.'

Agnes smiled as she gnawed gleefully on her treat like a giant beaver in a cartoon. 'Well then, if you must know it was Mary Jane Greenhut.'

'Harrumph.'

'Is that all you're going to say? *Harrumph?* Look, here is a photo of the two of us looking out through the pumpkin house windows.'

Agnes handed me a picture of an enormous orange vegetable – or was it a fruit? – that had a door and two windows cut into it. The windows were dressed with cute yellow curtains that were pulled back with blue ties. The 'roof,' which was just part of the shell, had been painted brown, but painted to look as if it were made from tiles. A black, crooked, stove pipe chimney, straight from a child's storybook, projected from one end. Indeed, I could see the images of Agnes and Mary Jane quite clearly, but they were dressed in prisoner's stripes.

'Agnes, that's plum disgusting,' I said.

'It's only a joke, Mags. Peter locked his wife up in a pumpkin shell, get it?' She crammed a

319

shortbread biscuit into her mouth, just in order to punish me.

'Better that Peter was penned up in the pumpkin than his wife,' I said. 'Those old nursery rhymes perpetuate sexist stereotypes.'

'Are you serious?' Agnes said.

'You bet your bippy, dear,' I said.

'What is a bippy?' Agnes asked.

'I have no idea,' I said. 'It's just a phrase that I heard someplace, maybe once, and latched on to it like a tick on a bird hound. Anyway, I have some more information to share with you about that awful night – well, leading up to that awful night.'

'What awful night is that to which you refer?' Agnes asked.

'What awful night is *that*, you have the *chutzpah* to ask?' I said. 'How about we start with the *day* that you got it into your shallow noggin to invite English nobility to Hernia but didn't properly vet your sources. Ergo, instead of getting the Duke and Duchess of Cambridge and the cutest children on the planet – next to mine, of course – you brought Satan back to Hernia.'

Agnes crammed four shortbread biscuits into her mouth, and when she spoke crumbs flew everywhere like a dust storm. 'L'esh not forget that you're Shatan's shibling,' she said.

I've heard meteorologists refer to hailstones as large as golf balls while at the same time holding up pea-size pellets for the television camera. Would anyone believe me, I wonder, if I said that Agnes really did begin to cry tears the size of ice cubes? Well, she did cry! She boo-hooed

320

and then hooed some more. I threw my gangly arms around my best friend, and in a move so not in keeping with who I am, I clasped her to my meagre bosom.

'It's OK, dear,' I said, although of course it was not. 'There, there, it will be all right.' What utter nonsense to say at a time like that. What does 'there, there' even mean?

But what mattered is that my dear friend found it soothing and she slowly slobbered to a stop. I realize this is not a delicate way to put it, but there is no way to describe the aftermath of teardrops the size of ice cubes (the old-fashioned kind from ice trays, mind you). While she tidied herself up a bit, I snatched the last biscuit from the plate and discovered three more in a tin above the kitchen sink. I stuffed the three biscuits into the pouches of my cheeks, like a squirrel. For an amateur ventriloquist, such as myself, talking with food in one's mouth is easy peasy.

'What is your bit of news?' she asked calmly, as if she'd never carried on akin to a child denied sweets in the cashier's lane.

'Do you recall how Pastor Diffledorf and his wife were less than warm and fuzzy to me on the day of – well, you know?'

Agnes is almost as good at sardonic laughs as I am. We have even joked that we should immigrate to the Island of Sardinia, and that once we were citizens we could help pass a law to change the name of the island to Sardonica.

'Ha! Warm and fuzzy? They treated you like chewing gum on the soles of new shoes.'

'Exactly. At first even Toy was toying – no pun

intended – with the theory that they had also been recruited by the menacing mantis. Especially Mrs Diffledorf, because she really seemed to have it in for me. Then my Sweetie Pie, Honey Pot, who's a doctor—'

'Would you stop rubbing that in, Mags?'

'Sorry. Anyway, he reminded me that in any given population one is a priori, predisposed to dislike roughly fifteen percent of the people whom one encounters. This is practically a biological fact, because it's based on tons of research. The cues for why we may dislike these individuals can be very subtle, ranging from how they smell to the size and placement of their eyes, or ears, the sound of their voices, etc. This works in reverse too and helps us to choose our mates. But, given that the underlying principle here is human evolution, I can't really buy into it. Still, it's nice to know that the Babester thinks that it was their genes that caused my pastor and his wife to dislike me so intensely, and that it wasn't anything personal that they held against me.'

My best friend reached across the glass top of her outdoor table to squeeze my hand in comfort. It was such a kind gesture, but *really*, after nearly fifty years of friendship (we were bathed together as infants) she should have known better, for my hands were safely back in my lap by then.

'Oh, you're so *English*,' she quipped.

'Really?' I said. 'As in British or the Amish sense of the word?'

'Whichever meaning will flatter you the most,' Agnes said.

'The former.' I was about to extol the virtues

of the United Kingdom in general when I felt something warm and fuzzy bump against my elbow. It probably wasn't the Diffledorfs, and I could see Agnes (who could frankly use a shave or a good depilatory), so I turned carefully and with a good deal of trepidation.

'Gruff!' I cried with immense relief when I saw that it was only Doc's old billy goat. 'What are *you* doing here? Who let you out of your pen?'

Agnes waved a plump hand dismissively. 'He doesn't live in a pen anymore. He lives in the house now – with me.'

'*Oh?*'

'Don't judge me, Magdalena.'

'I'm not – or maybe I won't. First, just tell me where Gruff sleeps.'

'He sleeps in my bed with me. What of it?'

I was flabbergasted. 'Agnes Miller Schafer! That is a Sodom-and-Gomorrah-class sin! That's exactly what Governor Tugwanker was warning us would happen if gay marriage became legal. You don't plan to marry this goat, do you, Agnes? You do remember your scripture, dear, don't you?'

'Don't be such a fool, Magdalena. In the first place, one marriage to an old goat was quite enough. In the second place, Gruff sleeps on the other side of the bed. And in the third place, this old goat's already been fixed, so he's always been a complete gentleman.'

'Oh. But then what's a dirty old goat doing in your bed?'

Agnes's eyes misted up. 'You hit the nail on the head. Gruff is old: at this stage he's only

323

partially housebroken, as I said. He's no longer sexually active, he smells of body odour, he passes gas all night, he belches nearly constantly and he snores loud enough to drown out the cicadas when I leave the windows open. To sum it up, having an old billy goat in bed with me is like having a little bit of Doc back.'

I nodded slowly, as I was forced to punch yet another hole in my judgement ticket. 'I'm sorry – yet again, I'm afraid. You do know that jumping to conclusions is how I manage to keep my girlish figure.'

'That and running off at your mouth.'

'Yes, I suppose that I deserve that.'

I scratched old Gruff between his two wicked horns. He seemed to really like that and kept nuzzling me for more attention. When I tried to stop he headbutted me with the front of his horns and knocked me out of my chair.

'Bad Gruff, bad Gruff,' Agnes said in the high-pitched tones of someone speaking to a baby or a *real* pet.

'Agnes,' I said, 'you do realize that you could well end up being impaled on those things. Those horns.'

'I'll take my chances.'

We sat in silence until the chill of an autumn afternoon forced us to make decisions. I was the first to get up and call it a day.

'Well, I had best be going,' I said. 'My family will be getting back from the fair with *their* tales of a giant pumpkin. I'll have to feign surprise.'

'Somehow I think that you'll manage,' she said. I didn't know how to interpret her comment, but in any case, she wasn't through speaking. 'Magdalena, are you happy with your life?'

'Am I happy with my life?'

'It's a simple question, Mags.'

'No, it's not. Let me turn it around; are you happy with *your* life?'

Agnes looked away to the gathering shadows along the edge of the woods. 'No. I am not.'

I was stunned. 'Why not?'

'I don't have a legacy. I'm half a century old, Mags, and I haven't done anything that will be remembered by anyone after I'm gone.'

'But that is so not true,' I said.

'Name one thing that I've done that's made a difference,' she said.

'You volunteer for the Suicide Prevention Hotline. You organized a local fund drive for victims of the earthquake in Nepal. You drive meals to shut-ins and you even clean the home of one of them, a woman who is too disabled to do it for herself. Oh, yes, and you read to those blind Amish who will not avail themselves of books on tape.'

'But who will remember *me* when I'm gone?'

'*My* children. The children in the Sunday school class that you teach, and which you've taught for the last twenty-five years. Your neighbours, and their children, will remember you. Just about everyone in the community will.'

At last, Agnes smiled. 'Thank you,' she said. 'But you still haven't answered my question. Are *you* happy?'

'I'm content,' I said. 'And I'm content with being content.'

Thirty

GLUTEN-FREE TOFFEE APPLE CINNAMON ROLLS

Dough
1 medium tart apple, peeled and chopped
1 tbsp thawed apple juice concentrate
⅔ cup plus 2 tbsp sugar (or equivalent), divided
1½ tsp ground cinnamon
2½ cups white rice flour
½ tsp xanthium gum (available at health-food shops)
1¼ tsp baking powder
½ tsp salt
1¼ cups buttermilk
6 tbsps butter, melted and divided
¼ cup toffee bits

Glaze
1½ cups confectioners' sugar
3 tbsp thawed apple juice concentrate
2 tbsp toffee bits

Directions
Pre-heat oven to 400 degrees Fahrenheit.
In a microwave-safe bowl, combine apple and apple juice concentrate; microwave,

326

covered, on high for 1–2 minutes until tender.

Drain; cool slightly. In a small bowl, mix ⅔ cup sugar and cinnamon.

In a large bowl, whisk flour, baking powder, baking soda, and salt and remaining sugar.

Stir in buttermilk and 2 tbsp melted butter. Turn onto a lightly floured surface; Knead ten times.

Roll dough into a 12 × 9 inch rectangle. Brush with 2 tbsp of melted butter to within a half-inch of the edges; sprinkle with toffee bits plus the sugar mixture and apple from Step 1. Roll up jelly roll-style, starting with long side; pinch seam to seal. Cut into eight slices.

Place in a greased 9 inch round baking pan. Brush with remaining butter. Bake for 22–28 minutes or until golden brown. Cool for 5 minutes; remove from pan. To make the glaze, mix confectioners' sugar and juice concentrate. Spread over rolls; sprinkle with toffee bits.

These rolls taste far better than store-bought gluten-free cinnamon rolls.